**Gabe folded his arms across his chest.
"I offered you a deal this morning."**

We were at a standoff. Both of us were stubborn as hell and putting our respective clients first. Janie might not be an actual client, but it was important to me to help her. It was important to me to make a difference in Lake Elsinore. "Tell me what's up with Dara first."

His gaze stayed on me. Cars whipped by. Blow-dryers turned on and off. Female chatter floated out the door. And Gabe didn't move. "You can't do it without me, babe."

"Is that a challenge?" I hated that Gabe didn't trust me enough to just tell me. He expected me to trust him that much.

His face hardened. "It's a fact. Go ahead, Sam. Try to solve this without my help." He turned and headed for his truck.

I glared at his back. "I will!" I didn't want to acknowledge the anger and fear rocketing through my blood. Once Gabe had fought to save me; now it seemed he was off saving another woman.

He wrenched open the cab door, then looked back at me. "You can try, sugar."

NINJA SOCCER MOMS

Jennifer Apodaca

KENSINGTON BOOKS
KENSINGTON PUBLISHING CORP.
http://www.kensingtonbooks.com

KENSINGTON BOOKS are published by

Kensington Publishing Corp.
850 Third Avenue
New York, NY 10022

ISBN: 0-7582-0449-3
Library of Congress Control Number: 2003112542

First hardcover printing: May 2004
First paperback printing: April 2005

10 9 8 7 6 5 4 3 2 1

Printed in the United States of America

For my sons, Matt, Gary, and Paul Apodaca. It's my joy and privilege to be your mom, and to watch you grow into the type of men I would cast as heroes in my books. Without you guys, I would have missed out on the pleasure of being a soccer mom!

Acknowledgments

The seed of the idea for *Ninja Soccer Moms* came from a story on the news about a parent stealing from a soccer league in another state. I was outraged by the story. I was a soccer mom myself for many years and that experience gave me a new respect for the hardworking parents who generously donated their time and money to give kids an opportunity to play organized sports. The soccer league I created in this book is fictional, as are all the characters. But to all the real soccer moms I have met over the years—a huge thank you. No matter how tired I was, you always made me laugh!

To my brother, Tom Roper, for sharing his knowledge about insurance agencies and trust funds. Thank you, Tom, for all your invaluable help, and for being my big brother. And to my sister-in-law, Bonnie Roper, for years of believing in me and loving the books!

Thanks to my incomparable editor, Kate Duffy. You have a brilliant mind, a quick wit, and you always "get it." You're the best.

1

The thing about revenge is that it takes a woman who is well and truly pissed to get it right.

That woman sat across from me in my cramped cubicle, wearing no-name jeans with an elastic waistband, and a pink Hanes sweatshirt. Janie Tuggle had yanked her gray-streaked brown hair into a ruthless ponytail. No makeup softened the lines on her face.

Right away, I knew that Janie wasn't here to sign up for a dating package at Heart Mates, my beloved and struggling dating service. But one look at Janie's determined hazel eyes, and my disappointment about not signing a new client was overshadowed by curiosity.

Besides, nothing else was going on this morning. It was Wednesday, and we hadn't had a new client all week. Quickly I stuffed the romance novel I had been reading to write a review for *Romance Rocks* magazine into the top drawer of my desk. I wrote several reviews a month under my own name, Samantha Shaw, but it didn't provide much income. Reviewing romances was my hobby. I loved the feisty, never-say-die heroines in those books.

Shutting my desk drawer, I gave my full attention to

Janie. We had known each other for years through soccer.

Ugh, I tried not to think about soccer. While I adored my two sons, I hated soccer. I'd spent years hiding from my marital problems by immersing myself in soccer and the PTA. I folded my hands and put on my best businesswoman smile. "So Janie, what can I do for you?"

She shifted in her seat across from my desk and brushed a piece of lint off her pink sweatshirt. "I need your help, Sam. I'll pay you. I know you do some private investigating."

"Uh, occasionally." Mostly when I trip over trouble. Then there's that whole not-being-licensed-to-investigate problem that I get around by having a hot, sexy boyfriend who is a licensed PI. "But Heart Mates is my career. You know, Janie, maybe it's time to think about dating again. It's been a year since your divorce and we really have some lovely dating packages." *Smile*, I told myself.

Janie looked down at her left hand resting on her jean-clad thigh and picked at the cuticle of her bare ring finger. "Dating is the last thing on my mind."

Well, I tried. "What is on your mind, Janie?"

She left off the cuticle and looked up at me with her hazel eyes. "Revenge."

I perked up. "Revenge?"

Her mouth tightened. "Damn right."

Good grief, I don't think I'd ever heard Janie swear. I'd seen her do the books for the soccer club, run the fund-raising candy sales, and deal with the irrational parents and temperamental coaches, all with a smile. Janie had always been the kind of easygoing woman who stayed in the background, while her more flamboyant soccer coach husband demanded attention. When Chad had dumped Janie for a younger model, the town promptly forgot her. This was getting more interesting than my romance novel. I leaned forward, putting my elbows on my desk. "Why don't you tell me what you mean by revenge?"

She clutched her hands tightly in her lap. "I mean I want to expose Chad for the petty thief that he is. He's stealing from SCOLE and I want you to prove it."

"Chad? A thief?" Stunned, I almost knocked over my cup of coffee. Grabbing the heart-stamped mug, I tried to grasp the idea of self-assured, athletic Chad Tuggle stealing from the Soccer Club of Lake Elsinore, or SCOLE as the locals called it. He'd been the head coach of the organization for years, so the idea of him embezzling sounded crazy. "Janie, what makes you think he's stealing from the soccer funds?"

"I know he is," she said quietly.

Her simple assurance had credibility, since Janie used to do the books for SCOLE. That had been taken away from her during the divorce by the soccer board. I tried to think this out. "Have you taken a look at the books?"

Her lips thinned. "They won't let me anywhere near those books. Ever since Chad left me for that belly-button-ringed tramp, the town took his side. He's the hero coach who led SCOLE to three consecutive championships. I'm the bad wife who deserved to be dumped."

It was true. Small towns took their team sports seriously. Our small Southern California town of Lake Elsinore didn't really have a lot going for it. An unstable lake that sparked huge fights to try to stop the rapid evaporation, but no real solutions, didn't attract big business or upscale residents. The average medium income hovered around the macaroni-and-cheese level. The neighboring towns of Temecula and Murrieta thrived and spawned stellar sports teams. Beating them became a source of town pride.

And the coach that led the team to victory became the town hero.

Now his ex-wife thinks the hero coach is embezzling from the team.

Janie wasn't going to get anyone to take her seriously without hard-core evidence. Business sense told me to run from this case. I desperately wanted to make Heart Mates a success in Lake Elsinore. But the wronged wife in me, the one I thought I'd buried under the madeover businesswoman, reared up. If it was true that Chad was embezzling, I wanted to help Janie show the town they were wrong to judge her the way they had. "What is it you want me to do?"

Janie leaned forward, her voice hopeful. "Chad's been keeping the books at his office ever since the divorce. If you could go in and convince him to let you have a look—"

I cut her off. "How would I do that? I'm not in soccer anymore. And even if I did get him to let me look, I wouldn't know what to look for." Given that I had bought Heart Mates without having the books audited, I probably wasn't the best woman for the job.

Janie picked up her Styrofoam cup of coffee and examined the contents. "Chad will let you look, Sam. When you started, you know, *improving* yourself, he talked about how hot you looked—" She broke off, leaning back in her chair and slumping her shoulders. "You know how men are."

Sure, I knew. And I knew that all the soccer moms and PTA folks who were supposed to be my friends never told me my husband was a cheating pig. But after my husband died and I'd found evidence of his cheating, I had done the unthinkable—I had my breasts enhanced. The shocked gossip that rippled through the soccer and PTA world was bigger than my new size C bra. At least Janie was honest. "Even if I can get him to let me look at the books, then what?"

She glanced up from her cup of coffee. "Send him on an errand or something and get me a copy."

"I can't just take the whole book to the copy machine and duplicate it. I'm pretty sure Chad would notice that." My charms didn't go that far. I'd be lucky to get him to let me look at the books at all.

Janie flashed me her first real smile since she walked into my office this morning. "He keeps the books on his computer. All you have to do is copy them to a disk. It'll only take a minute or two. Ask him to go to the doughnut shop and buy you a Coke. Something like that. Trust me, Chad's brain heads south around women."

"Oh." Now I felt stupid. I had been picturing an old-fashioned ledger book. We used a Peach Tree program for Heart Mates. Chad probably used something like that.

Janie sat forward in the chair. "Sam, please, I need you to take this case. I know Chad's a hero in town, but he's not who you think he is. This weekend was the last straw. He told the kids that he's hiring a private soccer coach for Mark, and sending Kelly to cheerleading camp next summer. Yet I just found out the health insurance on the kids was cancelled because he didn't pay the premiums. Never mind that Chad still hasn't paid me off on the house in the divorce settlement and pays hardly any child support."

God, I could see myself in Janie. The scared woman with two kids trying to survive and succeed. While married to Chad, Janie might have spotted a thing or two in the books that looked suspicious, but either Chad explained it away, or Janie let it go because she knew no one would listen to her. Then after the divorce, Janie had been just trying to survive. But now Chad had pushed her too far. Trying to prove he was the hero dad by giving the kids private soccer coaches and cheerleading camp, but he didn't pay for the basics. Hell, I knew Janie and the kids were living in a run-down little mobile home while Chad had the big two-story house.

Janie was ready for revenge. Justice. The truth.

Sort of made me feel like Robin Hood, stealing from the rich to save the poor. Or in this case, stealing from cheating, embezzling ex-husbands to rectify the wrongs done to the ex-wives.

I reached across my desk and took Janie's hand. "Tell you what. I'll go over to Chad's office and see if I can copy the SCOLE books onto a disk. Then we'll see what we can find." I walked Janie out of my office to where my assistant, Blaine, was busy reading a car magazine.

Janie stopped in the reception area and looked around. I followed her gaze over the metal folding chairs for waiting clients against one wall, the wafer-thin industrial gray carpet, and up to the water-stained ceiling tiles. Heart Mates was a work in progress.

Then Janie looked at me. "I'm going to have a place like this one day."

Cautiously, I said, "What do you mean?" I was pretty sure she wasn't lusting after the mold growing in the walls.

A shy smile carved years off her face. "I'm going back to school to finish my bookkeeping certificate. I sold my wedding rings and cashed in a bond my aunt had left me years ago. I never told Chad about that bond, but I hung on to it for an emergency. That's how I can afford to hire you. In a year or so, I'll be a businesswoman just like you." Janie went out the door.

Blaine said, "God help us."

I turned and looked at my assistant. He was munching on a hash brown patty from McDonald's. "What's that supposed to mean?"

Blaine closed his car magazine and brushed crumbs off his blue work shirt that was reminiscent of his days as a mechanic. "Two of *you* in a town the size of Lake Elsinore? Next thing you know, we'll have more dead bodies than Chicago and LA combined."

I made a face at him. "Very funny." Okay, maybe I'd sort of tripped over a murder or two. I knew Blaine had heard every word Janie and I had said since my office was basically half of the front office divided by a cubicle wall that Blaine had installed. So he was making fun of my little side career of private investigating. "There won't be any dead bodies with this case."

Blaine leaned back in his chair. "Famous last words."

I drove my 1957 Thunderbird across town to the Stater Bros. shopping center. Chad Tuggle had his independent insurance office squished between the Stater Bros. grocery store and Rapid Dry Cleaners. As I got out of my car, I looked down at my short black skirt that covered most of my thighs. Over my silk black camisole I had on a man's white shirt tied at the waist. My calf-high black suede boots added a little fun to the outfit.

It had been a long time since I'd seen Chad. I was going on what Janie told me about him. Before I could think myself out of it, I walked up to the glass-fronted suite and pulled open the door.

Sophie, Chad's part-time secretary, was not at her small desk facing the door, so she had to be off today. Chad's big cherry wood desk took up the right half of the office. It was a three-sided unit, like a rectangle with one end left open. The big desk faced out to see people coming in the door. Chad's computer sat on the small part of the desk lined up against a partition wall that separated the front and back of the office suite. Then against the far right wall was a credenza that had fancy office machines on the left side. The right side of the credenza had a bunch of soccer trophies. The three huge gold cups on fat bases took center stage—the championship trophies.

I didn't recognize the set of stone bookends that had been cut and painted to resemble soccer balls. Those must be new, probably a gift from his latest championship team.

The wall over the credenza had pictures of Chad with his teams, winning and appreciation plaques, and framed newspaper articles. The championship-winning hero coach was not necessarily a humble coach.

And where was the not-so-humble coach?

"Sam—that you? I didn't know anyone was out here. What brings you by?"

The loud voice yanked me from my thoughts. I'd forgotten about Chad's tendency to talk loud. The years of yelling directions to kids in a soccer game over screaming, insane parents had left its mark. He came out from behind the divider wall carrying an "Everybody Loves the Coach" mug. Obviously Chad had been in the back getting some coffee in the little kitchenette behind the partition. "Chad, how are you? I just stopped by to chat about insurance if you're not busy."

"I'm never too busy for you, Sam. Come sit down and we'll catch up. Then we'll talk insurance."

Chad walked around his desk with an easy, athletic grace. He wore dark gray slacks, and a light blue short-sleeved button-down shirt and tie. His forearms were muscled and tanned. Lots of time outdoors. Instead of fighting premature balding, he cut what hair he had into a buzz. With his light green eyes, he didn't need hair. Hovering on the back end of his thirties, he kept himself in good shape.

Chad set down his coffee cup on his desk blotter then said, "Hey, how about some coffee? I just made it."

Sitting in the barrel chair facing the desk, I slid my purse to the ground and crossed my legs. My black skirt slid up. "Uh, not right now, thanks." I flashed him a smile, only to find him staring at my thighs.

Finally, his gaze climbed to my face. "So, Sam, how's business at the dating service?"

"Well," I took a deep breath and pulled the tied ends of my white blouse down. "It takes time to build a client base. Word of mouth is helping us grow. In fact, I'm looking at getting a new computer program for book-keeping."

"Really? What program do you use now?"

He was making this too easy. "Peach Tree."

"Yeah, that's good, but I like using the Excel work-sheet. Here let me show you." He turned in his chair and called up a computer program.

I leaned across his desk, getting a whiff of coffee and strong spearmint. Did he have a lifetime supply of Altoids in his desk drawer? I had to fight a twitching smile at the mental picture of Chad popping Altoids for that minty-fresh breath all bellowing coaches needed.

Or was it cheating coaches?

He turned his head. "Can you see from there? Come around and you can see better."

I got up and looked down at my purse. The disk was in there. But first I had to get him to pull up the soccer program and think of a way to get him to leave for a few minutes. Up to now it had been easier than I expected. Luck like that wouldn't hold for long. Leaving my purse on the floor, I walked around the desk and leaned over Chad's right shoulder.

"See, here's the program." He opened files and de-scribed the functions.

I only half listened while my mind spun. How could I get him to open the soccer books? *Think!* "Chad, can you keep accounts for two businesses on there? I mean like say your insurance business, then another enter-prise of some sort?"

He leaned back to look at me, accidentally brushing his face against my breasts.

Resisting the urge to jump back, I forced myself to smile at him. I don't remember Chad ever being this ag-gressively carnal. Guess I didn't measure up to his cop-a-feel standards back in my team mom days.

"Sure, I use the same program to keep the SCOLE books."

Bingo! "You do? Could I see that?"

He closed the files for his insurance records and opened the one for SCOLE while chatting away. "You know Sam, it might be fun for the two of us to go out to dinner sometime. Or maybe have drinks at Don Jose's. Hey, after dinner I could show you my new digital camera. We could do some test shots and I'll show you how it works . . . for your dating service. Or we could use my new camcorder. I even know how to download videos to the computer."

And I bet you'd bring your spearmint Altoids or whatever was seeping out from his desk. "I thought you were dating—" I couldn't think of her name. I could picture her—the soccer mom slut. Every team had one. The mom that came to every practice in short shorts and tank tops and schmoozed with the coach while the other moms sat in a lawn-chair circle and chatted. This one had succeeded in getting the coach away from his wife. What was her name? She had a belly-button ring, which was too daring even for me. "Dara." That was her name.

His neck turned red. "Sure we date, but it's not exclusive or anything. Janie told some pretty ugly lies about Dara and me. Ah, here's the files for SCOLE." They opened up on the screen.

Lies, my ass. But I had a job to do here. And I was going to need money to promote Heart Mates and pay my bills. Then there was Blaine's salary. Plus, I really wanted to help Janie get a little revenge. "Yes, I see. You're very good at this stuff. Did you take classes? Go to college?"

His shoulders puffed up. "I taught myself. I can teach you how to do this, Sam."

Liar, liar, pants on fire. I knew for a fact that Janie took night classes to learn about bookkeeping and this program when she had been the treasurer. She taught Chad. "That's awfully nice of you, Chad." I leaned closer, brushing against his shoulder to study the files while I tried to think of how to get him out of the office for a few minutes. Or at least in the back. I saw his cup of coffee sitting on his blotter. "You know, maybe I will have something to drink."

He tilted his head back. "Coffee?"

There was a doughnut shop across the parking lot. "Actually, I'd love some hot chocolate." Would he be dumb enough to run to the doughnut shop and get me hot chocolate?

"I have hot chocolate in the back. Won't take a minute to nuke some water and make it for you." He reached toward the keyboard.

I laid my hand on his bare forearm.

His gaze snapped up to mine.

"Could I look at this while you make the hot chocolate?" Would that give me enough time?

"Sure. Look all you want and I'll explain how to use the software when I come back." He got up from the chair.

There wasn't much room inside the three-sided desk. I backed up to the credenza. Chad brushed so close to me that his spicy cologne mixed with my passion fruit lotion.

"It sure is nice to see you again, Sam. We've missed you in the soccer circles." His gaze dropped down to my breasts. "You're looking good these days. Real good."

I wanted to throw a drool cloth over my bust. It was a struggle to arrange my face into a simpering expression. "Uh, yeah, you too, Chad."

His grin radiated self-assurance as he reached up to touch my hair. "So is it true, do blondes really have more fun?"

I hear better lines at my dating service. "They get more thirsty," I said pointedly, to get him to leave.

He turned and headed around the desk.

Relief spread through me, but I had no time to enjoy

it. Once Chad disappeared around the partition, I raced to my purse, dug out the disk and went back to the computer. I would make a copy of the SCOLE books and then leave before Chad got back out with the hot chocolate. I'd claim I got a call on my cell phone, or another excuse. Jamming the disk into the proper-sized hole, I guided the mouse through the clicks to save the file to the 'A' drive.

The computer groaned and hissed. A little rectangle graph popped up, slowly filling with blue as it saved to the disk.

The blue stretched to the quarter mark. "Come on," I begged. From the back, I heard a short slam, like a microwave door, then beeps as Chad set the timer to heat water for the hot chocolate.

The graph hit the halfway mark. I squirmed on the chair. "Faster."

"Hey Sam, did I tell you that Mark made JV on the soccer team at school?" Chad's loud voice carried over the room divider.

Three-quarters done. The microwave beeped and I heard the microwave door pulled open. *Answer him!* "That's terrific, Chad. Mark's a great kid and a talented soccer player." Almost there. The blue stripe hovered only a millimeter away from the finish line.

Clinks and other sounds came from the back, followed by Chad's voice. "I really think he'll get a college scholarship. I've hired him a private soccer coach."

The blue line filled up the rectangle. *Done!* I yanked the disk out and heard more movement from the back. Was Chad coming out? Damn, no time to get to my purse. I whirled around to the credenza and the slim disk flew out of my fingers. It clattered against the glass front of a team picture then landed on the credenza behind the fax machine.

Heat burned up my face and prickled under my arms. I heard Chad moving around, so he must still be doing something in the kitchen. I had seconds. I leaned over a machine to reach behind the fax and get the disk.

Just as my fingers closed around the disk I heard the whirring of a machine starting up.

Freezing, I thought, *What the hell was that?* But I had no time to worry about it. I shoved the disk into the built in bra of my black camisole. I had to get out of here.

But that noise kept going. A grinding. Suddenly I realized I was being pulled down.

The paper shredder! Ohmigod, the tied shirttails of my white top were caught in the shredder! The machine was eating my shirt! Full-blown panic blossomed into fight-or-flight. I grabbed the knot in my shirt and yanked.

The shredder wouldn't let go. It was set flush into the credenza and kept pulling me forward. Cripes, now what?

Wait, there had to be a cut-off switch. I leaned forward, looking around the face of the machine. I couldn't find a switch. And worse, the plastic disk in my bra was slipping.

The grinding noise began to sputter in anger. The knot! The shredder was sucking in the tied lump, fraction by fraction, separating it and consuming it. I had to get out of the shirt or the machine was going to yank me down into its grinding blades.

"Sam! What . . ."

I turned my head to see Chad materialize next to me, holding a can of whipped cream and looking confused. "It attacked me!"

His face cleared. "Hold on," he said, then crouched down and put a hand on my leg to move me over. He opened a cupboard door and reached inside.

The machine stopped.

I let out a huge breath in relief and did a little test tug on my shirt.

The silent shredder held on tight. I could see tears running up from the mangled knot like runs in a pair of pantyhose. The disk slipped a fraction more in my bra. I blinked and hysterical laughter tickled my throat. Oh yeah, some slick private investigator I was—exposed by a paper shredder!

Hmm, and I appeared to have a stray hand wandering up my thigh. I glared down at Chad, crouched by the cupboards, and asked, "Could you help me here? I need scissors." I was going to have to cut away the blouse. Then I might cut off his thigh-exploring hand.

Chad took his hand off my thigh and rolled up to his feet, still holding the can of whipped cream. He stepped out of my view. From the rummaging sound, I guessed he'd opened the drawer to his desk behind me and was looking for scissors. Returning to my side, he set the can of whipped cream down by the shredder. "Hold still and I'll cut you free." He moved behind me.

"Give me the scissors, I'll do it."

Chad put both arms around me. "Better let me do it, Sam," he said into my ear. "You got yourself into quite a fix here."

Considering the slipping disk in my bra and his position behind me with his chin over my left shoulder, I had to silently agree.

Chad maneuvered his hands so that his forearms brushed the undersides of my breasts while he positioned the scissors on the fraying shirt. "Little hard to see over your rack. Nice work, by the way. Love your new look."

Jeez! I needed a shower, and Chad Tuggle needed a soccer ball hard-kicked into his groin. Some men had the idea that because a woman did a little self-improvement, she was suddenly a warm, breathing sex toy to be handled at will. "Cut me free, Chad." My anger sliced my voice into a breathless quiver that probably had Chad thinking I was hot for him.

He cut me free, leaving my shirt hanging in shreds around my rib cage.

I turned around and looked up into his green eyes.

"Don't I get a thank-you kiss?"

Well, I had to give him credit. He could have said a thank-you grope. "Sure, Chad. Close your eyes."

He closed his eyes. His breathing accelerated and he actually licked his lips, leaving his mouth open.

I snapped up the can of whipped cream and depressed the plunger, filling him up like a soft-serve cone. God, it felt good. Revenge for Janie, and payback for groping me.

Sputtering and spewing whipped cream, he opened his eyes and wiped a handful of whipped cream off his face. "What the hell are you doing?"

"What the hell are *both* of you doing?"

I looked over to see Chad's girlfriend, Dara, standing stone-still in the doorway. Her straight, choppy auburn hair framed a tightly drawn mouth and flared nostrils. The little zip-up sweatshirt she forgot to wear a shirt under didn't cover the glittering gold belly-button ring winking above the waist of her hip-hugging pants. I saw Dara's huge blue-gray gaze move over my shredded shirt, then shift to Chad's whipped cream–filled face. "Dara—" I used my calm mom voice as I edged toward the door, meaning to say something inane about old friends.

But the virulent hate I saw burning in her blue-gray eyes snuffed out my words. I slipped by her and made my escape, leaving Chad to deal with Dara.

2

Hurrying from Chad's office to my car, I thought that Dara Reed might need some anger management classes. Getting into the T-bird, I glanced over to Chad's office but didn't see Chad or Dara through the glass front. Chad had probably gone into the kitchenette to wash off the whipped cream. I rescued the disk from my camisole bra and tucked it into my purse. Then I started up the car and headed back to my office. I wanted to check the disk before I called Janie.

When I got to work, Blaine glanced up at me as he talked into the phone, then jerked his gaze back to me. After saying a quick goodbye, he put the phone down and said, "What happened to you?"

"I got caught in a paper shredder." I rummaged in my purse and fished out the disk. "Pop this into your computer and let's see what's on it." I held the disk out over his desk.

"Paper shredder, huh?" He took the disk, then bent down and put it in his hard drive. "Probably a good thing we don't have a paper shredder here."

I rolled my eyes. "Ha ha. What do you see on the

disk?" *Please don't let me have screwed this up. Not after all that.*

"Files. Looks like—" he began clicking things open, "—yep, looks like you got the files for soccer. There's Fees Paid, Expenses—all the usual boring stuff."

Smiling, I went to the coffeemaker on the TV tray at the end of Blaine's desk and filled my heart-stamped mug. "I've had a productive morning, even if I did ruin my shirt." Dang, maybe I was better at private investigating than I thought. Now if Janie and I could find proof that Chad was embezzling, I'd talk to Gabe to clear everything under his PI license, and then we could go to the police. Once Janie paid me, I could put some money into Heart Mates. I needed a really good promotion idea.

"Your hair looks sticky."

"What do you mean, sticky?" Setting my filled cup down on the brown TV tray, I reached up to my shoulder-length hair. "Ugh." It did feel sticky. Not the tame-the-frizziness-gels sticky but whipped-cream sticky. Thick chunks of my curly hair had clumped together. "Blow-back."

"Sounds dirty."

I glared at Blaine. "From the whipped cream I shot at Chad."

Blaine leaned back in his chair. "You're crossing the line into kinky, boss."

"I could fire you."

Blaine glanced out the window, then back to me. "Who'd take care of your T?"

He had me there. Blaine loved my T-bird. I was pretty sure he could get another mechanic job if he wanted to, but he stuck it out with me at Heart Mates. Together, we were going to build Heart Mates into a chain. I'd be the Jenny Craig of dating services.

Except I'd never use Monica Lewinski as a spokesperson. Although, I have to admit, she'd attract attention, which would be promotion for Heart Mates. Give her a cigar and . . . *Good God, what was I thinking?* Trying to assume a professional tone of voice, I said, "Any clients call while I was gone?"

"Roxanne Gabor. She sounded upset. I put her file on your desk."

I sighed. "She had a date last night. I guess it didn't go well. I'll call her back. Anyone else call?"

Blaine grinned. "Your mother."

A sharp pain stabbed at my temple. "Did she say what she wanted?"

Blaine leaned over to his hard drive, popped out the disk, and handed it to me. Then he picked up a message slip and read, "Tell Samantha to keep the last week of January open." He looked up. "And I am to clear your schedule here at Heart Mates. I believe you will be taking a trip, but your mother didn't share the details with me."

Wavy lines appeared in front of my eyes to accompany the stabbing in my temple. We were in early January now. "She's up to something. Something real estate-ish." My mother was the Real Estate Queen of Lake Elsinore and the surrounding areas. I hated real estate, but my mother determinedly ignored that little detail and schemed to pull me out of the dating service business into the more respectable real estate profession.

A shiver rolled down my spine. No way was I going to let my mother kidnap me for a week of God-knows-what kind of real estate torture. "I might have to leave town."

"The boys are in school."

I took a deep breath. "Right, TJ and Joel hate missing school. Well, then, all I have to do is avoid my mother for the next three weeks or so."

"That's what I admire about you, Sam. You don't let anything scare you."

I picked up my coffee cup and took a sip. "I choose

my battles, and choosing to battle with my mother is just plain stupid. But feel free to pick a fight with her anytime you want. You'll end up owning a house that should have been condemned, but you go right ahead." I turned to go into my office, hoping to find another shirt tucked away in one of my desk drawers. I didn't know what I could do about my hair.

Shutting the door to my cubicle, I spotted Roxy's file on my desk. I sat down in my chair and leaned over to put my purse in the bottom left drawer of my desk. Darn, no spare shirt or jacket in there. I started looking through the remaining drawers when I heard the front door open out in the reception area.

A client? It wouldn't do for me to meet a client looking like a sticky, shredded mess. I shut the last drawer and frantically looked around the office, hoping Blaine would stall whoever it was.

"Go on, she's in her office."

I was going to kill Blaine. I didn't hear the newcomer's voice, so Blaine obviously recognized whoever it was. If it was my mother . . . I stared at the door as it opened.

Gabe Pulizzi filled the doorway. Over six feet tall and packing two hundred pounds of pure muscle. "Gabe! What are you doing here?" I stood up, my pulse going from passive to red-hot lust at the sight of him.

Gabe lifted a single dark, winged eyebrow over his nearly black eyes. "Having a rough day?"

Naturally, he looked good. Damn good. Tan pants and a black shirt outlined his athletic frame. Gabe never looked like he lost a battle with a shredder and a can of whipped cream. "I . . . uhh . . . What brings you here?" My relationship with Gabe was complicated.

Sex tended to complicate things.

Gabe grinned. "I brought a surprise for you."

Cool. Although I could never tell with Gabe. His last surprise had been showing up naked while I was in the bathtub. That had been a good surprise. I leaned toward him. "What is it?" Sexy thoughts swirled in my brain—thoughts of an early lunch at Gabe's house, preferably naked.

He took a step into my office and then turned to one side. "I brought my mom to meet you. We're taking you to lunch."

"What?" It came out as a shriek. His mother? The phone on my desk rang, but I ignored it to stare at the woman in my office doorway. She had beautiful olive skin and dark eyes that resembled Gabe's intense gaze. A little taller than me, her weight had settled into her middle like an apple shape, but she had on pretty soft green pants and a flowing top that flattered her.

Damn, my sexy lunch scenario hadn't included his mother. *God, his mother!*

Realizing my reaction was a little rude, I tried to pull myself together. "I mean, how wonderful! I am really surprised!" And absolutely mortified to meet his mother dressed like a middle-aged Britney Spears with whipped-cream hair gel. I wished for my stun gun so that I could stun some sense into a certain Italian stud standing in my office right now.

Blaine yelled over the cubicle wall, "Boss! Line one for you! Says it's urgent."

"Thanks." I said, grateful for the interruption. "Excuse me." Nodding to Gabe's mom, whose name I still didn't know, I picked up the phone. With a clipped, professional tone, I said, "Samantha Shaw, how may I help you?"

"Sam!"

I pulled the phone away from my ear, then returned it. "Chad?" Uh-oh. Did he know I copied the soccer books?

"Hey, listen, Sam. Things got a little confusing here and you left before we could finish up our business. How about having dinner with me tonight?"

My head felt like someone pulled open my skull and poured in hot needles. "Sorry, I'm busy."

"Oh. Well then, why don't I come by your house, say around eight? I'll bring dessert. *A whipped cream dessert.*"

This wasn't happening. I glanced at Gabe, then looked at his mother. *His mother!* This is how Gabe introduces me to his mother? Badass PI or not, I was going to clobber him. "Listen, Chad, now's not a good time for me. I have to go."

"Right. Then I'll be over to your house tonight at eight."

"No!" I closed my eyes and rubbed the burning throb between my eyebrows. Some of those hot needles were trying to burrow their way out of my skull.

"Ah, come on, Sam. You know you want me to come over."

I slammed the phone down.

"Babe, you seem a little stressed."

No shit. I ignored Gabe. However dumb he was probably wasn't his mother's fault. Nothing I could do now but brazen this situation out. Moving around my desk, I went past Gabe and held my hand out to his mother. "It's a pleasure to meet you. I'm sorry about the circumstances. I've had a . . ." I looked into her dark eyes, then noticed her smile. ". . . I'd like to say unusual morning. But it's pretty typical for me."

Gabe's mom took my hand in both of hers. "I'm Iris, and my son is an imbecile. I told him so on the way over here." She nodded her head, her grip firm on my hand.

I liked her already. Her warm, dry hand felt strong and confident. She smelled like green apples. How could I not like a woman that smelled like green apples? "He's a man. They're all imbeciles."

"So we'll go to lunch? And you'll tell me about your typical day that leaves your clothes in shreds?"

"Why not?" I stripped off the shredded white shirt,

and then looked down at my calf-high suede boots, short black skirt and barely-there black camisole. Without the white shirt, I had crossed over from hip dating executive to aging biker chick. Just the look I had hoped to impress my boyfriend's mother with. I threw the ruined shirt on my desk. God, I wished for a nice tailored jacket. And Tylenol. Forcing a smile, I opened my mouth to say I was ready when I heard the front door open out in the reception area, then a woman crying.

"Excuse me." I slipped between Gabe and his mom and stepped out to the reception area. I recognized the crying woman. "Roxy?"

She lifted her head, her side-parted dark blond hair falling into sleek straight lines around her full face. Her red-rimmed, puffy eyes stood out, marring her natural beauty. "Oh Sam! It's just awful. I . . ."

She must have caught sight of Gabe and his mother behind me. Her face froze.

"Roxy." I put my arm around her shoulders. Roxanne had five or six inches and fifty or so pounds on me. But she was like a child and let me guide her past Blaine toward the interview room. "Why don't you go sit inside there and I'll bring us some coffee." I reached out and opened the door to the sound proofed room. "I have to finish up some business and I'll be right in."

She walked in and headed for the oak table where I liked to interview clients. I pulled the door shut and turned around.

Gabe and his mother. God, this was some day. "Uh, look, I'm sorry about lunch, but I have to talk to Roxy."

Iris stared at the closed door. "That poor girl—isn't she that new model? The full-sized one that I've seen on the morning shows?"

I should have known Gabe's mom would be as observant as her son was. Fixing an overused smile on my face, I said, "Maybe we can do lunch tomorrow if you are still here?"

Iris smiled at me. "Don't you worry a bit about us. You just go find out what's wrong with your client. You have important work to do." She turned and started walking out the door, then looked back. "Come on, Gabe."

I stared at her retreating back. My experience with mothers, my mother in particular, told me that was too easy. What was Gabe's mother up to?

"Babe."

Gabe stepped up to stand an inch from me. I looked up into his dark eyes under winged brows. "I could smack you."

His mouth quirked up. "Yeah?"

"Stop that," I whispered, knowing full well that Blaine sat four feet away listening to every word. "I can't believe you dropped your mother on me like that!"

"I thought you'd want to meet her." He arched a single eyebrow. I'd only seen him use that look on me. It usually meant, *What the hell are you talking about?* Or, *what the hell have you done now?*

"Right. Every woman wants to meet her boyfriend's mother looking like a biker chick."

A lazy grin rolled over his face.

"Go away. Just go away." I could not believe he didn't get it.

He reached out, cupping his large hands around my bare shoulders. "Why don't we change the subject and you tell me what that phone call in your office was about?"

Every once in a while, I underestimated Gabe Pulizzi. He'd been a street cop in Los Angeles until a couple of bank robbers decided to start shooting citizens and Gabe caught a bullet in his knee. He'd retired and moved out to Lake Elsinore, opening Pulizzi's Security and Investigating Services. Gabe moved in a dangerous world with the ease of James Bond.

I sort of tumbled into trouble going grocery shopping.

I should have known that Gabe caught every word I said to Chad on the phone in my office. His radar told him something was going on. "That was Chad Tuggle. His ex-wife asked me to check into something so I went to his office today. He apparently got the wrong idea."

"That happens to you a lot."

Blaine snorted.

I turned to glare at my assistant, but he busied himself rearranging the clipboard interview sheets we used for new clients. Looking back at Gabe, I gave in and told him the whole story.

His gaze riveted on me while one hand rubbed a bare shoulder. "You want to do this, babe?"

"Yes."

"All right. But you report to me, got it? If this guy really is embezzling, he could be dangerous. You be careful."

That easy? It took my breath away how much Gabe believed in me. "Okay. But Gabe, I've known Chad for years. He's not dangerous."

"You weren't looking for anything that might threaten him then, Sam. Now you are."

Touché. "I see your point. Okay, I'll be careful."

His mouth curved, and he lifted a hand off my shoulder to touch my hair. "So that's whipped cream in your hair, huh? Only you could make it look sexy." He leaned down and kissed me. "Later."

I stood there watching him walk out of Heart Mates and to his truck where his mother waited. Did his mother know that I was five years older than Gabe, and had two sons? What would she think of that? And worse, what the heck was a thirty-something professional woman doing worrying about what her boyfriend's mother thinks?

"Boss, you have a client waiting."

I turned and looked at Blaine. "Right. I just have to make a quick call." I ran into my office and picked up the phone. While dialing Janie's phone number, I searched the top of my desk and found Roxy's file.

"Hello?"

"Janie, it's good you're home. I went to Chad's office and got the disk. When would be a good time to take a look at it?"

"You did it? Okay, well, I have to run back to work now, but how about after school? I'll get Mark and Kelly to their practices, then come by your house at four-thirty. How's that?"

"Four-thirty at my house is fine. See you then." I hung up and rushed back out to the reception room.

Blaine held out two filled coffee cups and a couple of packages of fake sweetener for Roxy. "What are you going to do about Roxanne?"

I took a sip of one of the coffees and pulled my thoughts together. Roxy was a full-sized beauty. A couple of years ago she got tired of the whole diet thing. She made herself over with regular workouts, a good haircut, nice makeup, and new clothes, then sent her portfolio into some agents. She now had a blossoming career as a model. But I was worried about her. Roxy was desperately seeking love. She was a successful, intelligent woman, as well as beautiful, but she was looking for something in a man that I couldn't pin down. It frustrated me.

Every date was a disaster that left her devastated. But her professional life was flawless.

I said, "I'll talk to her. She keeps picking pretty boys who want to date a model and show off."

Since my hands were full of the coffee cups and Roxy's file, Blaine silently opened the door for me. I went in, determined to help Roxy see that she didn't have to prove anything to the town by dating good-looking shallow guys.

Roxy was bent over a photo album. She looked up,

her eyes shining. "Sam! How about this guy? He's into sushi, designer clothes, and upscale restaurants."

I set down the coffees and file, and looked at the still shot picture. A groan choked up my throat. Damn, another pretty boy. "Roxy," I sat down and pushed her coffee and the sweeteners toward her. "Tell me what happened last night."

She picked up the sweetener and tore it open. "At first it was fine. We had a nice dinner and went to play miniature golf. He kept looking around, but I didn't think too much of it until he practically jumped on me."

I groaned.

She stirred the sugar in her coffee and wiped fresh tears away. "It turns out his friends bet him that he couldn't get a date with me. They were waiting at the end of the golf course for him to prove he could bag the fat model."

"Dammit." I concentrated on making notes on Roxy's file while fighting the raw anger rushing through me. The guy from last night was going to be removed from our list. I put down my pen and took Roxy's hand. "I'm so sorry, Roxy. You deserve better than that." I took a breath. "You know, Roxy, finding a man isn't like finding your career."

She smiled. "You mean I'm too aggressive?"

I shook my head. "God, no. I mean that you are a goal-oriented person, which works well in your professional life. But in love, it doesn't work that way. You can't just set a goal of finding a man who is compatible with you and expect it to happen on schedule. And you have to factor in your rising visibility from your modeling career."

She looked up. "Sam, that's why I chose to come to your dating service. I don't want anything to do with the users that LA breeds. I want to find someone to share my life with. Someone who will stay with me for the long haul."

"I know." Roxy never knew who her father was—we both had that in common. Then her mom had died when she was ten and she came to Lake Elsinore to live with her Uncle Duncan. Duncan adored Roxy, but her childhood had left its mark. I couldn't grasp why she gravitated to the upscale pretty boys. What was it? I kept trying to lead her to the solid men that would give her the love and security she wanted. "Look Roxy, why don't you let Blaine and me run some profiles while you take a break from dating, okay?"

Roxy looked back down at the photo album. "What about this Kevin? He looks smart, and he's a financial consultant."

He looked like he should be on a billboard for Calvin Klein underwear. "Roxy, a financial consultant might have ulterior motives with you. You make a lot of money now. Besides, it says here that he drives limos, too. I don't think the financial consultant thing is working out." I sure as hell wouldn't take financial advice from someone who drove limos.

Roxy's beautiful eyes sharpened. "Sam, you know better than that. I have an agent and financial advisors."

True. Roxy was sharp in her career. She was professional and never broke down in tears while on a shoot. It was her personal life that cut her to the heart. I didn't think this was the man for her. In my opinion, Kevin was a nice guy who simply lacked enough success of his own and emotional maturity to handle Roxy's success.

"Can you just see if he's interested in a date, Sam? I only have a week before my next shoot."

I sighed. "All right, I'll call him. When do you want to meet him?"

She smiled. "Tonight."

Blaine and I closed up the office a little after four. We had snagged Roxy a date for drinks with Kevin tonight and worked at redesigning Roxy's profile to run a new set of matches.

I waved at Blaine and got in my car, hoping he wouldn't do anything stupid. I'd seen the dark look in his normally placid brown eyes when I'd told him of Roxy's experience with her date last night.

By the time I got home, I was tired. Pulling into the dirt road at exactly four-thirty, I saw Janie's car parked next to Grandpa's Jeep. I had hoped for a few minutes to change clothes and settle down.

I walked through the empty living room to the small dining room, which was nestled into the corner at a right angle to the long kitchen. Grandpa and Janie were at the table drinking iced tea. I put my purse down. "Hi, Janie, sorry I'm late." I turned to Grandpa and kissed his balding head. "Hi, Grandpa. Where are the boys?"

He waved to the sliding glass window. "Playing with Ali."

I looked out to the backyard to see the boys and our big German shepherd. TJ and Joel were playing keep-away with Ali's tennis ball on the big round trampoline. Ali apparently thought this was a terrific game.

Grandpa got up. "Want some iced tea, Sam?" He moved into the kitchen. "Janie was telling me that she's hired you."

"I'd love some iced tea." I pulled out a chair and sat down, then watched Grandpa get down a glass and open the fridge to pull out the tea. It didn't surprise me that he'd gotten Janie to tell him what she was doing. Grandpa was a retired magician, a pro at getting people to do or believe what he wished them to.

Since retiring, he'd turned into a big gossip and an Internet junkie. The boys and I adored him. We'd moved in with Grandpa after Trent died and we'd found out we were broke.

Janie got my attention. "Sam, weren't you wearing another shirt this morning?"

I looked down at my camisole. I'd been so busy today that I'd forgotten about it. "Yes, I had a little accident." Standing up, I dug through my purse and found the disk. "Here's the disk of the SCOLE books. Let me go change and we'll take a look at it." I put the disk down on the table and hurried to my bedroom.

I traded my skirt for a pair of jeans, added a black sweater over the camisole, and dragged a quick brush through my hair. Then I rushed back out to the dining room.

Grandpa was at his computer on the big rolltop desk right next to the dining room table. Janie had pulled up a chair next to him. They had already opened up the disk.

Leaning over Janie at the computer, I saw the same files I'd seen at Chad's office. "So? Are you finding anything?"

Janie pulled a calculator out of her purse and swiftly started adding up columns.

Finally, she sighed and sat back in the chair. Her shoulders slumped beneath her pink sweatshirt. "It's all there."

Frowning, I stared at the computer over her shoulder. Disappointment warred with relief. I wanted to get this right. On the one hand, being involved in exposing the hero soccer coach as an embezzler was not going to make me the best-loved businesswoman in town. On the other hand, if Chad really was embezzling, he deserved to be exposed. But Janie had seemed so certain. And watching her work the numbers in the SCOLE files, I believed she knew what she was doing. "You sure? I mean, you seemed so certain Chad was embezzling."

Janie looked over her shoulder at me. "I'm sure it's all correct in the books, but I don't know if the money that's supposed to be in the bank account actually is. Chad can write down anything he wants in the books.

But is the money shown in the books really in the bank? No one ever questions Chad, you know."

Two things struck me at once. First, she was right— the money could be missing from the actual account. I hadn't thought of that. But the last comment struck me deeper. *No one ever questions Chad.*

Including Janie? Was Janie scared? Is that why she had come to me? Was Janie telling me the whole truth? Gabe had told me once that clients tended to only tell us what they think we needed to know. I'd learned the hard way that secrets can be dangerous. I sure didn't know anything about getting bank records. "Uh, Janie do you know if anyone else is on the account? Maybe someone we can trust?"

She shook her head, her gaze on the computer screen. "No, I think it's just Chad."

"But that's—"

She turned her head, looking over her shoulder at me. "No one questions him, Sam. He's the hero coach."

Jeez. "Okay, let me talk to Gabe. He might know a way to find out how much money is in the bank account." I didn't know what else to do. And Gabe had warned me to report to him. I wasn't about to try messing with a bank.

Grandpa broke in, "I could find out for you."

"No!" I said immediately. Grandpa belonged to a group called the Multinational Magic Makers, or the Triple M for short. They were a worldwide network of magicians, and through them, Grandpa often got access to inaccessible places.

Bent over the keys, he typed with amazing speed. Years of magic had kept his fingers limber. "I bet I can get in there within a few minutes."

"Grandpa! That's probably like a federal offense! The Secret Service once raided a school for making counterfeit money! Do you want to go to prison?"

He laughed. "No prison could hold me, Sammy! I can escape from anywhere."

God, Gabe would kill me. I was supposed to be conducting this investigation under his direction. Not breaking into bank records via the Internet.

"Got it!" Grandpa said. "All I need now is the account number."

Janie pointed to the account number she'd written down on the pad of paper and Grandpa typed it in.

We all waited, leaning forward to watch the screen. The account popped open.

"Well lookie here," Grandpa said.

We all stared at the balance for the SCOLE account.

Janie grabbed the calculator and did the math. Then she looked up at me. "There's sixteen thousand dollars missing!"

3

Dang, I was getting pretty good at this PI stuff. "Janie, I think we have him." We had proof that sixteen thousand dollars was missing from the SCOLE account, and Chad was the only one with access to that account.

Janie kept staring at the computer. She shook her head. "He was sure no one would check. Sure that he'd get away with it."

I looked down at her. Janie had reason to be bitter. While we had both been soccer moms, the difference between us was that Janie truly liked what she was doing. She enjoyed the organizing behind the scenes.

I hid there from a bad marriage. Somehow I thought I could make up to my sons for a dad that was never around by being a supermom.

Once I faced up to reality, I had fled the soccer-mom life without a look back. But for Janie, having that life ripped away from her had really hurt her. I knew how much of the real work Janie did behind the scenes, and when she was thrown out of soccer, Chad had simply found others to do the work and still make him look good. Then he stole money. And no one knew, or if they knew, they didn't care just as long as he kept bringing home the championships.

"Sam," Grandpa broke in, "you can't exactly walk into the police station with your stolen disk and hacked-in bank account."

"We could take it to the newspapers," Janie suggested.

We wouldn't have to tell them where we got the information. Still, I made a face at the idea of going to the papers. So far, my experience with the press hadn't been real encouraging. But I did know a certain cop I could probably take this to. He would get the right people on it. "I have an idea."

Grandpa picked the papers he had printed out of the tray and looked at me. "Vance?"

I smiled. Detective Logan Vance and I had a past. We tangled over another murder in town, but once I discovered Vance's secret life, which he didn't want any of his fellow cops to know about, I managed to get more cooperation from him. Vance didn't exactly like me, but he would listen.

Or shoot me.

But I was betting I could get him to listen and get an investigation started on Chad. "I'll stop by the station tomorrow morning and talk to him. I'll tell him that a client of mine has information that Chad Tuggle is embezzling from SCOLE."

"Really?" Janie brushed her hair off her face, her hazel eyes brightening with hope.

Nodding, I said, "I'll call Gabe and clear it with him tonight. Then after I see Vance in the morning, I'll call you, Janie. All right?"

"Thank you, Sam. Thank you for believing me." Janie stood, her face shifting into seriousness. "And Sam, be careful. Stay away from Chad, all right?"

A warning tickled the back of my throat and skittered down my spine. Gabe had warned me to be careful, too. But I knew Chad. I looked out the sliding glass door to where the boys were playing with Ali, then back to Janie. "Do you think Chad's dangerous?"

She took a breath. "Probably not. But he's just so sure he can do anything and get away with it."

Fair enough. I nodded and walked Janie to her car. When I came back inside, the kids were coming in the sliding glass door from the backyard.

"Mom, what was Janie doing here?" Joel bounced in with the gawky energy of twelve-year-olds who were all arms and legs.

TJ strolled in with Ali. "I told you, Mom's on a case." At fourteen, TJ pretty much knew everything. Then his handsome face tightened. "Ugh, Janie wasn't here for your dating service, was she?"

"Dating services are for losers," Joel announced. "Being a PI is much better. Gabe is mega cool."

Speaking of Gabe, I headed for the phone to call him about Janie's case. "TJ, what makes you think I'm on a case?"

TJ leaned his tall, slender frame back against the counter. " 'Cause you were all huddled with Grandpa on the computer."

I smiled at my smart son. "Pretty observant, TJ." Picking up the phone to call Gabe, I spotted Ali with her slim German shepherd nose pressed into the seam of the refrigerator.

"Some guard dog you are, you big lush." Gabe had brought Ali to us when we were being threatened a while back. Turns out she'd been tossed out of the police dog program for stealing beer. She'd also saved my life more than once. We all adored her.

Ali barked.

"Later, Ali." I dialed Gabe's number while trying to think up something resembling dinner in my mind. "How about grilled cheese for dinner?"

Joel looked up from the bag of potato chips he had

his hand in. "With fried potatoes? The kind Grandpa makes?"

Grandpa shut down his computer. "Joel, you wash the potatoes and I'll slice them."

Gabe's phone rang four times in my ear, and then the answering machine picked up. I wondered where he was. "Hey, it's me," I said into his machine. Then I did a quick outline of finding the money missing from the soccer account and told him I was going to see Vance in the morning to get an investigation started. Hanging up, I stared at the phone for a minute. Had he taken his mother somewhere?

And what did his mother think of me?

The morning brought rain. Fat drops beat down on the windshield of my T-bird as I headed to the sheriff's station on my way to work. Gabe hadn't called me back last night, which probably meant he was okay with what I was doing.

At least, that was the theory I was going with this morning.

To the beat of the rain, I planned what I'd say to Detective Vance. Something like, *I have a client with direct knowledge of Chad Tuggle embezzling from SCOLE.* Yeah, that sounded . . . I snapped my head around to look through the rain at the doughnut shop on the edge of the Stater Bros. shopping center.

There was a green Ford Taurus covered in antennas. Detective Vance's car.

I pulled the T-bird into the double-yellow center divider and put my left blinker on. Vance was at the doughnut shop. This would be so much easier than trying to get him at the sheriff's station. When the traffic cleared, I turned in and parked my car next to the green Taurus.

I got out, pulled the hood of my long black raincoat up, and dashed for the door. Inside the doughnut shop was warm and yeasty.

Vance sat at the four-topped table made with twin rectangles hooked together and four chairs set into the unit. He had his little red notebook in front of him and a tired frown on his face.

When he looked up and saw me, his frown deepened. "Shaw. Just when I thought my day couldn't get any worse."

Not exactly the opening I was hoping for. "Morning, Vance. What are you doing here?" He had a large coffee but no doughnuts.

"It's a doughnut shop, I'm a cop. Where else would I be?"

Slipping off my raincoat, I made a face at him. "Get up on the wrong side of the bed, Vance?" Without an invitation, I tossed my coat on the chair closest to the window overlooking the street and sat down across from him. The smell of all those lovely doughnuts made my mouth water. I detected the scent of chocolate swirling above the yeast smell. What could one little chocolate buttermilk doughnut hurt? I looked down. I had on low-cut jeans and a tight red top with gathers at the bust line. One doughnut and I'd have a roll over the top of my jeans. Damn.

Vance snapped his notebook shut, picked up his coffee, and leaned back in the seat to study me.

I tried not to squirm and studied Vance right back. His sun-god looks were a little wilted. His close-cut sandy blond hair lay flat. No dimples decorated his square face, and his swimmer shoulders were slumped as if he were tired. I thought about asking him if he were all right, then decided to just get it over with. "I have something to ask you."

"Really?" He pulled the lid off his coffee and drank a good quarter of the large cup.

"I have this client."

His gaze met mine over the rim of his cup. "A dating service client?"

"Not exactly," I said, eyeing his coffee and thinking I should get some. "Anyway, she has information on her ex-husband. We know it's true, but we don't have any evidence. I need you to start an investigation."

"You working for the sheriff's office now? Giving orders?"

Lord, he was in a bad mood. "Look, Vance, this is serious. This guy has been embezzling money from the Soccer Club of Lake Elsinore. It's called SCOLE for short. That means he's stealing money from all the parents who pay fees for their kids to play. It's not right."

Vance snapped forward in his chair and thumped his coffee down. "That right? And who is this client of yours?"

"Uh, that's confidential. Will you look into this for me?"

His light brown eyes sharpened, ripping away the tired look. "What's the name of this ex-husband?"

Suddenly I had a bad feeling. A really bad feeling. My stomach got a hot pain, like a stone from a fire pit fell in there. Sweat prickled my back and underarms. Vance wasn't reacting like I expected. He was a robbery/homicide detective. I'd thought for sure he'd tell me to file a report or something. I hadn't even used my knowledge of his secret life to pressure him. "Vance, what's going on?"

"Shaw, what's the name of the ex-husband embezzling money?"

I knew I'd stepped in it. Somehow, I was in over my head. "Uh, it's Chad Tuggle. He's the head coach for SCOLE. He's sort of a hero in town." I stopped talking. Vance's face hardened.

"Well, now he's sort of dead."

"Dead?" The hot stone rolled in my gut, churning the cup of coffee and yogurt I'd had for breakfast. "But he can't be dead, I just . . ." *Shut up!* I screamed in my head.

"You just what?" He lowered his voice to a seductively smooth coaxing tone.

I'd just walked into a disaster, that's what I'd done. Damn. "Uh, look, you're obviously having a bad morning. Look at you," I stood up, "you're tired. Probably you were up all night with this—" My words froze when Vance grabbed my wrist.

"Sit. Down."

I sat. My brain wasn't working properly, so obeying was easier than arguing.

"I want to know everything. I've already talked to Dara, and she told me all about your spat with Chad. Were you and Chad dating?"

"What? You know better than that. I'm dating Gabe."

"Then why were you in Chad's office yesterday morning?" Vance pulled out a Bic pen and flipped open his notebook. "Start from the beginning."

I couldn't even grasp Chad being dead. Blinking, I tried to think. Dead. And Vance is a homicide cop. "Chad was murdered? Where?" Suddenly, the doughnut shop heated, and I had trouble taking a full breath. Tiny black spots danced in front of my eyes. Chad's office was a diagonal line across the parking lot. Vance was here. "Oh, Lord." I leaned forward, putting my hands flat on the cool, smooth surface of the table. "Was he murdered in his office?"

"Hmm, you seem to have a lot of knowledge for not even knowing he was dead." He wrote in the notebook.

"Stop it!" The words echoed in the shop. There were no other customers, but the little TV the owners watched in the back went silent. Great, my trauma was better than what was on TV.

And what about Chad? Yeah, sure, he wasn't a shining example of manhood, but dead? He didn't deserve to be dead.

"So Janie Tuggle came to you about her ex-husband. Why? She had evidence that Chad was stealing from SCOLE? Or just suspicions? Is that why you went to his office yesterday?"

God, what did I do? "I, uh, have you told Janie yet?"

"She's next." For a second, Vance's eyes lost focus and drifted out the window.

The dutiful, factual Vance was stalling. Any other time, I'd call him on it. But not for this. I couldn't blame him for not wanting to tell Janie her ex-husband was dead. And the kids! Mark and Kelly would be devastated. "Wait," I had another thought. "You said Dara already told you I saw Chad yesterday. So you notified his girlfriend, but not his ex-wife and kids?"

Vance pulled his lips thin. "She found him, Shaw. Last night around ten. He wasn't at home, so Dara went by work and found him." His whole face grimaced. "It wasn't pretty."

I closed my eyes. "How?"

"Looks like he had his head bashed in with something heavy."

I couldn't answer. Instead I concentrated on breathing and trying to still the nausea. "I'll go with you to tell Janie."

"First, you tell me what you were doing in Chad's office yesterday. I want all of it."

The way this worked, whenever I did a little investigation, it was under Gabe's license, so technically, Janie was a client of Pulizzi's Security and Investigations. There were rules and confidentiality stuff. "Tell you what, let me follow you to Janie's and I'll explain it there." Which would give me a chance to call Gabe on my cell from the car.

"No. Now." He stared at me.

With no way out, I told him part of the truth. I could fill in the rest later. "I went there to talk about insurance and we got to talking about bookkeeping software. Chad showed me his software for his insurance agency."

"Go on." He lifted his gaze from his notebook and waved his hand at me.

"That's it, really."

"Not what Dara says, Shaw."

The vision of Dara walking in right after I'd been caught in the paper shredder, then zapped Chad with the whipped cream, slammed into my head. This was not a good thing. "My blouse got caught in Chad's paper shredder while Chad was in the little kitchen making me hot chocolate. He ran out holding the whipped cream. He helped me get out of the machine and he got the impression that I was . . . *available.* I sprayed him with whipped cream."

Vance stared into my eyes, then slowly lowered his gaze. "Well, I wonder how he got that impression."

I wished I'd left my raincoat on. My red blouse was pretty low cut. Even tired, Vance looked good. His shimmery gray dress shirt was rolled up over his tanned forearms, but that made him look boat-casual, not cheesy or sloppy. I wondered if Vance thought he was better than I was. I lifted my chin. "He never tried that stuff when I was a soccer mom for his teams. Men are dogs. Just because I've updated my look doesn't mean I want every mouth-breathing male groping me."

"Maybe you weren't advertising the goods then, Shaw."

God, why did men think it was all about them? I changed the subject. "Are we done?"

"I couldn't get that lucky. Now tell me what you going to Chad's office has to do with Janie coming to you about Chad embezzling? What information does Janie have exactly?"

"Janie didn't have any evidence. Just that Chad had money to do things for the kids, but hadn't even paid her off for the house yet after the divorce. Janie lives in a trailer. It was just conjecture and I was going to check into it for her. I went to Chad's office to sort of re-establish contact with him."

"So you really didn't want insurance?"

I stared at his coffee. "Can't afford it."

"Fine," he snapped the notebook shut. "Let's go get this over with." He stood up.

I looked at him, surprised. "You believe me?"

He looked down at me. "Not a chance."

While Vance explained to Janie the procedure of holding Chad's body until they had all the evidence they needed, I held Janie's hand and focused on the small living room of her mobile home. The gold carpet and fake wood paneling faded into the background with bright floral throw pillows, baskets of silk flowers, and a couple of pretty blanket throws. The old nineteen-inch TV set had framed pictures of the kids on top. Janie had painted a cheap wicker hope chest a clean white with green scalloped trim, then topped it with scented candles and books to use as a coffee table. I admired Janie's talent of making the run-down mobile home feel cozy and inviting.

Vance's voice cut through my thoughts. "I have a few standard questions."

I looked at Vance sitting across from Janie and me in a white wicker chair with a cushion that matched the green couch. His tone hardened just enough to put me on guard.

He asked Janie, "When was the last time you saw Chad?"

"I guess that'd be when he dropped Mark and Kelly off Sunday morning."

"Okay, today is Thursday, so that's four days ago." He made a note. "Do you know of anyone Chad might have had problems with? Anyone who might harm him?"

Silence.

I looked at Janie.

She shook her head. "You mean someone who would kill Chad? No. Sure, there were rivalries with other cities over the soccer championship and stuff. But no one would kill him."

"Mrs. Tuggle, how long have you and your ex-husband been divorced?" Vance shifted his gaze around the mobile home. "I mean, it must be pretty hard for you now, trying to make it."

I snapped my head up. What the hell was Vance doing?

Janie answered in a soft voice. "We've been divorced about a year."

Vance wrote something in his notebook then looked up. "Now about paperwork . . . Do you know if Chad had life insurance or that sort of thing?"

"Yes, he did."

I was surprised at that. Since Chad had let the health insurance on the kids lapse, it seemed odd that he would keep paying on life insurance.

"Right. So do you know who the beneficiary of his life insurance policy is?"

Uh-oh. I didn't like where these questions were going.

"I am the beneficiary, Detective, since the kids are minors. We've had the policy for years."

"I see. And Chad kept paying the premiums after the divorce?"

She hesitated. Her fingers twitched in my hand. Finally, Janie said, "We split it. Sometimes he paid, sometimes I did."

"Sounds reasonable. Can you get me a copy of the policy today?"

"Uh," Janie looked around, as if she just woke up and wasn't sure where she was. "Yeah, I guess so."

Vance stood up. "You've been very helpful, Mrs. Tuggle. I appreciate it. And I'm sorry about your ex-husband."

Janie and I got up and followed Vance to the door.

Vance turned to look at me. "I need to talk to you, Shaw."

"Janie, I'll be right back," I slipped outside with Vance and pulled the door closed behind me. We stood on the porch covered in green indoor/outdoor carpet. The metal overhang protected us from the rain. Turning to Vance, I said, "What was that little show all about? You can't think Janie killed Chad!"

"You're not asking the questions here, Shaw. What exactly did you and Chad talk about yesterday?"

Vance was like a bulldog. "Just what I told you. We talked about bookkeeping programs, he told me Mark made the JV soccer team at school—stuff like that."

His gaze flicked over me. "I don't think so. First, you told me that Janie thought Chad was embezzling from the soccer club, and now you are talking about bookkeeping programs. Using logic," he paused, one side of his mouth kicking up just enough to flash a dimple, "which I know is completely foreign to you, I think the two are connected. I saw all the soccer trophies and other stuff related to soccer in Chad's office, Shaw. How accurate would I be if I hypothesized that the soccer books for the soccer club were on Chad's work computer?"

Damned accurate. Since I had a firm policy against incriminating myself—and I'm pretty sure that copying the soccer disks might be slightly less than legal—I tried a little straight denial. "I don't know anything about Chad's murder, Vance. Except that I didn't do it. And Janie didn't do it."

Vance regarded me for a long minute. Then he nodded once and said, "Stay out of my investigation, Shaw. I'm going to solve this case by the book, and I don't want to be tripping over you and your disasters. I'll be in touch." At the bottom of the steps, he turned back, "Oh, don't leave town, Shaw."

That did it. "Hey, Vance, wasn't that a line from one of your books? Your *romance* books?"

His shoulders stiffened and he whirled around, marching back up the steps.

Suddenly, I had a picture of myself stuffed into the back of a police cruiser.

Vance leaned in so that his face hovered an inch from mine. "If I hear one word, one *letter,* of a rumor that I'm a romance writer, I'll haul your ass in so fast you won't have time to say *lawyer.*" He took a breath. "And then I'll lose you in the system. It'll be at least a week before you're found, and by then, I'll have some serious charges to file against you."

He smelled of faint coconut mixed with rain and powerful anger. But I knew better than to back down in front of Vance. I'd reviewed a lot of cop-hero romance books. Those books were well researched—I knew cops. They had a thing about authority and control. Backing down was a mistake that would make me look weak in Vance's cop eyes.

I forced my gaze to stay steady on his. "Don't give me a reason to mention your secret life, Vance. I have a client to protect, to say nothing of myself."

His jaw twitched. His too-tight voice made me think of a guitar string ready to snap. "The more time I spend with you, the more I think Chad Tuggle picked up a rock and bashed himself in the head just to get away from you." He turned and stomped off toward his antenna-growing car.

"Sam?"

Whirling around, I prayed Janie hadn't heard that. But the door was still opening as she called my name. I don't think she heard. "What?"

"Uh, your cell phone was ringing in your purse, so I answered it." She held the small black unit out to me.

"Thanks." I reached for the phone, wondering what disaster this would be. "Hello?"

"Sam," Blaine said, "we have a new client. He's here right now and waiting for you."

"Uh, I'm kind of busy. Can't you do the interview?" Normally I liked to do the client interview so I could get a feel for the client. But I was in extraordinary circumstances right now.

"He's really counting on you doing it, boss. Oh, and Roxy Gabor's been trying to get a hold of you this morning. I couldn't make out what she was saying."

"Was she crying?"

"More like wailing."

I pictured Blaine's grimace when he said that. "Any idea what happened with Roxy?"

His voice softened a bit. "No, she wouldn't talk to me." Then his tone went back to brisk. "Nor will Mr. Davis who is waiting for you."

Heart Mates was my business and my baby. I needed to get to work. But Janie . . . I looked over at her. "I'll be there as soon as I can, Blaine. Give Mr. Davis some coffee and have him fill out the interview sheets while he waits."

"Gee, why didn't I think of that?" Blaine hung up.

I sighed and went back into the mobile home to get my purse. Janie stood looking at the pictures on top of the TV. Kelly, the older of her two kids, was in her cheerleader outfit, and Mark was in his soccer uniform. "Janie, I'm so sorry."

Lifting her gaze to me, she said, "I can't believe he's dead. Chad has always been bigger than life and everything always just slid off of him. Nothing ever stuck."

I thought of Chad taking up with Dara Reed and dumping Janie, and the whole town ignoring Janie.

Yeah, she was right. But we had a bigger problem. "Janie, you paid the life insurance, didn't you? Just like you did the health insurance."

She sort of caved in on herself. "Yes. And until Chad's murder is solved, the insurance won't pay." Taking a breath, she said, "Sam, you have to find who killed Chad. I'll pay your fee, whatever it takes. The kids and I, we need this solved. For more than just the insurance." She shifted her gaze to the photos of the kids. "We have to know what happened."

She wanted to know if the woman who took her husband killed him. Dara Reed. I got that. Janie needed to know who her ex-husband, the man she'd had two kids with, really was.

Why did so many of us women wait until it was too late to find that out?

I assured Janie that I'd help her and left. With my raincoat on and the car keys in my hand, I put my head down and headed into the rain toward my car, across the narrow street from Janie's mobile home. Not only had I promised to help Janie find who killed Chad, but it also sounded like I had a couple of problems waiting for me at work. At least the money I'd get from Janie for this case would help me improve and promote Heart Mates.

I looked up just before I ran into Gabe.

He leaned against the driver's side of my car, rain pouring over him. His arms were crossed over his worn denim jacket. The water ran down his granite face, plastering his dark hair to his head. "Gabe? What are you doing?" I looked around. His black truck was parked behind my car. Why was he standing in the rain?

He uncrossed his arms and pushed off the car. "We need to talk."

A dozen questions buzzed in my head. How'd he know where I was? Why was he standing in the pouring rain? If he tracked me to Janie's, why didn't he come to the door? Did he know about Chad Tuggle? Where was his mother? "What's wrong?"

"Unless I miss my guess, I'd bet my house you just told Janie that you'd look into Chad's murder."

That answered a couple of questions. "Well, I was going to talk to you about that."

His dark troubled gaze fixed on me. "No."

"What? You can't just say no." Well, he could since he owned Pulizzi's Security and Investigative Services, and since he had the license. "Gabe, Janie needs me."

"Here's the deal. I signed a client last night connected with Chad. I can't have you out investigating under my license unless we agree to do this together so there's no conflict of interest."

More questions answered. That was why he hadn't come to Janie's door, since he obviously didn't want to discuss this in front of her. The need to get to work pressed down on me. I had a client waiting, and another one who was upset. "Who's the client you signed on?"

Gabe pinned me with his gaze. "Dara Reed."

It felt like a gut punch. "The soccer mom slut? Have you lost your mind? She probably killed Chad!" Okay, I might be leaping to conclusions, but Gabe had to have checked Dara out. He was a damn good PI. He had to know that she broke up Chad and Janie's marriage. And she had walked in on Chad and me right after I'd whipped creamed him. She wouldn't be the first jealous girlfriend to kill a man.

Gabe sighed. He pushed his straight, wet hair back with his right hand. "Then you're out of it."

"Just like that?" All kinds of feelings collided inside, twisting around like life-squeezing pythons. I trusted Gabe. I did.

He turned and headed toward his truck. Yanking open the cab door, he looked at me. "Just like that."

4

I walked into Heart Mates and shrugged off my coat. It dripped all over the industrial gray carpet, leaving wet splotches that turned the color to the ever-popular soot shade. Looking around, I wondered where the client was and where I should put my coat. Rain always caught people in Southern California by surprise.

"Interview room," Blaine held out the clipboard with the information and security authorization sheets attached. "Nice of you to drop by. Want me to change our name to Heart Mates Private Investigations?"

I draped my coat over a folding metal chair and turned back to my sarcastic assistant. "Good morning to you, too." I took the clipboard, determined not to think about Gabe. All the lines were filled in with big thick printing. "Lionel Davis?" I looked up at Blaine.

"That's him. Waiting to speak to you, and only you."

I narrowed my eyes. "What's the matter with him?" I whispered, running my eye down the information sheet. Worked as some sort of biochemical tech at a big corporation in Temecula. That screamed nerdy scientist to me, but that's what Heart Mates was for—to help those who might not be adept at romance on their own.

So why was Blaine smirking at me?

"I didn't do the interview, boss. He's waiting for you—that is if you're not too busy, you know, nosing around someone's life until they end up murdered."

I slammed the clipboard down on Blaine's desk. The loud thwack felt good. "You got a problem with me, Blaine?" Okay, I was pissed. First Vance, then Gabe, now Blaine. What was it with all the men in Lake Elsinore today?

Looking up from the clipboard, Blaine leaned back in his chair. "Roxanne Gabor is a mess. I could barely understand her. She wouldn't tell me what's wrong, wouldn't tell me where she was. She just *cried*. Then Romeo comes in and insists on talking to you. No, I don't have a problem with you, but maybe your clients do. Maybe they need you and you're too busy trying to be Super Sleuth to worry about them."

Ouch. "Okay, I get it." He was right. Blaine liked car engines. He understood them, and if they broke, he knew how to fix them. Crying women weren't that easy. You couldn't just feed them oil and tweak a part. Our deal was that Blaine dealt with difficult clients who got physical and I dealt with difficult clients who got weepy.

Trying to gather some dignity, I picked up the clipboard. "I'll be in the interview room with—" I looked down at the information sheet—"Mr. Davis." I walked around Blaine's desk and paused at the door to the interview room. Just to prove I was doing my job, I said, "Pull the file on Roxy's date last night. I'll call her as soon as I'm finished with this client." I opened the door and slipped inside.

Oh, boy. An overgrown cowboy, complete with a little string tie, sat at the oval oak table and fiddled with a palm-sized spray bottle of some kind. Pasting on my businesswoman smile, I strode forward and held out my hand. "Hello, Mr. Davis, I am—"

He jumped up. "Samantha Shaw!" The spray bottle

slid across the table and plopped onto the carpet at my feet.

"Oh! Sorry about that!" He came around the table.

"No problem." I bent over to pick up the little bottle and smacked heads with Mr. Davis. "Ouch!"

"Ooof!"

Forgetting the spray bottle, I slapped my hand over the right side of my forehead and stood up. Stars flashed over the romantic travel posters on the walls. It took me a few seconds to blink away the weird pops of distorting light.

Then I noticed blood pouring from big boy cowboy's nose. "Oh! Mr. Davis!" I looked around for something to staunch the bleeding.

Oh, crap, was his nose broken? Hysteria pounded at my headache. All the blood made me think of Chad with his head bashed in. I hadn't actually seen him, but my imagination vividly filled in the blanks. Closing my eyes, I struggled to breathe. The interview room felt hot, the air heavy.

Get a hold of yourself! I had a bleeding client. I'd seen worse than this with my own kids. Opening my eyes, I saw Mr. Davis just standing there. Quickly, I ran over to Blaine's cameras at the far end of the long interview room and grabbed a blue sheet he used to drape the stool. Rushing back, I shoved it under Mr. Davis's nose. "I'm so sorry!"

He had to be about five eleven or six foot, with the build of a teddy bear. A teddy bear dressed up as a cowboy. White shirt with black ribbing tucked into jeans over his cuddly middle and some shit-kickin' boots. Probably some kinda snake or crocodile hide. He looked down at me with teddy-bear eyes. "No, it was all my fault. You got a lump on your head."

I touched the spot directly over my right eyebrow and winced. That'd be colorful. Sighing, I said, "Mr. Davis—"

"Lionel." He put his hand over my hand holding the blue sheet up to his nose.

"Right." Taking my hand away, I let him hold the sheet to his nose and stepped back. Something crunched and squished under the heel of my boot. Lifting my foot, I looked down. Instead of leaning over, I did a deep knee bend that tested the seams of my jeans to pick up the item.

Nose spray. Dear God, we'd practically traded brains for a bottle of nose spray. Looking up at Lionel, I said, "Do you have a cold?"

"Allergies."

I suspected his nasal tone was from his nosebleed. "Why don't you sit down, Lionel, and let's see if we can get your nose to stop bleeding. Do you think it's broken?" Did I have insurance to cover this kind of thing?

He sank down in the chair, still holding the sheet to his nose. I set the nose spray down on the table. "Here, let me take a look." TJ and Joel had regular nosebleeds. I pulled back the sheet. The bleeding had stopped. His nose didn't really look swollen. "I don't think it's broken."

"You smell good."

Huh? I glanced at his soft eyes. Lord, I hoped he didn't have a concussion. "Uh, Lionel, listen could I get you some coffee? Or maybe some ice for your nose?"

"Nah, my nose is just sensitive. My doctor says it's all the nose spray, but I have to use the nose spray. I can't breathe if I don't, and I have to breathe to line dance."

"Line dance?" Maybe I had the concussion, because I was having a hell of a time following this conversation. I went to the door to the little storage area and tiny bathroom behind the interview room. Pulling open the door, I tossed the bloody sheet in. I'd take it home and wash it tonight or whenever I remembered. "You line dance?"

He fidgeted with the nose spray. "I have awards. I dance a lot in contests. When I go to bars, women gather around and ask me to teach them to line dance."

Blinking, I wondered why the heck I was standing here talking about line dancing with a teddy-bear cowboy. Roxy was desperate and miserable. Janie was desperate and miserable. This guy was . . . well, weird. Nice weird, but still weird. And let's be realistic—if women gathered around and asked him to teach them to dance, why would he be at a dating service? I sat down across from Lionel and picked up the clipboard. "Why don't I tell you a little bit about our dating packages? We have the basic package that—"

Lionel held up a blood-smeared hand. "I already paid Blaine for the Temecula wine tasting dating package. I thought you'd probably like that. I've read all about you in the newspapers, so I guessed you'd like wine tasting."

Blaine's smirk flashed before my eyes. I didn't know what was going on with Lionel, but Blaine did.

And he thought it was funny.

Oh, boy.

I studied Lionel. He'd gone red around the ears, either from the head banging, embarrassment, or he had romantic feelings about me. Sheesh—he knew about me from the newspapers? Sure, why not fall in love with a woman he only read about in the newspapers? This could only get better, since I'd been in the newspapers from my tendency to stumble onto dead bodies.

Blaine was so dead.

Deep breath, I told myself and tried for my most brisk and professional voice. "Lionel, it doesn't matter what kind of dates I like. You should choose a package that will fit the type of entertainment best suited to you and the date you choose." *Which won't be me,* I added silently.

"I choose you." A huge smile slathered across his face.

I dropped the clipboard onto the table. *Whoa, cowboy!* "Uh, Lionel, I'm afraid there's been a mix-up. You see, I own Heart Mates. I can't date the clients." But I can fire my assistant.

His big brown teddy-bear gaze shone with hurt. "I'm only your client so that you can get to know me." He dropped his gaze to the table where he was twirling the crunched bottle of nose spray. "Ladies don't always take the time to get to know me. Sure, they'll dance with me, but . . ." he trailed off, then stood and scooped up his nose spray to tuck it in his shirt pocket. "I just have to prove to you how much you need me." He walked out the door.

I grabbed the clipboard and scrambled up after him. "Lionel, I don't date clients!"

Lionel stopped by Blaine's desk. "You sure she likes the wine tasting package the best?"

Blaine looked up from the ranch dressing he was dipping his French fries in. "Oh, yeah, Sam loves wine tasting. Don't tell me she's playing hard to get?"

"Blaine, you know I already have a boyfriend." My voice sounded reasonable, but visions of the pepper spray on my key ring danced in my head. I could feel my finger depressing the nozzle and zapping Blaine.

Lionel whipped his head around to look at me, his soft face spilling into surprise. "What kind of boyfriend?"

"Uh—" After Gabe's stunt this morning of ordering me off Janie's case, our relationship was a little murky. But I was kind of desperate here. I lifted my chin and announced, "A detective."

A focused intelligence solidified in his gaze. "Police detective?"

This wasn't going as well as I hoped. "Private."

"Ah."

I closed the distance between us and glared up into Lionel's brown-bear eyes. "What exactly does that mean?"

Lionel smiled. "That's how I found out about you— the newspapers. You're always in danger. But you won't need a PI to protect you. I'll do it." He used his big hand to thump his chest. Then he turned around and left.

I stared after him while Blaine burst out laughing.

Putting my hands on my jean-clad hips, I said, "You think that's funny? Have I ever sicced a client on you? Don't think I won't!" I turned to stomp away into my office, when I remembered Roxy. Turning back, I tried to look like an intimidating boss. "I need that file on Roxy's date."

Blaine held out a few sheets of paper. "I printed it from the electronic file. You could pull it up yourself on the computer. Nice shiner on your forehead."

Setting the clipboard down on Blaine's desk, I touched the mushy lump. "It shows, huh?"

"Right through your frizzy bangs." He jiggled the papers in his hand.

I took them and huffed off toward my office.

"Boss, what about the security check? Want me to fax this to Gabe?"

Gabe did routine background checks on all our new clients. That was how I met him. I'd hired him right out of the Yellow Pages. Right now I was in the mood to smack him with said Yellow Pages. Stalking back to Blaine's desk, I held out my free hand. "Give it to me."

Blaine took the security release form out from under the interview/info sheet on the clipboard and handed it to me.

I took the security sheet and went into my office. Settling into my desk, I leafed through the pages of Roxy's date. I summoned up Kevin in my head. Nice guy, young and brash—frankly, I couldn't see him doing what her last date had.

I picked up the phone and dialed Roxy's number at the home she shared with her uncle. No one answered. Cutting the connection, I looked at Kevin's file and dialed his phone number. Maybe he could tell me something. Getting the answering machine, I left a brief message telling him that I was doing a follow-up review of his date with Roxanne Gabor. "At Heart Mates, we periodically check with our clients to make sure we are providing the quality of matches to make our clients happy. I'd really like to hear back from you, Kevin." I hung up.

Now what? Looking under Kevin's file, I found Roxy's. Flipping through it, I found her cell phone number and dialed. When she answered, she was out of breath and whispery. "Hello?"

It sounded like I'd caught her in the middle of a rousing round of sex. "Uh, Roxy? It's Sam. Blaine said you called."

"Sam. Uh, I'm looking for something right now. I have to go."

"Wait! Roxy, at least tell me how your date went last night." Hmm. Kevin hadn't answered his phone—maybe they were together right now. But then why would she have called Blaine crying?

Her breath caught. "Why did he do it? Why?"

"Roxy?" My hand tightened on the handset of the phone. She wasn't crying now. She sounded desperate. "You mean Kevin? Look Roxy, whatever has happened we can fix it, okay? Where are you? I'll come to you." A crying Roxy I understood. This almost robotic, whispery, distracted Roxy scared me.

Silence, then, "Can't talk now."

"Don't hang up!" I yelled in frustration.

I heard her sniffle. Then she said, "Meet me at the nursery. I'm almost done here." She hung up.

I set the phone down. Something weird was going on with Roxy. But meeting her at her uncle's nursery made me feel better. Roxy loved plants and flowers. She had worked at Duncan's Nursery just up the street from Heart Mates since she came to live with her uncle. I really liked and admired Roxy. I wanted to help her find someone to love.

I dug my purse out of my desk and went out to the reception area. Before I could say anything to Blaine, the front door opened.

Grandpa and Ali came in.

"Grandpa, what are you doing here? Are the boys okay?"

Ali strolled up to me for a quick hello, which meant I was allowed to pet her for about five seconds. Then she jumped up to put her front paws on the edge of Blaine's desk to stare at him.

He stared back.

Ali barked.

Blaine opened his desk drawer and pulled out a box of animal crackers that he kept especially for her. He tossed her one at a time.

My dog had her people well trained.

Grandpa laughed, then turned to me. "I forgot I had the exterminators coming, Sam. Remember the ants? And tomorrow night is that party you are doing for Angel."

"The lingerie party!" I hadn't forgotten, exactly. My best friend was starting a new career in mail-order lingerie. I was hosting her premiere party.

"I have story hour at the library. I don't want to leave Ali home while the house is being sprayed. Is it okay if she stays here with you? I'll pick her up when story hour is over."

Grandpa was a favorite of the town children. He did magic tricks and made balloon animals when he read stories. I wasn't sure who loved it more, Grandpa or the children. "Sure, Grandpa. Ali can go with me over to Duncan's Nursery to talk to Roxy." Ali was never a problem.

Grandpa went past Ali, still perched with her paws on Blaine's desk, to the TV tray with coffee. He poured himself half a cup and said, "What's up with Roxy, Sam?"

"Dating disaster."

He shook his head. "Duncan just adored that girl

from the second he brought her back to Elsinore. She's his only family since his sister died. Roxy's the best thing that ever happened to Duncan."

I smiled. Roxy had it tough with no dad and her mom dying, but having someone love her so much healed the deep wounds, or at least helped her cope with the wounds. "Maybe that's it, Grandpa. Maybe no man can live up to Duncan for Roxy. I sure don't know any man who could ever live up to you."

"Sure, Sammy, you really lowered your standards with Gabe." He kissed me as he walked past. "Gotta go. Those kids don't like to be kept waiting." He carried his coffee out the door.

"Grandpa, you be careful driving with that coffee."

In the doorway he turned back and grinned. "I'm a magician. I can make it disappear." Then he drank it all and held out the empty cup.

I went to get the Styrofoam cup. "You're a riot, Grandpa," I said as I watched him walk across the wet pavement to his black jeep.

I went to the folding chairs and picked up my coat.

"Boss, Ali can stay here," Blaine said.

Ali got down from the desk and went to the door.

I looked at Blaine and shrugged. "She likes to go in the car. She can come with me."

He waved us off. "I'm entering Lionel's information in the computer. Can't do more than that until Gabe clears the security check. See ya."

Gabe. Ouch, that was a sore spot. "Right, I have the form in my purse. I'll get it to him soon." Ali and I left.

In the T-bird, Ali sat up on the red passenger seat, with her head hanging out the opened window. She loved it in the summer when I took the hardtop off and we zoomed around town topless. But on a rainy January day, Ali made do with the opened window.

Heading right on Mission Trail, we made it to Duncan's Nursery in a few minutes. I made a left into the dirt parking lot, shut off the car, grabbed my purse, and got out. Ali jumped out after me. I figured enough time had passed that Roxy would be here by now, but I didn't see her black Jaguar.

Ali dropped her nose to the muddy parking lot and sniffed around. Her ears twitched. So many scents. Wagging her long tail, she got busy chasing down the smells.

I spotted Duncan Baird. He was a slim rectangular man who looked like he should be out on the range breaking ponies. Right now, he was lifting heavy bags of manure into the back of a Toyota pickup with the easy grace of a man who lived his life outdoors in the sun.

I leaned against the side of the car and watched Ali. She raced back and forth across the parking lot, and then she spotted a few birds that had ventured out now that the rain had stopped. She barked and chased them into a row of trees lined up in ten-gallon cans. Water dropped from the leaves onto her nose. She stopped and sneezed, then shook her head.

I laughed at her. She was having a blast. God, I loved that dog. She was so well behaved that we hardly even thought to take a leash with us anywhere. Now Ali was sniffing along the edge, between the parking lot and the plants. Long railroad ties marked it off. Ali wandered up toward the trailer office when she froze.

Uh-oh. I pushed off the car and started toward her. I'd seen that intent look before. It usually meant she found something important. Maybe a hurt kitten or a nest of baby birds. Or a snake . . . Wait, it was the wrong time of year for snakes. I felt one of my boots sink in the mud and stopped. These were suede boots, not meant for mud walking.

"Sam, what can I do for you today?"

I jumped and turned to look into Duncan's craggy face. "How are you, Duncan?"

His peeling lips twitched in a smile as he looked down to my boots. "Can't complain. We needed the rain. And my boots are waterproof."

"Waterproof never crossed my mind when I shopped for these." I lifted a foot to show him my black suede boots. We both looked down to see the brown ooze staining the delicate suede. Damn. Setting my foot down, I said, "Is Roxy here yet? She told me to meet her here."

"Roxy? No I haven't seen her. But I need her to call back that computer guy. Can't make heads or tails of what he's saying."

"She's probably on her way. What's wrong with your computer?" Roxy had dragged Duncan into the computer age. She worked with some computer techie to get everything at the nursery computerized. Duncan had enough basic knowledge to work the system, but he turned glitches and problems over to his niece. I could relate to that. Computers and I don't exactly communicate.

"Can't get the customer receipts to print—" His gaze slipped past me. "Hey! Get out of there!"

I whirled around in time to see Ali jump up on one of the three plastic trash cans set out by the trailer office. "Ali!"

The trash can went over, and the lid popped off. Ali barked and started digging through the rubble.

I forgot about my boots and ran across the mud, anchoring my purse underneath my right arm. "Ali, no!"

She ignored me, digging through plastic bags, newspapers, dead leaves, and other assorted junk. I got to her, slid to a stop and grabbed Ali's black collar with silver studs. "Ali!"

At eighty pounds of pure muscle, my one hundred and twenty-nine-and-a-half pounds of not enough exercise barely caught her notice. She kept digging and barking.

"Get that dog out of here!" Duncan roared from behind me.

I had both hands on her collar. "I've never seen her like this! I don't know what's gotten into her!" I yanked hard on her collar. My purse slipped down my arm, but I focused on my dog. "Ali, come—ugh!" My feet slid out from under me and I landed on my butt.

In a pile of trash. Slimy, wet trash.

Duncan closed one big hand around Ali's collar and pulled her back.

She growled.

Getting on my knees, I turned around to face my dog. "No, Ali!" I couldn't believe she would bite Duncan, but I didn't want to chance it. She wasn't looking at Duncan, though. Her long nose and intelligent eyes focused on that trash can.

Weird. While Duncan held her collar, I got up, grabbed my purse off the ground, and slung it over my shoulder, then piled the trash back into the can.

She didn't like that, alternating between whining and barking. I put the lid back on the can and did the only thing I could think of—dragged it into the trailer office, then shut the door.

I went back out to my dog. Getting down on one knee, I took her face in my hand. "What has gotten into you?"

Duncan let go of her collar. "Get that dog out of here."

I looked up at him. "I'm sorry, Duncan. But you know Ali, she's never done anything like this before." I thought he was overreacting.

"I don't have time to take care of your dog, Sam. Roxy's not here, and I have work to do."

I knew an invitation to leave when I heard one. Besides, I was worried about Ali. She never acted that way without a reason. I stood up. "Look, Duncan, I'm concerned about Roxy. She's acting awfully emotional, even for her. Have her call me when she gets here. Please." I took Ali's collar and went to the car.

Blaine was going to have a fit when he saw all the mud Ali and I tracked into the car. My boots were toast. Fortunately, my purse had landed on top of the trash pile, not in the mud. I set it down on the floor of the passenger side.

And what the hell was wrong with my dog? What was in that trash can that she wanted so badly? Driving on Mission Trail toward work, I looked over at Ali. She was curled up on the seat, her sad eyes watching me. "What, Ali? What am I missing?"

My cell phone rang. Watching the wet road, I leaned across to the floor in front of Ali's seat and pulled my cell out of my purse. "Hello?"

"Sam, it's me."

"Angel, what's up?" My mind was on Ali, not my best friend.

"I'm at Mom's shop. I think you'd better get over here right away."

"Now's not a good time, Angel. I'm—"

"Sophie Muffley is here, Sam. She's getting her hair done. And she's telling everyone who will listen not to talk to you about Chad Tuggle's murder."

5

I dropped Ali off at work, then shot up Railroad Canyon and turned right at the Cocoa's restaurant on Casino Drive. I went past the Sizzler and made a left into the pink stucco strip mall.

None of this made sense. Sophie was Chad's part-time secretary at his insurance office. Her husband was the president of the soccer club. No one was tighter with Chad. So why the hell would Sophie tell people at Angel's mom's beauty shop not to help me find out who killed Chad? Knowing Sophie, I was surprised she wasn't in Detective Vance's face insisting that he find the killer immediately.

I parked in front of Glam4Less, then remembered that I'd fallen into a pile of trash in the muddy parking lot. Crap. And here I was at a beauty shop full of women.

I got out of the car and grabbed my long raincoat from the back. I solved the problem by slipping that on. I knew how to improvise.

Inside, the smell of peroxide and perm solutions was tossed around by busy blow-dryers. The noise level rivaled my house when Grandpa and the boys turned on wrestling. On my left was the counter with the booking receptionist. Angel sat there on a high stool admiring her freshly painted nails.

They were black with colored sparkles. Cool. I wasn't quite sure what I thought about the black tips in her waist-length red hair. "New look?"

Angel lifted her vivid green eyes. "For my premiere party. Tempt-an-Angel Lingerie is all about sexy fun. I needed a new look."

It was a burden to overlook my best friend's long-legged beauty, but I was up to the challenge. "You and your lingerie will be a hit." No matter what else happened, I was determined to pull this party off for Angel. We had a girlfriend pact about finding our careers and men. I found my career—okay, maybe I wasn't a success just yet—but I wanted Angel to find her career, too.

Men were another problem altogether. I wasn't sure that telling Angel about Gabe's stunt this morning was a good idea. Sure, Gabe was a tough guy right off the streets of LA, but Angel was in a class by herself.

I focused on why I came running over here. "So what's the story?" I asked, glancing around behind me. The shampoo bowls were nestled in the back right corner of the shop, and behind there was the back room for employees. The front of the shop had the hair stations. The manicurists worked next to the receptionist station. The shop had a black-and-white Fifties look to it. Framed posters from TV shows like *I Love Lucy*, and movies like *Grease*, decorated the walls.

"Sophie Muffley, over there at Mom's station, heard Joanna telling Mom that Janie cancelled her nail appointment this morning."

I looked over at Angel's mom. She was easy to spot, with Lucy Ricardo red hair that was teased on top with a flip at her shoulders. Trixie wore her usual—overalls paired with a busy printed T-shirt, and tennis shoes that had glitter and sequins glued on them. She looked up in the mirror at me and waved with her scissor hand.

I waved back.

That's when Sophie Muffley, sitting in Trixie's chair beneath a black cape, caught sight of me. Sophie and I had worked many, many soccer functions together. In her late fifties, her kids were grown and she was a career volunteer. Her awards were numerous—local clubs and newspapers had honored her. If I had a dime for all her acceptance speeches about how she gave up her career—and she never exactly said what that career was— to dedicate her life to children, I would be rich.

Trixie worked the foot latch on the chair to lower it. Sophie got up, stripped off the black cape, and turned her gaze on me.

My arms itched. More than once, I'd been browbeaten by Sophie into doing back-breaking jobs. But I was now a professional woman. I could stand up to Sophie.

She stalked over to stand two feet from me. Her narrowed gaze ran down my length, taking in my raincoat and mud-spattered boots. "Samantha Shaw, how dare you pass yourself off as a private detective to poor Janie Tuggle! Now you come sailing in here dressed like a female Columbo?"

I blinked. Female Columbo? Oh, my raincoat. Sheesh. No way was I telling her the real reason I had on the raincoat. "Sophie, this is a raincoat. It was raining this morning. And I never lied to Janie." Not exactly. I never told Janie I was a private detective. I just wanted to help her. I looked around the shop. The two ladies getting their acrylic nails filed stared at me. A lady under the hair dryer turned it off. Blow-dryers went off. Everyone froze.

And stared at me.

Sophie lifted her chin. She kept herself ruthlessly thin, which made her face slightly pointed. Attractive enough, but severe. When dry, her hair was blond and styled close to her head. "Janie Tuggle told Joanna that you are investigating Chad's death. I'm warning you, Sam. Stay out of this, or I will be forced to take this matter to the police."

One of us had inhaled too many fumes. I didn't think it was me. Sophie was a hundred-and-twenty-pound bulldozer, but she wasn't crazy. So what was going on? "Sophie, I work for Pulizzi Security and Investigations part-time." Remembering the scene with Gabe this morning, I wasn't so sure about that. But I could help Janie as a private citizen with no pay. That was legal, and I would do it if necessary. "But I never told Janie that I had a license myself."

"You implied it. Janie is one of ours, and I don't want you getting her into trouble. She needs friends now, not trouble."

Anger shot up from my gut right to my mouth. "Right. And you stood by her when you threw Janie off the SCOLE board. Took away the books. Protected Chad. What friends." Fury roiled in my chest. They had abandoned Janie when Chad took up with Dara. Now they claim her? What was that about?

Sophie ran her long thin fingers through her wet hair. "You don't understand. There are things we have to do for the good of the soccer club and the kids. Can't you get that? You used to understand. What happened to you?"

That was a clever trick and one that cooled my anger. Sophie was skilled at turning everything she wanted into "for the kids," then asking me why I didn't care about the kids. So what did she want, exactly? Sucking in a breath to bring down my heart rate, I studied her. She did look tired, upset. The truth was that Sophie had suffered a horrible shock this morning. She was close to Chad. Both as his part-time employee and through soccer. Hell, her husband, Jay, was the president, and Chad

had been the head coach. They ran SCOLE. I tried another tactic. "Look, Sophie, I'm so sorry about Chad. This has to be awful for you and Jay."

Her thin shoulders beneath her silk print shirt relaxed. "Yes, it's awful. Of course, Rick Mesa will step in for Chad as head coach, but Chad will be missed."

Shocked, I said, "You already talked to Rick?" Rick was Chad's best friend and assistant coach.

She nodded.

That seemed kind of premature. Sophie couldn't have known for more than a couple of hours that Chad was dead. I thought about it. Maybe this had to do with the missing money from the soccer account? "What are you going to do about the soccer books? Is there someone else who can take that over for Chad?"

Sophie looked blank. "Uh, I don't know. What difference does it make?"

Interesting. She talked to Rick about stepping into the head coach position, but she wasn't worried about the books. So did she know there was sixteen thousand missing from the account? "I was just thinking that Janie could help out."

Her face hardened. "Sam, stay out of it. I mean it. You aren't going to make this tragedy into one of your newspaper headlines." She turned and stalked back to her chair.

I blinked and looked at Angel.

She picked up her purse behind the counter and followed me out into the parking lot. "You know, Sam, I get the feeling that Sophie cares more about keeping you out of Chad's murder investigation than finding out who killed him."

A gazillion thoughts raced through my head. Sophie had already talked to Rick Mesa this morning, and they were trying to get Janie under control. I recognized that Sophie more or less pulled rank to stop people from Lake Elsinore's soccer world from talking to me. And I'd bet money Janie didn't know about it. Sophie was controlling things. Why? I looked at Angel. "They are closing ranks around Chad and his death for some reason."

"What do you think she meant by the newspaper headline crack?"

We were standing out on the sidewalk in front of Angel's mom's shop. I looked around the parking lot. "I think she's hiding something. Maybe the missing soccer money? Maybe they don't want anyone to know Chad stole money from SCOLE because it would look bad."

Angel's green eyes glittered. "He stole money?"

Quickly, I caught her up, from finding the money missing from the soccer account last night, then finding out this morning that Chad had been murdered. I ended with Gabe tossing me off the case.

"No shit? Gabe's taking this Dara's side over you?"

I winced and looked away, out to the cars scattered around the parking lot. Leave it to Angel to cut to the chase. "Guess so."

Angel didn't let me off the hook. "Uh-huh. And what are you going to do about that? What do you think Dara wants with Gabe? Besides his hunk of a bod?"

Bile rose up the back of my throat. I couldn't control Gabe or what he wanted. If he wanted Dara the slut . . . I brought my hand up to rub my face. "I'm going to help Janie find out who murdered Chad. Given Sophie's reaction, I'm more determined to help Janie. I'm not going to let Sophie and SCOLE run over her like they did when Chad dumped her. But—" I turned and faced Angel, "—Gabe preached at me about being partners, but he didn't trust me enough to tell me what Dara wanted."

She tilted her head. "Confidentiality?"

I took my coat off. I didn't need it to cover my butt in the car. "It wouldn't be a problem if he trusted me, would it?"

Angel looked past me and said, "How about we put a

tracking device on Gabe's truck? Then we could see what he's up to."

"Angel!" Laughing in spite of my rotten day, I said, "Stalking your ex-husband is one thing. He couldn't find a tracking device if you painted big red arrows pointing the way. But Gabe would find it in no time. Then he'd kill me."

She shifted her stare back to me. "Guess we'll find out." She grinned.

Uh-oh. Now I heard the engine. I looked back over my shoulder and both of us watched the big black truck slide to a stop next to my T-Bird. Gabe jumped out of the cab and shot toward us. The passenger door opened, and for a minute I thought maybe it was Dara.

Then I saw the dark-haired, apple-shaped woman get out. Gabe's mom, Iris.

"Sam," Angel whispered, already digging through her expensive leather purse. "Keep them busy while I get this on his truck."

I stared at the doohickey in her hand. "No!"

Gabe's voice slammed into me from behind. "Sam, what are you doing here?"

Shifting my gaze from Angel and the thing she held in her hand, I turned to look at Gabe. His black hair fell straight over his broad forehead. The brown gaze he fastened on me darkened even while I watched. Flared nostrils and a tight jaw radiated anger. Shit. "Uh, well," *Lie!* "I need to get a manicure."

He arched one brow. "Looks like you are coming out, not going in."

Oh, hell. "I forgot . . . something. What are you doing here?"

"He's taking me to the beauty parlor," Iris said, as she strode up beside him. "I understand this shop is the best in town."

I forced my gaze to stay on Gabe and his mom even though I knew Angel was putting a tracking device on his truck. Angel had all kinds of tracking equipment she used to torment the man dumb enough to leave her for a manicurist named Brandi. My fearless best friend was trying to help me, in her own twisted way.

Gabe's mom started turning her head toward Angel putting the device on Gabe's truck. "Iris!"

She turned back to me, her brown eyes wide.

I started babbling, while hugging my coat to my chest. "Oh, yes! This is the best beauty shop in town. Ask for Trixie. She owns it, and she's my best friend's mom."

"I'll do that."

Gabe took a step closer. "How did you get that bruise on your forehead?"

I reached up and winced when I touched the lump. "An accident with a client this morning."

"One of Heart Mate's clients, or were you out snooping around under my license?"

Gabe's mom stared at me. Anger thrummed around my other raw emotions. I was getting damned tired of accusations from people. Why was he challenging me in front of his mother? I tilted my chin up. "A Heart Mates client." Taking a breath, I caught a glimpse of Angel's head popping up over the back end of Gabe's truck. To keep his attention on me and away from Angel, I said, "I'm not investigating under your license." Yet.

Gabe stepped closer and caught hold of my arm. "The mud all over your ass says differently."

Cripes, I'd forgotten about that. With my coat off, Gabe and his mom had full view of my dirty butt from my fall in the trash and mud while struggling with Ali. Unfortunately, getting involved with a case usually meant ruining clothes, and Gabe knew it. But this time, my mud-covered butt had nothing to do with the case. "Ha!" I tried to pull my arm from his hold, but that was useless. "I was at Duncan's Nursery looking for Roxy, *my client*. But Ali took it into her head to get into Duncan's trash can. I slid on the mud fighting with her."

Gabe's mouth twitched. "So you were putting your ass on the line for your client?"

Embarrassment climbed up my neck to splash all over my face. I jerked on my arm.

Gabe let go.

I overbalanced and almost fell backward, but Gabe caught me by wrapping both his hands around my upper arms. "Easy, Sam—" the rest of his words were lost in the revving of an engine. With Gabe's hands still on my upper arms, all three of us turned to find the source of the noise.

A tan Ford extended-cab truck sprang out of a parking space by the street, squealed toward us, and skidded to a halt behind my car and Gabe's truck.

Lionel Davis threw open the cab door and jumped out, grabbed something out of the bed of the truck, and ran toward us up on the sidewalk.

"Let her go!" He waved something in the air.

Oh, God—he had a tire iron! He waved it madly as he plowed between Gabe's truck and my car, straight at us.

"Christ." Gabe let me go, whirled around into a crouch, and launched himself, hitting Lionel hard in his gut. They both flew down on the blacktop between the cars. The tire iron clanged down on the sidewalk where Gabe tossed it. Then he flipped Lionel over on his stomach, yanked a pair of handcuffs out from the small of his back beneath his jean jacket, and cuffed him.

I stared at it all with my mouth hanging open. Then I heard the murmur of voices behind me and turned around. The entire beauty shop had come outside to see what happened. I heard Sophie say, "It's always trouble around her." I turned back.

With his knee in Lionel's back, Gabe looked up me. "Let me guess. He's your accident-prone client from Heart Mates."

"Uh, yeah." Lord, could I look any more ridiculous in front of Gabe's mom? In my best professional voice, I added, "I have the release form in my car for you to run a security check."

"He failed." Gabe stood and pulled Lionel up with him.

Lionel lifted his gaze to me. "Samantha, are you okay? Did I get here in time? I saw him attack you!"

Attack me? Gabe? "Lionel, what are you doing here?"

"I followed you. To protect you. Been watching you since you pulled into the parking lot after going to that nursery." His big brown eyes were wide with sincerity. His nose dripped blood onto his white shirt to mix with the oil smears from the blacktop.

"You followed me? Are you nuts?" No, really, I just wanted to know. Was he a lunatic? 'Cause I collect lunatics. Swear to God. Other women collect jewelry, purses, Cabbage Patch dolls. Me? I collect lunatics.

"I'm not nuts. After leaving your office this morning, I heard about the murder that happened last night. Seeing as how you're always in the paper involved with murders and all, I decided to protect you. Once we start dating, I can protect you all the time." He stopped talking and wiped his nose on the shoulder of his shirt. His cuffed hands clanked together.

I didn't know what to say to that.

Apparently Gabe did, though. He was laughing.

"Stop that!" I ordered him. Embarrassment blew hot through my body.

He laughed harder. Bent over with his hands on his well-cut thighs, he roared with hilarity.

I glanced over at the tire iron on the sidewalk. If I picked it up and whacked Gabe, he'd stop laughing. I was not going to be laughed at—especially in front of my boyfriend's mother.

But Iris got to the tire iron first. She picked it up off the ground, stood over her son and banged the tire iron in her hand. "Gabe Pulizzi, I didn't raise my sons to be disrespectful."

Gabe stopped laughing.

Now there was a woman I could admire. Turning to Gabe, I glared at him. "Uncuff Lionel."

His dark gaze flashed. "Let the cops deal with him, Sam."

With his mom watching? I didn't think so. First, I wanted to show her I was capable. Second, I really think that from Lionel's point of view—he did see Gabe grab my arm, let go, then grab me again—it looked like I was in trouble. While I knew I was in no physical danger and that Gabe had grabbed me to keep me from falling, I suppose Lionel could have misinterpreted what he saw. "He's *my* client. Uncuff him."

Gabe sighed and pulled out a small silver key. He undid the cuffs while his mom walked over and tossed the tire iron into the bed of Lionel's truck

"Go home, Lionel. We'll talk later. I'm really not sure that Heart Mates is the right place for you."

"But . . ." He threw up both arms, looking teddy-bear sincere.

I was tired. This case was confusing as hell, my boyfriend was trying to push me out, and Angel had reappeared with a insane smile that promised bad things for me. On top of that, I had a missing, hysterical client and a dog acting weird. How many disasters did I have to deal with at once? I started with Lionel. Putting my no-nonsense mom stare in place, I said, "Go home. Now!"

Wiping his nose with his arm, Lionel shuffled over to his truck. He got in, took out his nose spray and did a few nasal whiffs, then put the idling truck in gear and drove away.

I looked at Trixie, Sophie, and the rest of the women staring at Gabe. Not Lionel, not me, Gabe. Like he was some kind of scrumptious chocolate snack. My temper crackled. "Show's over."

"All right, ladies, let's go back to work." Trixie shepherded everyone back inside.

Iris touched my arm. "Samantha, Gabe says you have two sons."

Uh-oh. I was a mom. I knew that look. She was worried about her son dating me. But would she pick right here in the parking lot in front of a beauty salon to tell me I was all wrong for her son?

Why not? Lionel picked here to prove his love.

"Yes, TJ and Joel." I didn't know what else to say.

Iris pulled her shiny black vinyl purse off her arm and undid the clasp. "We can't have you getting hurt then. Here—" she pulled out an object—"take my gun."

"Gun!" I shouted, then clamped both my hands over my mouth and looked around. These days, screaming *gun* was a lot like screaming *fire*. Instant panic.

"Cool!" Angel materialized between Iris and me.

Gabe caught Iris's hand. "Mom, put that away."

"Yeah, Sam's afraid of guns," Angel whispered, like it was shameful.

I looked at Gabe. "Your mother carries a gun?"

"I was all the kids had left," Iris answered, "after their father was killed. I wasn't about to let some thug leave my children orphans."

That I could relate to. "Iris, I can take care of my sons. I'm not going to leave them orphans." Gabe's father was killed? I knew he'd died young but . . . God, he never told me anything. I wondered: was that why Gabe had become a cop instead of a firefighter, like his dad was? His brothers became firefighters, too. He has one sister, who is a paramedic.

Iris seemed to consider that. "Well if you need a gun—"

"Do not give Sam a gun!" Gabe hissed.

I glared at him. "Stop making decisions for me."

His jaw twitched, and I saw a lump forming on his right temple. Gabe looked at Angel. "Will you take my mom inside? Mom, this is Angel." He waved his hand to introduce the two women. Then to his mom, he went on, "Call me on the cell when you're done. I'll pick you up."

Angel grinned her thousand-watt smile. "Hi, Iris, your son is quite a hunk." Their voices faded as they entered the shop.

I looked at Gabe. "You never told me your father was killed."

"My father was killed. Feel better?"

I stared at him. "You're a little testy today."

His jaw twitched. "Sam, you are in over your head. This case isn't just about some small-town embezzling now. It's murder."

"Yeah? Well, thanks to your client's version of my meeting with Chad yesterday, now Vance considers me a suspect." Gabe had once told me that the police had their own agenda and I'd better look out for my sons and myself. I wasn't going to tell him about Janie and the insurance on Chad. We weren't sharing that kind of information.

Gabe narrowed his gaze. "Vance is blowing smoke to get you to cooperate with him."

Gee, his concern and caring were overwhelming. "I'm not backing down. Sure, I won't get paid, but Janie's my friend. And something about this thing smells. Bad." I tilted my head up and dared him to argue.

Gabe folded his arms across his chest. "I offered you a deal this morning."

We were at a standoff. Both of us were stubborn as hell and putting our respective clients first. Janie might not be an actual client, but it was important to me to help her. It was important to me to make a difference in Lake Elsinore. "Tell me what's up with Dara first."

His gaze stayed on me. Cars whipped by. Blow-dryers turned on and off. Female chatter floated out the door. And Gabe didn't move. "You can't do it without me, babe."

"Is that a challenge?" I hated that Gabe didn't trust me enough to just tell me. He expected me to trust him that much.

His face hardened. "It's a fact. Go ahead, Sam. Try to solve this without my help." He turned and headed for his truck.

I glared at his back. "I will!" I didn't want to acknowledge the anger and fear rocketing through my blood. Once Gabe had fought to save me; now it seemed he was off saving another woman.

He wrenched open the cab door, then looked back at me. "You can try, sugar."

6

That was the second time today Gabe got the last word.

Then drove off.

I stomped to my T-bird and got in. I needed a plan. Gabe Pulizzi was not going to win; I was not going to fail. I pulled my cell phone out of my purse and dialed Janie's number. When she answered, I kept my eye on the beauty shop and said, "Janie, it's Sam. Did you talk to Sophie Muffley yet?"

"No. What's going on, Sam?"

I explained Sophie telling everyone in the beauty shop not to talk to me, and accusing me of misleading Janie. "You know I'm not a licensed private detective, right, Janie?"

"Yes, I know. But I want you to find who killed Chad, Sam. Sophie and them, they are part of the problem with Chad. They let him get away with whatever he wanted as long as he brought home the championship for SCOLE. I knew you'd be different."

I could hear the desperate anger in her voice, but I wasn't sure at whom the anger was directed. Once, I'd been angry at all the people I'd thought had been my friends in soccer and the PTA who never told me about my husband's hobby of women. But eventually I understood whom I was really angry at—myself. I had the feeling Janie was in that same place. "Okay, Janie. I've actually got an idea of how to get started. But I want you to be prepared. Sophie and some others may try to pressure you to leave things alone."

"You think they are hiding something? Like they knew Chad was embezzling?"

"Could be. Are you up to it?" I heard her breathing for a few seconds.

"I have to be. Yes, I'm up to it. Sam, what do I do about that detective? Should I give him the paperwork on Chad's insurance?"

I bit my bottom lip, thinking. Gabe would know the answer to that. I figured it would be best to go strictly honest. The thing about Vance was that he was a by-the-book guy. If I found evidence that led him away from Janie, he would follow the evidence. "Give him a copy of the policy when he asks again, but don't volunteer anything."

"Okay. And Sam, thanks."

I jumped when the passenger side car door opened. I'd been so engrossed in my thoughts that I forgot to watch the beauty shop.

Angel slid into the passenger side and pulled the door closed. "Three guesses who Gabe's mom started chatting up real friendly-like in Mom's shop."

I looked through the window into the shop. There were Iris Pulizzi and Sophie Muffley with their heads together. "He sent his mother to spy on Sophie. But the question is, why? What is Gabe after? What does Dara have to do with this whole mess? She's the one that found Chad . . ." I trailed off, thinking. "It has to have something to do with the missing soccer money. And

Sophie worked for Chad in his office, where the soccer books were kept. She's a logical person to talk to. Damn sneaky sending his mother, though."

Angel lifted a delicate red-tinged eyebrow. "Almost as sneaky as putting a tracking device on Gabe's truck."

I smiled and started the car. "Pull out your tracking stuff, and let's follow Gabe."

It took a little bit of driving around, but we spotted Gabe's truck parked in a housing tract on the corner of Machado Street and Lincoln.

It was the same housing tract where Chad Tuggle lived. Or had lived. "I think Gabe's doing a little breaking and entering."

Angel put her GPS screen, which she had been tracking Gabe's truck on, back in her large purse. "Why?"

"Don't know, but it's something to do with why Dara hired him. Chances are good that it's information connected to Chad's murder since it's Chad's house." I realized I had several reasons for desperately wanting to solve this case. Helping Janie was number one, but proving myself to Gabe ran a close second. We had been building a sort of loose partnership, both personal and business. That came to a screeching halt with his demand that I work with him without knowing the facts of Dara's case. I meant to find out what Dara hired Gabe for.

I slowed down as we passed the street Chad lived on. His two-story house was three houses up the street. There were no cars in the driveway or in front. Gabe had parked two streets over.

Two could play at this game.

I went one street the other way and parked. "Come on, let's see if we can find out what Gabe's doing."

We got out of the car. We walked around the block in

the cool after-rain sunshine. "How do we get in?" Angel asked.

I considered that. "My guess would be the side garage door. Chad always left that unlocked during his soccer games. When I'd been team mom for him, he sent me back to his house lots of times to get stuff he'd forgotten."

Quickly, we passed the first two houses on the street. Chad's house was cream stucco with a peach trim. Approaching on the garage side of the house, I motioned to Angel to follow me. Quietly I went up to the six-foot wood fence and pulled the string to release the latch on the gate.

The rain had made the wood swell, and I had to shove to get the gate open. I prayed Gabe didn't hear anything. We stood on the long strip of cement that ran the length between the house and the fence. Straight ahead opened up into a small yard. I could spot half of the fishpond. There was a built-in pool hidden by the house from were we stood. Janie had hosted many team swimming parties so I knew exactly how the backyard was laid out.

Our goal was the door on our left, which led into the three-car garage. Walking softly in my boots, I reached out and tried the doorknob.

It turned.

My blood started pounding in my ears. What if Gabe was in the garage?

What if the killer was in the garage?

What if a vicious dog was in the garage?

"Sam?" Angel whispered behind me.

"Right." I needed to find out what Gabe was after. No more stalling. I reached into my purse and pulled out a canister of pepper spray. Then I turned the knob and slowly pushed the door open. The garage was dark and smelled like a wet blanket.

I stepped inside, followed by Angel.

As my eyes adjusted, light from the opened door showed a workbench, tools, and on the far side of the garage, one of those all-in-one weight things bolted to a support pillar. It looked like it came straight off an infomercial. All that was missing were the male and female hard-body models discussing how they only used the machine five minutes a day for a week.

No cars were in the garage. Chad's Explorer must have been at work when he was killed. Had the police impounded it? Would he have hidden the soccer money in his car?

I turned to the white door that led through the laundry room into the house. Glancing at Angel, I whispered, "Maybe we should have some kind of plan."

Angel gathered her long red-with-black-tips hair into a ponytail, then twisted it up on her head and somehow made it stay there. A few stray wisps floated down around her face. "We want to sneak up on Gabe, hide, and see what he's doing. How much of a plan do we need?"

I glared at her. "What do you think the chances are of us pulling this off?"

She grinned, practically lighting up the garage. "He's not expecting us to be here. And don't forget, he's got to go back and pick up his mom. He'll be distracted."

This might actually work. I hoped. "Okay, why don't you look around downstairs, and I'll look upstairs? All the bedrooms are upstairs, so I'd think Chad would have an office or something up there."

"Sure." Angel waved her hand to the door.

I reached for the door handle. Chad never had a house alarm when he was married to Janie, but now that he had taken up embezzling from SCOLE, maybe he'd put in an alarm.

But if Gabe was in there, he would have disarmed the alarm.

It was hard to get a full breath.

"Sam, are you going to let Gabe have the last word?" Angel whispered behind me.

"Hell, no." Squaring my shoulders, I tucked my purse back behind my hip, clutched my pepper spray, and turned the door handle.

It wasn't locked. Slowly, we eased open the door and went into the laundry room. The washer and dryer were on the right. Carefully we closed the door.

We were in. No alarms blared, and so far, Gabe hadn't caught us. I headed straight to where the laundry room turned left into a small hallway that led to a downstairs bathroom and family room.

This was probably breaking and entering. Maybe even crime-scene tampering. But there had been no crime here. And since Janie was the ex-wife and probably inherited everything as the kids' guardian . . . I turned off my spinning thoughts. If I had a hope in hell of outsmarting Gabe at this, I had to focus.

A squeak overhead froze me to the tile. Angel stopped beside me. We were on the threshold of a large family room. I looked up at the ceiling.

That squeak had to be Gabe up on the second floor. Had he heard us? I glanced at Angel.

She gestured for me to go on. I knew she'd keep watch down here. Quickly I looked around to get my bearings. We were facing the family room. It had a big black leather couch with recliners built in, facing a huge big-screen TV. Chad had redecorated. I wondered how much that TV and couch cost. I remembered the clean but worn furniture in Janie's mobile home. Chad still owed her money for the house and didn't pay the kid's health insurance premiums, but he bought new stuff for himself. What a guy.

The kitchen was through the family room. On my left was the stairs, then the living room. Quietly, I headed for the stairs.

Naturally they went straight up. No little turns to

hide in while climbing up. I took a deep breath, tucked my can of pepper spray back in my purse, and started up the stairs while straining to listen.

Halfway up I heard clicking. Familiar clicking. I strained to place it. It sounded like . . . Grandpa on the computer! Was Gabe on Chad's computer? What was he looking for? Something to do with the missing soccer money? At the top of the stairs, I stopped.

The stairs opened to a balcony on my right that overlooked the living room, filled with a pool table. I wondered where Angel was. Probably snooping through the kitchen. I went left, where I had my choice of either going left again to the master bedroom or right to the three remaining bedrooms.

The clicking stopped.

If Gabe walked out of any room, he'd see me. *Quick, where to go?* The kids had the two bedrooms past the bathroom, so I guessed Gabe was in the bedroom with the door just to the right. It used to be Janie's sewing and craft room, but I was sure Chad had changed it. I tiptoed to the wall and quietly edged to the door. Holding my breath, I listened.

Nothing. Maybe he wasn't in there. There was only one way to find out for sure. I took a deep breath to control my pounding heart and calm my breathing.

Quietly, I put my left hand on the door molding and inched my body around so that I was pressed up to the opening. Then I leaned around, took a quick peek into the room, and pulled back.

Leaning back against the wall, I thought about what I saw. There had been a big desk for computers sitting in the middle of the room. It had been black and tubular with a flat-screened monitor sitting in the middle.

Had the monitor been on? I'd seen the back of it, so I didn't know. I saw the window across from the door with the shade drawn down. A gray chair pushed back from the desk and nothing else.

No Gabe.

Maybe Gabe was in the master bedroom. There could be another computer in there, or maybe the clicking I'd heard wasn't a computer at all. Quickly I glanced right. One of the double doors to the master bedroom stood open. I could see a dresser and past that, a sliding glass door that led out to a balcony that overlooked the backyard. No sign of Gabe.

Crap. Maybe he wasn't even here. Maybe all I'd been hearing was the house settling.

But that had been his truck outside a couple of streets over. Where did Dara Reed live? Did she live in this tract, and Gabe was seeing her?

Screw it, I was going in the room. It looked like Chad's office and right now, I needed all the help I could get.

I leaned around the doorjamb and looked into the room. The desk was set in the middle, sort of catty-cornered facing the door. I thought I saw a glow from the monitor. If it was on, then Gabe was probably in the house somewhere. Maybe even in the room. I scanned the room from the right all the way to my left and almost screamed.

Gabe grinned at me. He stood flattened against the wall with his head turned to watch me.

Damn.

"Looking for something?"

I stepped into the room and put both hands on my hips. "Why are you hiding? You almost gave me heart failure!"

Gabe pushed off the wall. "Why are you skulking around a dead man's house?"

I tried for an exasperated look. "I'm not skulking. I'm . . ." I trailed off and tried to think. Why would I be in a dead man's house? "Uh, I'm here to get Chad some burial clothes and . . . I heard a noise." I turned my back on Gabe and looked at the desk. There was a stack of newspapers, and the top one had a picture of Chad. In the middle of the desk, the flat-screened computer monitor was on. There was a picture of a soccer team, with Chad and Rick Mesa beaming beside them. What had Gabe been doing? "Your truck's not parked out front, so I didn't think anyone was here."

I jumped when Gabe put his hand on my shoulder. "I didn't hear your car either, babe. Seems to me you might be breaking and entering."

"Actually, I walked in the garage door." I stared at the computer, trying to figure out what was wrong. The picture on screen was called wallpaper or something like that, but it seemed to be missing something. Gabe's hand kept me pinned.

"Not bad," Gabe said. "Same way I came in."

"Hmm." I tried not to let Gabe's compliment distract me. CDs were scattered on the desk. Gabe was looking through the CDs. What for? I shrugged his hand off my shoulder and went to the desk. I picked up a CD. It was for Microsoft Word.

That was it. I snapped my gaze up to the screen.

"Someone's already been here." Gabe said as he came up behind me and leaned over my shoulder. "The computer is wiped clean."

Just a few stray icons were left on the computer, like My Computer, Recycle Bin, and the Printer icon, but there were no files for Excel or things like that. "Nothing left?"

"Nothing."

"Why?" I couldn't begin to figure it out. The killer wiping the computer clean was the obvious answer, but why? "Did you go through these CDs to see what had been on the computer?" I thumbed through. I recognized Power-Point, since my kids used that for reports and stuff. Scanner programs. All kinds of stuff. Turning my head, I looked at Gabe.

He didn't answer.

It made sense that Gabe had been trying to figure out what had been wiped off the computer by looking at the CDs. Maybe. Unless Gabe had been the one to wipe all the files off the computer. Why would he do that, though? To protect Dara? From what?

I turned around. "Gabe, did you do it? Wipe the computer clean?" Gabe and I had done that once before. We'd broken into a house to get some personal sex videos of clients off the Internet.

"No. Look, Sam, this is getting dangerous. Someone bashed in Chad's head, and they are going to a lot of trouble to cover their tracks."

I stared up at him. He had on his jean jacket over a dark shirt stretched tight across his chest. His deep, intense eyes watched me. "You know something."

He did the hard cop stare.

Frustration tightened the back of my neck. My insides turned over. Had I lost Gabe? *Don't,* I warned myself. *Stay focused on the case.* Unless . . . Maybe I could convince Gabe to tell me what he knew.

I wasn't exactly dressed for seduction, with the drying mud on my butt, and frizzy hair. But it was worth a try. "Come on, Gabe." I put my hand on his arm. It was rock hard under the jean jacket. Moving in closer to his body, I slid my other hand inside the jacket and around his waist. I leaned my head back, looking up into his face. *Look sexy,* I thought.

I ran my tongue around my lips and said, "Tell me what you know about Chad's murder."

He arched a brow.

I moved my other hand beneath his jacket, running them both around his back and down his hips. He had a tight butt. I clutched both cheeks. "Tell me what you know. Just a little hint . . ." I left off suggestively.

"A hint?" His voice was thick, almost choked.

I nodded my head, leaning my breasts into his chest. "Just a hint." Dang, I was getting kind of hot. Who am I kidding? Gabe always makes me hot.

In a husky voice, he said, "Okay, here's a hint—try it naked next time."

Naked? Gabe naked sprang into my mind. All long hard limbs, flat stomach, excellent package . . . I jumped back. Gabe's voice wasn't husky with lust. He was holding back laughter. I glared at him. "You knew!"

He burst out laughing.

I whirled around and stormed over to the computer. Gabe's arm shot around my waist and yanked me back against him. Still laughing, he said into my neck. "Practice, babe. You'll get better."

Humiliation burned my face. At least he couldn't see that from behind me. But Gabe had taught me a thing or two. "You think?" I asked in a purr, while I quickly locked my hands together and shifted enough to my left to send my right elbow flying backward into his stomach.

His breath blew past my ear in a foul word, and he let go of me.

I whirled around. "Suck eggs, Pulizzi." Not my best line, but I straightened my spine and headed for the door. I had a couple of clues I could work with. Like the computer being wiped clean. My thoughts were cut off by Gabe's arm around my waist. Again, he dragged me back against his chest.

Did he want a fight? I stuck my hand in my purse and latched onto my defense spray.

Gabe put his mouth to my ear. "Shh, someone's in the house."

I froze. I felt the coiled tension in his body behind me. He wasn't playing now. Fear washed over me, humming in my ears. Since my hand was already around the defense spray in my purse, I pulled it out.

Then I remembered Angel. All the hard lines in

Gabe's body were pressed into my back. I could feel his tension as he strained to listen. Finally, I enlightened him. "That's just Angel."

He barely grunted and tightened his arm around my waist. "No, Angel is in the kitchen. Someone's coming in the front door."

Well, that was disappointing. He even knew Angel was downstairs. We hadn't put anything over on Gabe. Then I heard it, too. The scrape of a key in a lock.

"Stay here." Gabe let go of me and headed out of the door.

God, what if it was the killer? Angel was down there! I rushed out of the room and down the stairs.

The front door pushed open just as I stepped off the last step. Gabe was flush up against the wall. He reached out and yanked whoever was on the front porch inside and then flung them down.

I leaped off the bottom step and aimed my defense spray at the intruder on the ground. "Don't move or I'll spray!" I shouted, then looked down.

Rick Mesa, Chad's best friend and assistant coach, was sprawled on the floor. His eye darted between the can of defense spray in my hand and Gabe at my side. "What the hell?" Fast and athletic, Rick kicked out, knocking my hand aside, and got to his feet. He crouched for a fight.

My can of defense spray hit the carpet and rolled to a stop about six feet away. I looked back at Rick.

He had totally disregarded me as a threat and was sizing up Gabe. At about five-ten, Rick was tight and wiry, but no match for Gabe. Though he did look pissed enough to try to take him. "Rick," I shouted, throwing myself between the two men.

Rick dropped his gaze to me. "Sam? What are you doing here? Who is this clown?" He waved a hand past me toward Gabe.

"That's Gabe Pulizzi. He's, uh, a private detective. I'm helping Janie out. What are you doing here?"

Rick stared at Gabe for a long minute and then looked back at me. "Janie didn't say anything about you being here."

Of course she didn't, since I hadn't told her where I was going when I had her on my phone. To get past that little problem, I went on the offensive. "What are you doing here, Rick?"

Rick looked around the house. "Getting some clothes for Janie to bury Chad in."

"Humph," Gabe grunted behind me.

Apparently, that was a popular excuse. I ignored Gabe. "Oh, I see you have a key."

Rick gave me a deadpan stare. "Look, why don't you guys just leave? I want to . . . you know . . . take care of this job for Janie and get out of here."

Remorse slithered around in my belly. "Yeah, uh, Rick, I'm really sorry. I know Chad was your best friend. It's really terrible."

"Yeah, it is. Don't make it worse, Sam."

"Make it worse? How much worse could it get?" I'd never heard easygoing Rick so much as raise his voice. He was calm in dealing with kids and extraordinary at handling crazed parents. I had a great deal of respect for Rick. So his almost belligerent tone surprised me. Were the lines of strain around his eyes and mouth grief, or something else?

"It could get worse. Sophie called me and told me you were stirring up trouble. Stay out of this, Sam."

This was getting way out of hand. Anger rushed into my blood, bypassing my brain to pump words straight out my mouth. "What are you hiding, Rick? Is SCOLE trying to hide that Chad embezzled money? Well, it's too late. We already know about that." God, I was pissed. Another thought leaped in the fiery mess in my brain.

"Is that why you guys removed Janie as treasurer last year? You didn't want her to expose Chad's embezzling?" God, would they sink that low? I didn't want to believe it. I nearly jumped out of my skin when I felt Gabe's hand on my shoulder. In my anger, I'd forgotten he stood behind me. I had to calm down.

"What are you talking about? What money?" He stared at me as if I'd popped out a third breast.

He didn't know. A sense of relief spread through me. I liked Rick. Always had. He's one of the genuinely nice guys, and I didn't want him to be a liar and a cheat. "I don't get it, Rick. What's the big secret that you all are trying to hide?"

"We're not hiding anything." He sighed. "Look Sam, it's bad enough that Chad was murdered. We don't want bad publicity to make this worse." He set his jaw.

I knew he wouldn't tell me anything else.

"Why, Rick." Angel walked out of the kitchen, her smooth seductive voice breaking the tension. "Hello." She flashed a killer smile at Rick.

Rick's grim expression melted in a shy smile, making him look like a teenager instead of a thirty-something-year-old man. His coloring deepened. "Hi."

Angel looked over at me. "I finished cleaning the perishables out of the fridge, Sam. Nothing to worry about in the freezer, either."

Decoding Angel's message, I knew that she didn't find anything interesting in the kitchen, like, say, sixteen thousand dollars of missing soccer money in the fridge or freezer. "Thanks, Angel. I know Janie will appreciate it."

Gabe dropped his hand from my shoulder and moved to my side. "Now that you ladies are finished, why don't you run along and I'll lock up?"

I smiled. "We're not finished. But you can go. Your mom's probably waiting for you at the beauty salon."

Rick finally tore his gaze from Angel to look at me. "I think you should all get out of here. Now." He looked pointedly at the front door.

I decided to try one more time. "Rick—"

"Sam." Gabe's voice interrupted.

I held my hand up, trying to keep Gabe out of this. I wanted to find out what Rick knew.

"Behind you," Gabe said.

I turned and almost screamed. "Mom! What are you doing here?" I couldn't believe it. She had obviously walked in the sliding glass door across the family room. Wasn't anything in this house locked? My mom looked like she'd just arrived to show the house. She had on a winter white skirt and jacket, with a black silk shell beneath. Her blond hair sat in a perfect wedge cut, and she carried a slim black briefcase.

"Chad had been thinking of putting his house on the market. According to my sources, Janie Tuggle, as guardian of the kids, will inherit. I came by to make sure the house is in shape to sell."

I stared at my mom. She did not get to be the real estate queen of Lake Elsinore by being squeamish, but that was a little too ghoulish, even for her. "Mom, that's gross."

"That's business, Samantha." Unzipping her black case, she went on. "I'm not even going to ask what you and—" her gaze traveled to Gabe, tightening her perfectly lined mouth—"he are doing here. Ah, here it is." She pulled out a glossy brochure, walked a few steps on her black heels and waved it at me. "This is the resort in Phoenix we will be staying at the last week of January. In between studying for your real estate license, we can network to build your resources. We will also work on your wardrobe. I suppose there's a reasonable explanation for the dirt all over your backside?"

I'd been ducking my mom all day, and she caught me in a dead man's house. Figures. Shaking my head, I ignored the brochure in her hand and said, "Mom, the boys are in school. I can't go with you." I hated real estate.

"Nonsense. Dad will watch the boys, and Blaine will run the office. I already told them."

God, she arranged my life with Grandpa and my employee before even asking me. In fact, she wasn't asking me now, she was telling me. "Mom!"

Angel's voice cut through my wail of frustration. "Attention, boys and girls!"

We all turned to look at Angel, who was peering between the green slats of the blinds of the front window. "Detective Logan Vance is parking his car in the driveway. He is accompanied by a locksmith van."

"Oh, shit." I looked at Gabe. "What now?"

"Run."

We all headed for the sliding glass door like a massive hive of bees. After getting out to the backyard, Gabe slid the door shut. Just then we heard a car door slam.

Vance. On his way to the front door.

Gabe grabbed my elbow. "Can you jump the fence?"

"Yes." Maybe. My mom had disappeared around the corner, heading toward the back gate. "My mom!" I whispered.

"Can handle Vance." Gabe tugged me between the pool and the fishpond on my right. I looked up. Angel and Rick were going over the back fence, using a two-foot retaining wall to give them a leg up.

We ran over the rain-dampened cement between the pool and fishpond. I focused on the fence, praying I could get over it. I didn't want to get caught by Vance—"Oh!" My boot heel slid on the cement edge of the pond. My elbow slid from Gabe's grasp. Teetering for a long second, I flung out my arms to get my balance.

My left arm swung into Gabe's hand reaching for me, knocking it away.

I fell sideways into the fishpond. Cold, mucky water

closed over my face. Sputtering, I shoved myself up on my elbow.

Gabe and I locked gazes for a long second. Brackish, fishy water seeped through my red top and jeans and dripped from my hair. Then he said, "Good luck explaining to Vance," and jogged to the fence.

I got to my knees. Ugh, the bottom of the pond was slimy. "Don't you dare . . ." I trailed off when I saw Gabe grab the top of the six foot fence, pull himself up, and leap over. Gone, just like that.

He'd left me to escape or get caught by Vance.

This was war.

7

Gabe Pulizzi was going to pay.

Somehow, I pulled myself out of the pond, snatched up my purse off the ground, and got over that fence before Vance and the locksmith got into the house.

Sheer anger drove me.

Landing in a backyard, I glanced at the one-story house with blinds tightly closed and guessed the owners were gone. No sign of Gabe, either.

Making my way through the backyard to the street I was parked on, I didn't worry. Thanks to Angel's nifty state-of-the-art tracking device, I'd find Gabe. He might be from the dangerous streets of Los Angeles, an ex-cop and a hot-shot PI, but I was a pissed-off woman.

He was going down. Preferably in a dirty fishpond with one or two hungry piranhas swimming around.

Angel sat on the hood of my white 'bird watching me. With every swing of her leg, the slit in her long jean skirt parted right up to the top of her thigh. How the hell had she gotten over the fence in that skirt?

"I didn't know we were stopping for a swim."

"Shut up, Angel." I wrenched open the door and got in the car. Blaine was going to have a double heart attack, first from the mud at the nursery and now fish-pond water all over the car.

Angel slid in beside me. "Why did Gabe stalk off like that? Did he push you in the pool?"

It took me a good three breaths to get the words out. "I fell in the fish pond and Gabe abandoned me. He's going to pay."

Angel whistled between her teeth. "This is getting fun."

I rolled my eyes, started the car, and headed for home. I loved Angel, but even I couldn't deny that her idea of fun was twisted.

"What do you think your mom was doing there?"

My shrug turned into a shudder when cold, brackish water slid down my back and into the seat of my jeans. "Could be she really was checking out Chad's place. I'll track her down and ask her." I frowned, thinking about that. My mom had left a message with Blaine this morning, then stopped tracking me down.

Whenever my mom got a new plan to change my career, she never stopped trying to contact me and convince me. Ever. Could it be my mom was distracted?

By Chad's murder? How?

It took only about five minutes to shoot up Lincoln, turn left on Grand, and get to our house. After I parked the car, Angel followed me onto the porch. I sat in a chair and yanked off my boots, then pulled off my wet socks. I looked like the Bride of Frankenstein and smelled like day-old tuna.

Shower first.

Revenge second.

Fury and frustration snarled together inside my head. Getting up, I said, "I'm going to take a shower. Then I'll run you back to your car at your mom's shop." We both went into the house.

Grandpa looked up from where he sat at his computer.

"Hey, Sam, hi, Angel. Exterminator is gone. Blaine said Ali was acting weird, but she's been fine with me."

Ali got up from her blanket by the sliding glass door. She padded over to me and started sniffing. I'm sure the fishpond water gave her lots of scents.

I stopped by the hallway to quickly pet my dog. Grandpa was right. She seemed perfectly normal now. "Ali took it into her head to dump over a trash can at Duncan's Nursery. We had to pull her off. I'm going to take a shower." I left Angel to explain things to Grandpa and hurried down to my bedroom.

After my hot shower, I pulled on a short black skirt and a cream-colored V-necked sweater. Gabe's laughing at my seduction-for-information attempt stung, so I dressed to feel better. I stepped into some black heels, did some makeup magic, and went back out to the kitchen.

Grandpa and Angel were fixing sandwiches. I went up to Grandpa and kissed his weathered cheek.

He grinned. "You're looking better. Angel told me about your investigating. Gabe really doesn't know you have that tracking device on his truck?"

"Nope." I got a couple Diet Cokes and a bottle of iced tea out of the refrigerator and took them to the table. "We discovered that someone has already been in Chad's house and wiped his computer clean there. And more people showed up while we were there—Rick Mesa and Mom." I'd thought about this in the shower. "I think they are looking for something."

Grandpa brought a plate of egg salad sandwiches and set them down in the middle of the table. "Like the missing sixteen thousand dollars of soccer money?"

"Maybe. But I don't think Gabe would look for stolen soccer money for Dara. He was a cop." Though he did have a code all his own. I went to the pantry to get paper plates and napkins.

"Unless Dara hired him to find it and put it back so that she doesn't get into trouble," Angel said, as she set out a bowl of canned peaches.

I turned from the pantry and saw the blinking light of the answering machine. "We have a message." Holding plates and napkins in one hand, I hit the play button and went to set the stuff down on the table.

A muffled voice said, "Stay out of Chad Tuggle's murder. He got what was coming to him. So will you if you get too nosy." Click.

I straightened and whirled around to stare at the answering machine. Adrenaline poured into my bloodstream, and I broke out in a sweat.

Angel stood with one hand on the back of a chair. "Play it again."

I walked a step to the phone and hit *play*.

"Stay out of Chad Tuggle's murder. He got what was coming to him. So will you if you get too nosy." Click.

"Did I just get a death threat?" I mean, jeez, most people get stupid sales calls. Me? I get death threats. This day was just unbelievable.

Grandpa had stopped right beside me with a box of frozen brownies in his hand. "Some kind of warning, maybe?"

"It was a man's voice. Lowered and disguised, but a man."

Angel said, "What about Rick Mesa? He seemed awfully eager to get you to stay out of Chad's murder. He was at the house looking for something. Maybe he knew Chad was stealing the soccer money and they had a falling out or something."

Gentle Rick a killer? Well, strange things were happening. And who else could it be? Not Gabe, I knew that. It wasn't his style. Besides, Gabe knew that warning me off would have the opposite effect.

Grandpa looked over at Angel, then back at me. "What other men have you talked to about this, Sam?"

I went back over my day. "Detective Vance, obviously. Then I saw Duncan at the nursery, but that had to do with Roxy, not Chad's murder, and hmm . . ." I trailed off, thinking about getting Angel's phone call, then going to the beauty shop. "Oh wait. Don't forget Lionel Davis. He tried to attack Gabe." Lionel had a screw loose somewhere, but how could he be connected to Chad? Although he did show up at Heart Mates on the day I found out about Chad's murder.

Grandpa met my gaze. "Looks like you stirred something up today."

"Guess so." I took the box of brownies from his hand and went to the microwave. I fished out three frozen squares of chocolate, arranged them on paper towel, and set them in the microwave. I set the timer for a couple of minutes at half power. Then I went to the table and sat down. Grandpa sat on my right, Angel was across from me, and Ali kept watch from her blanket by the sliding glass door. During a long minute of silence, we arranged plates and food.

Angel took a bite of her sandwich and asked, "What are you going to do, Sam?"

I looked up at Angel. "I'm going to track down Gabe Pulizzi and make him tell me what the hell is going on." I took a bite of my sandwich, barely tasting it. He knew this case had turned dangerous. He'd told me it was dangerous in Chad's house. But he wouldn't tell me why.

That might have been okay.

If I hadn't just gotten a death threat and had two sons and the most loved Grandpa on earth who could get hurt. That was unacceptable.

After a bit of discussion with Grandpa and Angel, we decided that I'd have better luck sneaking up on Gabe under the cover of darkness.

I dropped Angel off at her car, then went to Heart Mates and tried to find Gabe the conventional way. I called his house, cell phone, and pager, and left messages on his voice mail.

Nothing.

I killed the next couple of hours by trying to track down Roxy and my mom. No luck there, either. Then I worked on a new computer profile for Roxy. Once I found her, I'd get her to approve it and we'd run new matches. I wanted to find the right kind of man for Roxy. The new profile would match her with more mature and stable men—or so I hoped.

Done with that, Blaine and I closed up Heart Mates and I headed to Stater Bros. to pick up the essentials for Angel's lingerie party tomorrow night. I stocked up on margarita mix, munchies, and a few other things we needed at the house, then headed for home.

I parked my car in front of our little house and got out, carrying a bag of groceries. Joel was sprawled on the floor playing a video game, while TJ did homework at the coffee table. "Hi, boys. Go get the rest of the groceries from the car, please."

"Hi, Mom. Did you get ice cream?" Joel turned off the video game.

"Ice cream sandwiches." I kicked off my black pumps and headed to the kitchen, with Ali running circles around me trying to sniff what was in the bag.

TJ strolled past me. "Got an A on my science report."

I stopped and managed to grab the back of his T-shirt. "TJ! That's great." Shifting the bag of groceries in my arm, I hugged my son. "I'm so proud of you. You worked on that report a long time."

His blue eyes lit up, and then he raced out to help Joel bring in the groceries.

Grandpa came in the kitchen from the hallway. "Hey, Sam, TJ tell you about his report?"

I smiled. "Yes, he did. All real casual-like, of course."

Joel came in with more groceries. "Mom, what's for dinner?"

"Spaghetti. How did you do on your book report?"

"Got a B." He fished out the ice cream sandwiches and put them away.

"Good, Joel." I nodded and got a pan out to start the water boiling for spaghetti.

TJ came in with the last bag. "The news about Coach Chad is all over school."

Dropping ground meat in another pan for sauce, I grabbed a paper towel to wipe my hands and looked at TJ. Chad had coached one of TJ's teams and I'd been the team mom. "About Chad's death?"

"Yeah." He started folding the plastic grocery bags. "Are you investigating his murder, mom?"

I walked across the kitchen to him. "I'm looking into it for Janie, yes. TJ, are you all right?"

He looked up at me. "Mom, I haven't even seen Coach Chad in a couple of years. It's just that rumors have been going around about Coach for a long time. You know, how he left Janie for Josh's mom."

"Dara? You know her son?"

TJ smoothed the bags. "Yes. He's at school. He's quiet. I'd heard that Coach Chad got friendly with Josh and that's how he met his mom. But, Mom, Josh is like—"

He looked up at me and I watched my smart, too-old-for-his-fourteen-years son struggle to put his feelings into words. I made myself stand still and give him time.

"Josh is sad, Mom. He doesn't say much. I don't think Chad was really being a friend to him. Not like Coach Rick would have been. I think Chad just used Josh to get to his mom or whatever."

I got it. Maybe Josh had even said something to TJ about it. Being used to get into your mom's bed was sick. I knew it 'cause a few men had done that with me. Be nice to the kid and Mom thinks the man is a knight in shining armor. "TJ, do you know Josh well?"

He shook his head. "Talked to him a few times at school. He doesn't have many friends, Mom."

I reached out and hugged TJ. "Thanks for telling me. Go ahead and finish your homework and I'll have dinner ready soon."

When the boys left, I went back to making the sauce, while Grandpa got two cups down and filled them with coffee. My thoughts centered on what TJ had said. I'd always thought that Dara set her sights on Chad. But what if it had been the other way around, and Chad persuaded her? What did that mean?

What did I even know about Dara Reed? She'd moved to Lake Elsinore a while back with her one son.

"Grandpa, do you think you could look around on the Internet, you know, with your connections, and see what you can find on Dara Reed?"

He handed me a hot cup of coffee. "Sure, Sam. I'll get started right now. Maybe by the time you get home from looking for Gabe tonight, I'll have some information."

Gabe. He still hadn't called me back. But Angel had shown me how to use her receiver to the tracking device she put on his truck. As soon as I got dinner done and the boys settled, Ali and I were going to find out just what Gabe was doing that was so important he couldn't return my calls.

My plan was to find Gabe and surprise him, then demand answers. I counted on him being so impressed with my ability to find him, since he didn't know about the tracking device, combined with my short skirt and deep V-neckline, to compel him to talk to me.

Okay, maybe the short skirt and plunging neckline were about my miffed pride over Gabe laughing at me.

Ali and I went by Gabe's house first, just to make sure he wasn't there. Ali recognized where we were and whined low in her throat, hoping we could stop and visit Gabe. "His truck is not in the driveway, Ali. He's not home." I glanced over at her. She had her nose pressed against the passenger-side window watching Gabe's house slide by. "We'll find him."

I studied the screen of the GPS receiver while driving. It wasn't much harder than talking on the cell phone and driving. Fortunately, the residential streets in Gabe's neighborhood were empty. If I was using this right, it looked to me like Gabe was hanging around the Stater Bros. shopping center on Lake Street. He could be shopping.

Or he could be nosing around Chad Tuggle's insurance office. Looking for what? It seemed weird to me that somebody wiped off Chad's home computer to *get rid of* something, while others broke into Chad's house *looking for* something. Was it all the same something? What did Dara hire Gabe for? I had to find out what Gabe was looking for.

One way to find out. I turned left on Broadway, then left on Grand Street, and went up to the signal to make a right on Lakeshore.

Gabe's truck stayed in the same place on the receiver.

I went past the Machado Street stoplight and turned left into the Stater Bros. parking lot. I looked around for Gabe's black truck and didn't spot it. But I did see a thin beam of light moving around in Chad's darkened office.

Bingo. Gabe was using a flashlight to snoop around. He probably parked in the alley behind Stater Bros. and the adjoining strip mall that held Chad's office. I parked in front of the Stater Bros., where Gabe wouldn't spot my car if he looked out Chad's front window. I looked at Ali. "I know Gabe is your good buddy, but this time I want you to stay with me and be quiet. No more stunts like you pulled at Duncan's Nursery today, okay?"

She shifted impatiently on her front paws.

I'd have to chance Ali not giving me away. I wasn't going to be stupid and go in Chad's dark office without her. The beam of light was gone now; either Gabe had turned it off, or he had moved back to the small kitchen area where I couldn't see it.

I held my car keys in my hand. We both got out of the car and went up to the office. Crime-scene tape stretched across the door. I ducked beneath it and reached out to test the door.

It opened.

Briefly, I paused with my hand on the door. Why was it unlocked if Gabe went in the back way?

One way to find out. I touched the fake pager unit filled with defense spray that I had clipped to my skirt and eased the door open. I whispered, "Let's go." Ali followed me in. The glow of the parking lot lights bled into the office, barely outlining the shapes. No humans, just furniture.

The thought of Chad with his head bashed in and sprawled on the floor froze me. *Where had he been killed?* I wondered. *By his desk?* I shook the thought off. I had to go on—to see if Gabe was here, and why.

I bent down and whispered, "Ali, sit and stay right here."

She sat. My heart kicked up. I'd checked and double-checked Angel's tracking device. I knew it worked because we'd tracked Gabe to Chad's house with it.

Gabe was snooping around looking for something.

But my heart hammered. That damned answering machine message spooked me. What-ifs played in my brain. What if the killer . . .

Stop it, I told myself. I needed information from Gabe and I needed to tell him about the threat. I knew he'd tapped his sources to find out about Chad's murder, and I was going to get that information from him. I needed to keep my kids and Grandpa safe. Getting a grip on my fear, I pictured the office in my head like a map and started in, walking softly toward the back.

The deeper into the office I went, the darker it became. The glow from the parking lot lights didn't reach this far. Dark silence surrounded me, giving me that disconnected feeling.

I made it to the divider wall and stopped. My chest hurt and felt raw from my fear. A dull thud drummed in my ears. I checked my pager/defense spray hooked at my waist.

No sound except my breathing and the thudding in my ears. The faint sound of Ali's steady pant reached me. That made me feel safer. Quickly I pictured the little kitchen in my head—a small square about two-thirds the size of Chad's front office. The remaining third was a bathroom on my left, leaving most of the kitchen to my right. Green painted cupboards lined the wall directly to my right, then turned on an L shape where there was a stainless-steel sink next to a small white refrigerator. At least that was how the kitchen looked a couple of years ago. Plenty of cupboards to hide something, like money, in.

I held my breath, determined to find out what Gabe was looking for. I took a step into the dark kitchen.

A hand closed around my arm, yanked, and swung me around. I was stunned, a scream locked in my chest as my car keys flew out of my hand. My butt rammed into a countertop. Before I could move, a solid arm slammed into my neck, snapping my head back into a cupboard. I was unable to breathe; terror washed over me. I stared into the darkness, only able to make out the shape of a man.

A hard man.

The man who killed Chad? Was I going to die? Horrible fear washed a bile taste up the back of my throat. My two sons, TJ and Joel, they needed me. I couldn't die.

A low, vicious warning growl cut through my terror. Relief swept over me. *Ali!*

In spite of the pressure against my windpipe, I croaked out, "My dog will kill you. She'll—"

"Shaw?" The pressure on my windpipe eased.

Ohmigod. "Ali, down girl." I called out. I couldn't believe this. Detective Vance? Ali knew Vance, which was probably the only reason she hadn't attacked him flat out without any warning.

The growling stopped.

"Let go of me, Vance."

The pressure on my windpipe lifted completely. A light flashed on overhead.

I squinted through the sudden fluorescent glare to make sure it was Vance.

He stared at me with his hard-cut, lifeguard face. No dimples. In fact, he looked more tired than he had at the doughnut shop this morning. He had on tan pants and a black sweater, his usual casual elegance. He reached behind his back and pulled out a set of handcuffs. "Samantha Shaw, you have the right to remain silent—"

"You can't be serious!" I pushed off the countertop. "You can't arrest me! I didn't do anything!"

He took another step toward me. "Anything you say can and will be used against you."

Panic shoved against my breastbone.

He reached for my arm.

I twisted away to my right. "Vance!" I had my back to a small refrigerator. Ali sat down and watched this show with perked ears. She apparently didn't see any real threat here. Having spent some time in the police-dog academy, she was used to handcuffs.

Vance moved fast, snapping one cuff around my left wrist. Before I could register that, he spun me around and snapped the other behind my back.

My God, he was arresting me! My mother would kill me! Cripes, what was I thinking? I had two sons to worry about. My mother was the least of my problems.

Then I pictured her reaction if I was arrested. No, Mom was my biggest problem.

Vance pressed in from behind me. "If you cannot afford an attorney—"

"Vance! Listen to me!" I rested my forehead against the cool white of the fridge. It hurt my bruise, but that didn't seem important right now. Now that I was breathing actual oxygen instead of my own fear, I knew exactly what happened. "This is a mistake. I thought you were Gabe. He switched the tracking device."

Vance turned me around so that I faced him. The usual gold flecks in his brown eyes look flat, like floating flotsam. He smelled of male frustration tinged with coconut suntan lotion. "Shaw, what the hell are you babbling about?" His gaze flicked up to my forehead. "Dammit, you're hurt."

"Nah, that's not from you. Got that earlier from a client." I felt my mouth twitch and knew I was on the verge of hysteria. I needed sleep and probably a new life. Oh, and a new boyfriend. My old one would be dead soon.

Vance's mouth quirked up so that his dimples made an appearance. "A client?"

"Never mind. But I believe there's a tracking device on your car."

"What?"

Sure, why not confess all to the police? "It was on Gabe Pulizzi's truck. I thought Gabe was in here and I came in to—" okay, maybe I should lie a bit, "—warn him that it's illegal. But it turns out Gabe's not here. No, it's my favorite detective." The sarcasm rolled off easily. "I bet Gabe is laughing his ass off."

Vance's brown eyes sharpened. "I smell trouble in paradise."

I shrugged. "That's because you're a cop. You always smell trouble. Come on, Vance, you're not going to arrest me." I tried to inject confidence in my voice. Vance and I had an understanding—we agreed to blackmail each other, use each other, and dislike one another.

A change slid over Vance. His entire stance shifted from angry aggressive cop to—*uh-oh*. Heat flared to life in the gold chips in his brown eyes. Leaning in closer, his gaze skimmed down to my chest. With my hands cuffed behind me, my breasts were prominent in my low-cut, tight sweater. Okay, I'm a grown woman, a business-woman, a mother of sons—I could handle a man.

But a cop with handcuffs?

My chest constricted like I'd been exercising. I sucked in a deep breath, then realized my mistake when his nostrils flared watching my breasts swell.

Vance dragged his gaze to mine. His voice dropped to a thick whisper. "I can see the outline of your bra."

I was in big trouble. This was Gabe's fault. He made me so damned vulnerable, and I hated being vulnerable. When I knew things were going well between us, I could handle the sizzle between Vance and me.

But Gabe was keeping secrets from me and protecting Dara's skinny butt. He'd left me in the fishpond.

Vance and I were adversaries that used each other. For information. I ignored the hissing of my libido. "Get these cuffs off, Vance. This kind of abuse might work in the romances you write, but I won't put up with it." I threw in the romance stuff to remind him I knew of his secret life.

A sun-god grin carved out his dimples. Lifting his hands, he put them against the fridge over my head and leaned down. His black sweater pulled across his swimmer's chest. "Ever read my books, Shaw? Of course you have. You always give them five stars for sensuality. I don't need handcuffs to bring a woman bone-melting pleasure."

My breath hitched in my throat while my bones tried to melt to his hypnotic suggestion. Caught up in his gaze, his words, some of the scenes Vance had written stirred in my head. He always pitted tough heroes against feisty, smart women. Those women knew what they wanted, and often as not, they wanted the hero. They thought they were in control—right up until the sex scene. Heat and friction did things in my body.

"Ah, I see you remember, Shaw. You know I wrote those scenes. Now you're wondering if I am that good of a lover in the flesh, aren't you?"

I followed his sensual voice, thinking hot sizzling thoughts until my brain slipped in a little icy truth. Vance wrote romances. Most romances were written for women. Detective Logan Vance, aka R.V. Logan, knew the language of women. He was using that on me right now. "Damnit, Vance, knock it off. You can write porn for all I care. I'm more interested in finding who killed Chad than discovering if your dick is as big as your ego."

His eyes hardened. "Turn around and spread your legs, Shaw. You are under arrest for tampering with a crime scene."

Shit. He was arresting me.

8

Vance couldn't be arresting me. This wasn't happening.

But the angry throb in Vance's voice told me otherwise. "Not only breaking into this active crime scene, but also a dead man's house. What are the chances that the prints on the can of defense spray I found on Chad Tuggle's carpet will match your prints? You are going to jail, Shaw." He grabbed my shoulders and spun me around to face the refrigerator.

Shit, I'd completely forgotten about the defense spray. Rick had kicked it out of my hand. Pushed up against the refrigerator, I desperately tried to think. "I didn't break in anywhere!" Technically true. The doors were unlocked both at Chad's office and at home.

Vance stuck his foot between my shoes and pushed my legs apart. "No one breaks into my crime scenes and fucks with my case." He ran his hands up under my arms then around beneath my breasts.

"I don't have a gun in my bra!"

"Not enough room with all that silicone? Or is it saline?"

God, I could feel his fury. I was in real trouble here.

"Vance, I'm helping out Janie. Call her; she knows I was in Chad's house. She'll vouch for me. The house goes to her as the kids' guardian!" Panic wound through my words and pounded in my head.

His right hand stopped at the fake pager clipped to my skirt. "What's this?"

God, this only gets worse. I didn't dare tell him that it was actually defense spray after he'd found the can of defense spray at Chad's house. "It's just a pager."

Vance slid it off and set it on the counter.

I struggled to think rationally. Vance was pissed. Tired of his case being fucked with. Things started clicking into place. The front door unlocked, Vance hanging out here in the dark. "You were staking out Chad's office."

"Little late now to figure that out."

Did Gabe know that? Had he sent me here on purpose to get me arrested and out of his way? The thought made me sick.

Vance put his hands back on my hips to continue his pat down.

"Look, you gotta believe me. I really thought Gabe was in here. I came in because I needed his help." The raw truth hurt, but being arrested would hurt more. "Vance, I had a phone message. A threat." I hadn't admitted it to myself, but I was running to Gabe. Who probably set me up to be arrested. When would I learn not to rely on a man?

His hands stopped and lifted off my butt. "When?"

"Let me turn around." I was thinking fast. Okay, the truth was out, or some of it. I had to bargain with Vance.

He stepped back.

I turned, leaning against the fridge. The handle bit into a sore spot behind my hip. That was where I slammed into the counter when Vance grabbed me. Sucking up a breath, I told him about getting home earlier today and finding the message.

"Did you recognize the voice?"

"No, it sounded fake. Like muffled and lowered." My breathing started returning to normal.

He looked at me. "What did you stir up to get threats?"

I summed up my day. "I sort of ran into Sophie Muffley and Rick Mesa and talked to them about Chad. That's it. Otherwise I was at work, went by the nursery, and, uh, the grocery store."

He pulled his little red notebook out of his shirt pocket and flipped through it. "What did Sophie and Rick tell you?"

It didn't surprise me that Vance knew who Sophie and Rick were. I knew from experience that he did his homework. "They didn't tell me anything, except to stay out of it." I left out the part about Rick being in Chad's house, probably looking for something.

Vance ran a hand over his face and tucked the notebook away. "Shaw, you broke into a crime scene, a dead man's house, and now you are probably investigating without a license since your boyfriend looks to be protecting the interests and assets of one Dara Reed. How do you get yourself into so much trouble?"

Hormones? But the real question was how did I get myself *out* of so much trouble? "Are you going to let me go?"

Vance put a hand on the fridge over my head and leaned down. "I think we can work something out."

Suspicion splashed over my brain. Quickly I tried to figure out Vance's angle. He had people breaking into his crime scenes—that was evident from his little trap. His quick arrest of me showed his anger. But was the anger from something more than crime-scene tampering? I was getting the runaround, and apparently threats, about investigating Chad. If everyone involved in soccer had closed ranks against me, then that probably meant . . . "You want me to spy for you?" I worked hard to summon up indignation. "You want me to talk to the people in town to find out information they won't tell you, the outsider cop?"

He raised both eyebrows and looked down into my face. "Your outrage would have more impact if you hadn't bugged your boyfriend's truck. And need I remind you that he put that bug on my car? If that's the truth, of course—something that I will find out shortly."

I really didn't like hearing the facts from him. "Look Vance, I don't have a license to investigate—"

"I'm not asking you to investigate. Besides, we use informants all the time."

I wanted to scream *no*, but I was handcuffed and Vance might be able to make a case to arrest me. I stared up at him and tried to keep my priorities straight, which meant I needed to know what Vance thought about Janie. "Do you think Janie Tuggle killed Chad?"

"I go where the facts take me. Janie Tuggle had reason to be pissed at her ex-husband. He got everything out of the divorce and stiffed her on payments for the house. Then there's the fact that she paid up his life insurance. The evidence shows a struggle took place behind Chad's desk by the paper shredder. It's possible that Janie and Chad had an argument and it got out of hand."

I tried to process all of that. "You think Chad's death was an accident? But why would the person leave?"

"Could have been a lot of things. According to your story, you got your shirt caught in that paper shredder. How did that happen?"

A thread of deep fear coiled in my stomach. "I told you, it was an accident! Chad was getting me some hot chocolate here in the kitchen, and the bottom of my shirt hit the automatic mechanism on the shredder. Chad had to use scissors to cut me loose. It was just an accident."

His brown eyes studied me. "You are an accident, Shaw. Look at you now, caught red-handed breaking into a crime scene with a lame story. Hell, if I find a bug on my car, how do I know you didn't put it there?"

Shit. He had me in a corner. "What do you want from me, Vance?"

"First, I want to know what you saw on Chad's computer yesterday morning here in his office."

I was in a really tight situation here. I had never admitted to Vance that I had a disk of the SCOLE files, so to tell Vance about that now would probably piss him off more. "Uh, can you take the cuffs off first?"

He looked down at me. "No."

An involuntary shiver rolled between my shoulder blades and sank into my belly. "First Chad showed me his program for the insurance business. Then he showed me his SCOLE files."

"Soccer Club of Lake Elsinore?" Vance asked.

I wished he'd move back. "Yes."

"What was on there?"

Okay, time to come clean. "Actually, I sort of have a copy of those files on a disk."

His gaze flattened. "I want that copy."

Which meant he didn't have the files on Chad's computer. I thought of the computer at Chad's house. "The computer files—they are all gone, aren't they?" So whoever killed him wiped out the files. That must mean the murder had something to do with the missing soccer money.

"I want that disk, Shaw."

"Fine, I'll get it for you." Right after I ask Grandpa to make us a copy of it.

"Do you know who might have had the skills to delete files from the hard drive, Shaw?"

"No." Maybe. Janie was the one who taught Chad how to use the bookkeeping system, but why would Janie delete the files? For one thing, she knew I had a copy, and secondly, they were her proof that Chad was embezzling.

Janie had Chad where she wanted him, so killing him made no sense. Who else could it be? Sophie? She worked with Chad part-time, so she might know how to wipe the computer clean. Rick? I'd seen a side of him I hadn't seen before at Chad's house today. I didn't really know.

"I don't think you get the rules here, Shaw. You are going to start helping me or you are going to jail. Which is it going to be?"

My head throbbed. The fact that I stood here with my hands cuffed behind my back indicated just how serious Vance was about blackmailing me into helping him. The fact that I once used Vance's secret life as an author of romance novels to blackmail him into helping me prove a man innocent of killing his wife proved that Vance held a grudge. I didn't see any choice since I couldn't do a thing for Janie from jail. "Fine. I'll be your narc. Just get me out of these handcuffs and get away from me."

"I want the disk, too. First thing tomorrow morning, you drop that disk off at the station, got it? If it's not there by nine in the morning, I'll find you."

Oh, just great. I was now at war with Gabe Pulizzi and working against my will with Detective Logan Vance.

Gabe wasn't home and didn't answer his cell phone. Ali watched me silently as I drove home and slinked through the front door. It took all my willpower not to take the tracking device Vance took off his car out of my purse and put it through the food processor. Then I could force-feed it to Gabe.

I pulled up short in the living room when I spotted Grandpa and the boys looking over several computer-generated greeting cards laid out on the coffee table. The TV blared a cop show. Ali raced over to check in with TJ and Joel.

TJ petted Ali, then picked up a card. "Mom, I think we should give Coach's family this card."

The red haze of fury blurring my vision made it hard to see. "Tell you what, TJ, let me make a phone call, then I'll look." I stormed to the kitchen and yanked the phone off the hook. I punched in Gabe's pager unit.

I watched the boys rolling on the floor with Ali while listening to Gabe's taped voice explaining my options for leaving a message. "You are a dead man, do you hear me, Gabe Pulizzi? Vance damn near arrested me tonight. He handcuffed me and—" I sucked in a breath, fighting down the sensation of sick anger. Of betrayal. I'd let Gabe into my life. I trusted him. "Don't call me!" I slammed the phone down.

Don't call me? I groaned at my weak finish. I wanted to bang my head against the wall, but my forehead wasn't up to the abuse. Maybe I should call him back and say something clever.

I was too mad to think of something clever.

Grandpa walked into the kitchen. "Vance almost arrested you?"

"I don't want to talk about it." I went to the pantry and pulled out a bag of food for Ali and headed for her dish by the sliding glass door. Ali beat me there and stuck her nose into the dog food bag. "Back up, Ali."

She stepped back and sat down to watch me pour her food. I smiled at my awesome dog. Husbands and boyfriends should be so well trained.

Grandpa filled up her water dish at the sink and set it down by her food. "I couldn't find much on Dara Reed. Found her son registered at high school. But nothing about her except a driver's license. Couldn't even find a credit card."

I put the dog food away in the pantry, and then leaned back against the stove. Oh, boy, I was going to have a bruise on the back of my hip from Vance whipping me around in Chad's office kitchen. Thinking about Dara, I said, "Are you sure? No credit cards?" What kind of self-respecting woman didn't have credit cards? It was unnatural.

"No history before she moved to Lake Elsinore."

Idly rubbing the back of my hip, I met Grandpa's gaze. "What do you think it means?"

"I think Dara Reed doesn't want a lot of info floating around the Internet about her. I suspect she came to Lake Elsinore from out of state, which means I'd have to dig a little deeper. I put out some discreet feelers through my Triple M group."

That caught my attention. I looked across the narrow kitchen to where he was leaning against the sink. "Discreet?"

Grandpa went to the refrigerator and took out a of couple of beers. "Well, it looks to me like Dara might not want to be found. I don't want to send up red flags if she has a good reason."

That never occurred to me. A good reason? As in hiding? Dara showed up in town with a son and no man. The first thing that popped into my head was, "Like hiding from an abusive husband?"

"Crossed my mind." He handed me a beer.

I twisted off the top and took a drink. "This whole case is just weird. Like a huge puzzle with missing pieces."

Grandpa studied me with his crafty blue eyes. "Who do you think might have some of those missing pieces?"

I ran through my thoughts out loud. "Everyone seems to have secrets. And I think those secrets led to Chad's murder. There's the missing soccer money, which may or may not be what everyone is looking for. Everyone being Gabe, Dara, Rick, Sophie . . . " I trailed off. Ali barked and gave me her pleading look. Big eyes, ears laid back. I went over and dumped some beer into her licked-clean food dish and added, "You know Vance isn't getting any answers, either." I gave him the short version of Vance's demand that I help him and turn over the copy of the SCOLE disk.

Grandpa's blue eyes turned speculative and he lifted his beer bottle up to examine it. "He's not asking at the right time. Like, say, at a lingerie party when the alcohol is flowing."

I looked at my own beer bottle and thought of the margarita mix I'd stocked up on for Angel's Tempt-an-Angel lingerie party the next night. Sophie had already told Angel she was coming to the party. I shifted my gaze back to Grandpa. "You're a genius. I'll ply Sophie with margaritas and get some answers."

Grandpa beamed at me. "Always good to get your audience in a cooperating state of mind before you trick them."

I laughed, then went over and hugged Grandpa. "I love you, Grandpa. And not just because you are clever and devious. Now let's go look at the cards the boys made on the computer."

The boys and I spent an hour and a half picking a card, then chatting and watching TV. They talked me into eating an ice cream sandwich. Once they went off to bed, I pulled out my Rolodex phone tree. The phone tree began life as my soccer mom tool, then segued into a rich source of information when I moonlighted as a private investigator.

I'd been toying with the idea of calling a few people and asking what they might know about Chad and Dara. But something held me back.

I wasn't sure what Dara Reed's secret was. What if she was hiding from an abusive husband, ex-husband, or boyfriend, and my snooping through my phone tree contacts somehow led the guy right to her?

I didn't know what questions to ask yet. Though protecting TJ and Joel was uppermost in my mind since the telephone message threat, I couldn't risk exposing Dara until I knew her story.

I set the phone tree back in the kitchen. I walked through the house and made sure all the doors and windows were locked. I double-checked to make sure the alarm system was on.

Then I looked in on the boys. TJ slept in the bottom bunk. He was on his side facing the door, his blanket tucked carefully around him. He looked so much like his handsome father that it made me pause. But TJ was more of a man at fourteen than Trent had ever been. He had the sensitivity to spot a quiet sadness in Dara Reed's son, Josh. And to worry that Chad had somehow used the boy. I smiled in the night, looking at TJ. He had a good heart to go with his father's good looks.

I shifted my gaze to Joel sprawled out on the top bunk, with his covers tangled around his legs. He looked more like me than his dad. He had inherited Trent's charm, along with his grandfather's craftiness. Watching Joel just beginning to cross over into manhood made my heart swell and ache at the same time. I felt nostalgia for the happy, chubby baby that lingered in my memory, and pride at the young man he was becoming.

Lord, I must be getting old.

I glanced at Ali on the floor, spread out on her side. She opened one eye to assure me that she was on the job looking out for my two sons, then closed it again. I pulled the door halfway shut so Ali could get out if she wanted to and continued down the hallway to my room. Grandpa's light was still on, so he was reading in bed.

Which is exactly what I planned to do. I had started a really hot romance novel yesterday morning when Janie came into my office. I couldn't wait to finish it and get started on the review. It was a fabulous book, funny and sensual at the same time. Once in my room, I shut the door almost all the way. I got undressed, washed the makeup off my face, put on my "Romance Rocks" T-shirt and socks, then climbed into bed. I opened the book and slipped away from murders, crying clients, black-mailing detectives, and annoying boyfriends.

I don't know how long I had been reading when the book was suddenly ripped from my hand.

Adrenaline and confusion slammed into me. I opened my mouth to scream while trying to figure out what was going on.

"Don't scream." Gabe stood over me in his black T-shirt and jeans, holding my romance novel.

Finally, my terrified lungs relaxed and I demanded, "Give me that! They were just going to do it!"

Gabe's face changed. Male interest practically oozed from his eyes. He dropped his gaze to the page I was on. "Damn, that's not the reading I had to do in high school." He looked at me.

I refused to be embarrassed. I loved romance novels. I loved the heroines, and right now, that was more than I could say for Gabe. "What are you doing here?"

He dropped his gaze to my breasts.

Uh-oh. That romance novel had me so into the char-acters, I was practically a walking sex act waiting to hap-pen. Definitely a five-star rating for sexual tension. To Gabe, I said, "It's late and I'm going to sleep. You obvi-ously know your way out. And give me my book."

He tossed the book across the room so that it landed on my desk.

Okay, we weren't going to do this the easy way. I threw back the covers, swung my legs out of bed, and stood up. My right hip balked at that. Boy, it was going to hurt tomorrow. I ignored the pain and turned to Gabe. "Okay, you broke into my house, bypassed my guard dog, and appeared in my bedroom at—" I glanced at the green dials of my bedside clock—"almost midnight. I'm im-pressed as hell. So what do you want?"

"Let's start with why Vance almost arrested you."

I glared at him. "First tell me how you found the tracking device on your truck." I'd been so sure we'd gotten away with it.

"My mom told me she saw Angel skulking around my truck." He crossed his arms, waiting.

Gabe's mom was too smart, just like her son. I took a deep breath. "Your little stunt of moving the tracking device led me right to Chad's office. I thought you were in there. Turns out Vance was in there waiting for someone to break in. He had me handcuffed before I could talk him out of it."

The ends of Gabe's mouth twitched. "It looks like you talked your way out of it eventually."

"Once he blackmailed me into spying for him." I had to swallow that down.

"Who are you supposed to spy on?"

"Rick Mesa and Sophie Muffley." Why was I telling Gabe this? We weren't working together, so I didn't need to feed him information.

"What about Dara?"

I made a face. "No. Vance correctly surmised that you and I were not working together or communicating. I believe the tracking device on his car was the tip-off. He's really a good detective. Now if you are done playing twenty questions, will you leave?"

Gabe's intensity settled on me. "But I'm not done, sugar. Why are you favoring your right hip?"

Shit, they were both good detectives. "When Vance caught me, I hit the counter in Chad's little office kitchen. Now that you are fully informed, maybe you can lock the door on your way out."

In the light from my nightstand, I saw his face tighten with a dark anger. "Let me see."

I used my hand to wave him off. "My hip is the least of my problems."

An eyebrow went up. "You want to do this the hard way?"

My temper snapped. "Where were you tonight? You were so big on teamwork until Dara the slut showed up in your life. Now you are secretive, and God only knows what your mother is doing here!"

Gabe stepped forward until he towered over me. "I asked you to work with me, Sam."

"You demanded that I leap without a net! You wouldn't tell me anything! I saw Dara yesterday morning, Gabe. She looked mad enough to have killed Chad." I'll never forget the way she looked at Chad and me when she walked into the office and saw Chad sprayed with whipped cream.

"She didn't."

Anger throbbed in my head. "Then what is she hiding? What are you hiding? And why am I getting threats on my answering machine?"

Gabe's voice dropped to deadly. "What threats?"

I stared back at him. "I was looking for you tonight to tell you about it. It was just a message on my answering machine. I told Vance. All it said was 'Stay out of Chad Tuggle's murder. He got what was coming to him. So will you if you get too nosy.' "

"That's why you went into Chad's office? To tell me about the threat?"

I looked away. "It doesn't matter. I have it under control. I told Vance about it." I would take care of the boys and myself. Tonight had been an abject lesson in why I shouldn't rely on a man.

"Babe—"

I cut him off. "You know what pisses me off the most? I'm starting to get the feeling that I am wrong about Dara Reed. That I misjudged her. But the whole town is keeping some secret and you"—I turned back and looked at him—"are keeping it from me, too."

"Christ." He raised his hand to drag it through his hair. "Sam, I'm caught here. I have to protect Dara. You have to understand that. Especially if you are working with Vance." He dropped his hand and fixed his gaze on me. "But that doesn't change what's between us."

We were both caught. Probably by more than either of us was admitting. "I can't do that! I can't separate out—"

"Yes, you can," he reached out and took a hand full of my shirt, pulling me into him, into his hard body, and his mouth.

Oh yeah. I could.

"Mom!"

Startled, I pried my face from Gabe's and looked at TJ standing in my doorway. God. "What?" I tried to sound like it was no big deal that I was standing in my bedroom at midnight fusing tongues with Gabe. I'd sworn to myself that my sons would never see this.

TJ's face was pale. "Mom! Ali's growling. There's someone on the front porch!"

9

Ohmigod! Someone was on the front porch! I could hear Ali's vicious growls peppered with an occasional bark now. I raced out of the bedroom.

Gabe caught me at the door to TJ and Joel's bedroom. "Stay here with the boys." He reached behind his back and pulled out a gun. Then he disappeared around the corner.

"Mom?" Joel's huge sleepy eyes looked up at me. "What's going on? Why is Gabe here?"

I reached out and pulled Joel into my arms. "TJ and Ali heard someone on the front porch." I didn't answer the part about Gabe being here.

When Gabe came back, he had a prisoner.

"Lionel!" I shouted.

"Mom, who is that?" Joel leaned into me.

"It's all right, Joel. He's a client."

"Sam! Tell this buffoon to let go of me. I'm taking up watch over you." Lionel rolled his gaze down to my bare legs. "You shouldn't have him here when you're dressed like that."

"He was asleep in the chair on the porch," Gabe said. "He doesn't have any weapons, just nose spray."

Sometimes I wondered if all the crazies had some kind of homing device that made them zero in on Heart Mates and me. "Lionel." I let go of TJ and Joel and walked over to him. He had several inches and many pounds on me, but I made up the difference with my fury. "Did you leave me a phone message today?"

He looked down. "No, ma'am. You were kind of cranky today, you know . . . Maybe it's your woman's thing or something, but I decided that I couldn't reason with you. So I thought I'd just come over and sit a spell on your porch to make sure you were safe. Hey, are these your sons?"

"*Woman's thing?* Did you say I was cranky because of my *woman's thing?*" I looked back at Gabe. "Where's your gun?"

Gabe's whole face twitched. "Babe, you can't shoot him."

"Are you sure? He's an intruder in my house." *Woman's thing?* I was unreasonable? He's the lunatic who tried to attack Gabe.

Lionel said, "I kind of hate to point this out, Samantha, but you are acting irrational right now. Do you want me to get you some Midol?"

TJ and Joel both snickered.

That did it. "All right, boys, both of you back to bed. Ali, you stay with the boys. Lionel, go home."

He widened his big brown teddy-bear eyes. "But what about your Midol?"

"Gabe, give me your gun!"

Lionel held up his hands. "Okay! I'm going!" He turned and hurried out the front door.

I turned to Gabe. "You too. Leave."

He grinned at me. "Do you need Midol?"

First raging hormones, then raging adrenaline with no relief, had me tense enough to chew glass. "Get out, Gabe."

"I don't think so, babe. I tend to agree with you that

Lionel's not a real threat, but then again, I think you'd drive Gandhi himself to violence. I'm staying."

I grit my teeth. Every time I got close to working it out in my head with Gabe, he changed. "I thought you were protecting Dara."

"Mom's with her."

Hard to argue with that. Gabe's mom scared *me*. "Can your mom really shoot that gun?"

"She's won awards."

I didn't know what to say to that. Really, I didn't. I turned away from Gabe and went into the kitchen for Tylenol. Reaching up to the top of the cupboard, I yelped when I felt Gabe's hand on my waist. One hand pinned my stomach against the counter, the other lifted my shirt. "What are you doing?"

"Checking your hip." His index finger slid into the waistband of my panties, tugging it down.

I shivered.

"Bruised." He said, leaning into me. "I can kiss it better."

TJ had walked in on us. I couldn't do this. I wanted TJ and Joel to know I was there for them, not out man-chasing somewhere. Not even Gabe-chasing. "Gabe, the boys—"

He pressed his body into me. "I'll sleep out on the couch." He let go of the back of my panties, slid his hand around my hip and between my legs. "After."

"Sammy," Grandpa's voice broke through my lust haze. "What's all the noise?"

"Fuck," Gabe snarled into my ear. "Want me to shoot *him*?"

The phone woke me from a restless sleep. "Hello?"

"Sam? It's Roxy. Are you awake?"

Her voice sounded thick and tearful. "Roxy!" I sat up and swung my legs over the side of the bed. My clock glowed a green six-thirty A.M. "What happened yesterday? Why didn't you meet me at Duncan's Nursery?"

"I got held up. Uncle Duncan . . ." She started to cry.

"Roxy, what's the matter?"

She took a shuddering breath. "Sam, can you meet me this morning? I'll tell you everything then. I need someone I can trust."

Her voice wavered, but she sounded like she had gotten control. "Is Duncan all right?"

A beat passed, then she said, "He just loves me so much. But he's okay. Duncan wants me to be happy, Sam. I told him I could trust you. Is nine this morning at Smash Coffee okay with you?"

I was confused, but that's pretty normal for six-thirty in the morning. "Yes, I'll be there, Roxy." Hanging up the phone, I realized that maybe it wasn't such an odd conversation. Roxy was man-miserable, and Duncan might blame me for that since she was using my dating service. But Roxy trusted me to help her figure out what she really wanted. Okay, I'd meet with Roxy and find out what was bothering her, what happened on her date with Kevin (the financial advisor who drives a limo), and then talk about a new profile for her.

I stood and tried to stretch out the kinks from a restless night's sleep. I had tossed and turned, knowing that Gabe was sleeping on my couch. I was having trouble balancing my boyfriend and my sons.

Then there was the case. My working with Vance was a problem for Gabe, which meant he and Dara had something to hide from Vance. What?

I threw on a pair of sweatpants and headed down the hallway. I needed answers from Gabe.

The couch was empty, with a pillow and a neatly folded blanket at one end. "I just can't catch a break."

"Hey, Sam."

I turned around to see Grandpa sitting at the kitchen table reading the paper. "Morning, Grandpa." I went into the kitchen, poured a cup of coffee, and started the process of making lunches for the boys. "I see Gabe left."

"Gone when I got up."

I put together sandwiches and took out some frozen brownies. "He's doing that a lot lately. I forgot to give him Lionel's background check."

Grandpa looked up. "Gabe said he was going to check into Lionel, Sam. He was concerned."

I put the lunches on the end of the counter for the boys, then got out bowls and spoons for their breakfasts. "I thought you said he was gone when you got up."

"I talked to him last night when he went out on the porch to cool off."

Heat splashed over my face. "Uh, good. I mean, good that he's looking into Lionel." Part of me was glad Gabe was overheated, but I was a mother first. "Gabe came by because—"

"Probably was a good thing he was here. Make that Lionel realize you got someone looking out for you." He turned the page of the newspaper.

This was the hard thing about being a single parent. I didn't have the other half of the parental unit to discuss this stuff with. "Grandpa, I don't want TJ and Joel to get the wrong idea. Gabe slept on the couch last night."

He closed the paper and looked up at me. "TJ and Joel like Gabe. They respect him. They almost busted a gut laughing when they realized that when you had put a tracker on his car, he switched it to a cop's car."

I thought of the two of them rolling around on the floor playing with Ali. I had attributed their laughter to their silliness, not mine. I sighed and said, "I'm glad they enjoyed my folly."

"Oh, they did, but they were also impressed. Not only because you managed to get the device on Gabe's truck, but also because Gabe treated you just like he would anyone else by moving it to Vance's car. He doesn't pull his punches with you. He doesn't treat you like a little woman who needs a man to hold her hand. What do you think you are teaching TJ and Joel about men and women?"

I sipped my coffee. "How to laugh at their mother."

Grandpa grinned. "That. But look at it from their point of view. Gabe's an ex-cop, a PI and a cool guy, right? And he knew you could handle him switching the tracking device. He had faith in you, Sam. If Gabe Pulizzi has faith in their mom, then their mom must be pretty capable."

"Yeah, but when TJ came running in my room last night—" I winced, remembering times I'd gone in my mother's room and she had a man there. She had been angry.

"Did you or Gabe get mad at TJ?"

"No, of course not! God, Grandpa, TJ was scared. There was a strange man on the porch. I would never be mad at him for that. Gabe all but shoved me into their room, told me to stay with the boys, and went outside to check it out."

"So you both took TJ seriously. TJ felt like he did the right thing."

"He did do the right thing."

"There you go. TJ knows he can come get you any time he needs you." He got up, coming over to me. "The truth is the boys accept Gabe. He treats them, and you, with respect. Honey, no one is asking you to stop being a woman."

I met his gaze. "Thanks, Grandpa. Me and the boys are lucky to have you."

He grinned, then moved past me to get some more coffee. "I made a backup of the SCOLE disk for you. I want to take a closer look at that and see if there's something we missed."

I nodded. "That will help. When do you think you'll get more on Dara?"

"Today or tomorrow at the latest." That was the last

thing we said as the boys and Ali blew into the kitchen. Breakfast, lost shoes, parent signatures, and general before-school chaos took over the rest of the early morning.

I was inching my way through the heavy fog in the general direction of the sheriff's station, and running late. The SCOLE disk was in my purse, but it was already ten minutes to nine. I didn't want to be late for my meeting with Roxy at Smash Coffee.

Frankly, I didn't trust her to wait for me. She was too weepy and on edge.

I was on Lakeshore and came to the fork in the road. If I veered right, that would take me along the edge of the lake and to the sheriff's station.

The left fork put me on Graham Street. Then I could turn left on Main Street, hop on the 15 Freeway, and be at Smash Coffee by nine.

I had a second to decide. I took the left fork and headed for Smash Coffee. I'd run the disk back to Vance at the sheriff's station after I saw Roxy.

From the 15 Freeway, I took the Railroad Canyon off-ramp and turned left. Then a right on Grape Street. Smash Coffee was located in the Wal-Mart shopping center. I parked the T-bird and got out into the cold fog.

I felt my hair spring out of gel mold and into a frizzy twist. So much for my grooming this morning. I gave up and went inside.

The aroma of fresh ground coffee mixed with the yeasty smell of baked goods pulled me into the shop. The right side of the store had a counter built over scads of glass containers filled with coffee beans. A bakery case rose up at the end of the counter, displaying muffins and cookies.

"Sam!" Dominic Danger rushed around the counter

and came toward me. "You have got to see Anastasia. She's a beast, but of course I adore her." He engulfed me in a bear hug. Releasing me, he kept hold of my hands. "Anastasia is at the groomer's today, though. She's having her nails done."

I blinked up at the onslaught and laughed. "You are spoiling that cat." I had acquired a kitten a while back sort of by default while investigating the death of a friend of mine and Dom's. It had turned out that Dom's business partner was the killer. Once all the drama was over, Dom surprised me by taking the kitten. I looked Dom over. Spiky blond hair, hazel eyes, flawless skin, and tight leather pants paired with a sheer black shirt that fell beautifully around his golden pecs. Dominic was an actor in the small community theater. Speculation on Dom's sexual preference was a favorite topic of gossip. I think Dom purposely dressed to keep people guessing and interested.

"And how are you, Sam?" Still holding my hands, he spread my arms to look at me. "Interesting. Suede skirt with . . . Is that a Nordstrom's T-shirt? It's divine. I would have sworn suspenders were over, but they work on you, luv. With those boots, it's a sexy jockey look."

Smiling, I managed to get my hands back. "You look fabulous, as always."

"Of course," Dom waved his manicured hand and headed around the counter. "What can I get you this morning?"

"Actually, I'm meeting Roxy here, Roxanne Gabor. Do you know her?"

Dom started grinding some coffee beans. Over the noise he said, "Roxy? Sure I know her. She has the love-liest collection of silk scarves. Not many women can re-ally pull that off, you know." The coffee grinder stopped. "Try my Mocha Bounce, it's fabulous. It will get your blood running."

"How many calories does it have?" I asked while following Dom's movements as he put the grounds in a space-age-looking machine and added water.

From behind me a voice said, "That skirt does look a little tight, Shaw. I'd go with black coffee if I were you."

I spun around. "Vance! What are you doing here? Are you calling me fat?" His mirrored sunglasses hid his eyes, but his face looked relaxed.

Pulling off his shades, he flashed his dimples. "It's all a matter of taste, Shaw. Some men like the . . ." he dropped his gaze down my body, "full look."

Fat. He was calling me fat! I looked down. My stomach didn't pouch. Much. Okay, maybe just a little, a tiny had-a-couple-of-babies pouch. And I did have sturdy thighs, but I wasn't fat. Glaring at Vance, I looked down his dark suit paired with a pale yellow shirt and darker tie. Damn, no belly on him. "Yeah, well some women like men with no butts, too." I turned my back on him. "I'd like a muffin with that coffee, Dom."

Grinning at me, Dom set a foaming coffee on the counter and went to the bakery case. "What kind, Sam? We have blueberry, cranberry, cream cheese, banana nut, chocolate chip—"

"Chocolate chip." If I had to deal with Vance again so soon, I needed courage. Chocolate courage.

"Add a black coffee, please." Vance said. He reached past me to set a ten-dollar bill on the counter. Then he got my foaming coffee and his boring black coffee and went to a table. I collected my muffin and said, "Keep the change, Dom. Vance probably has a secret source of income." *Like writing romance novels.* I went to sit down at the wrought-iron table. I wanted to face the door so I could watch for Roxy, but Vance already had that seat.

I put my muffin down, reached for my purse, and pulled out the disk of the SCOLE files. "Here," I slid it across the table. "This is the file I took off Chad's computer."

Vance's gaze flashed around the room. then he took the disk and stuck it in his jacket pocket. "What else?"

I took a cautious sip of the Mocha Bounce coffee. Mmm. It had a chocolate, nutty flavor and was rich enough to make the chocolate chip muffin unnecessary. Blaine was going to love me if I took him the muffin. Finally, fueled by the caffeine and chocolate shot, I looked up. "I don't have anything else."

He fixed his gold-flecked brown eyes on my face. "What about Rick and Sophie?"

"It's barely nine in the morning. I haven't talked to them yet."

He crossed his arms over his chest. "You better not hold out on me, Shaw. I'll haul your full figure in for investigating without a license and crime-scene tampering."

"You know, Vance, you ought to consider some antidepressants. Might help your suspicious attitude." Actually, with his attitude, Vance was telling me what I'd already suspected. Something else was going on beneath the surface of Chad's murder. A hunt for something. Maybe the soccer money, but . . . I don't know. I just had a feeling.

He stood and picked up his coffee. "What are you meeting Roxy Gabor here for?"

"How long were you standing behind me eavesdropping?"

He smirked. "You put a bug on your boyfriend's truck. I don't think you can throw stones, Shaw. Answer the question."

"Business. Heart Mates business."

"You expect me to believe that Roxy Gabor, the model, needs your dating service?"

I looked over Mr. Sun God with dimples. "You got a crush on Roxy, Vance? She's way out of your league. But if you sign up at Heart Mates, I'll put in a good word for you. Oh, by the way, she is a *full-sized* model. Doubt she'll be interested in your skinny butt." I picked up my Mocha Bounce and ignored him, trying not to worry about my own full butt while I waited for Roxy.

By nine-thirty, I'd finished off the Mocha Bounce coffee and the chocolate chip muffin, and had scarfed down countless pieces of a sample pumpkin cheesecake muffin that Dom had cut up to inspire customers to buy more.

No Roxy. I reached into my purse to call her again when my phone rang.

"Boss, I have a new client here who's under the impression you actually work at Heart Mates. What do I tell her?"

Damn. "Her? It's a her? Not Lionel?" I couldn't deal with Lionel. If he said the word Midol once more, I'd hit him with his own tire iron.

"Missy Zuckerman. She's anxious to find her Heart Mate and she just knows that you can help her."

"Are you laughing?" I narrowed my eyes and stared at my thighs. Blaine was laughing at something. Hell, he was laughing at me. "Is Missy Zuckerman another lunatic?"

"No. How far away are you?" Blaine asked.

I gave up on Roxy. "Ten minutes at the most. I'm at Smash Coffee."

"Oh, boy. I'll tell the troops that the boss is paying us a visit." He hung up.

Dom was busy with customers, so I did a quick wave and left. It only took me about four minutes to make my way to work. I couldn't imagine why Roxy was acting so flaky. Could her uncle be sick or something? She did seem kind of worried about him this morning.

I parked the car and decided to worry about Roxy

later. Right now, I had to focus on work. Putting on my businesswoman smile, I sailed through the door and stopped short.

It smelled like a funeral. Flowers filled the office. Loose flowers. Not vases of flowers, but single roses, daisies, and carnations were strewn everywhere. I looked up and saw baby's breath stuck into the aging, water-stained ceiling tiles.

"Uh," I turned to Blaine. "What happened?"

Blaine grinned, used his right hand to smooth back his feathered hair, and reached beneath his desk. He pulled out a white poster board that had the words, "Hope you feel better soon" written in red ink across it.

A bottle of Midol was taped to the bottom with a big red heart around it.

A woman's voice said, "Oh, that is so sweet. A man who understands about women."

I turned around to face the woman who said that. She looked like a rational enough woman, so I chalked her comments up to nerves. "Hello, I'm Samantha Shaw." I tried to pretend that Blaine wasn't still holding the poster board up and smirking. "You must be Missy Zuckerman."

"Yes, I am. I am so excited about finding a man here at Heart Mates. My horoscope says that romance is a strong possibility."

Uh-huh. "Well then, we must get you signed up right away." I took quick stock of Missy. She wore an olive-drab gauze skirt with a yellow gauze top that draped down to her hips. She'd twisted her dried-grass-colored hair up into twin buns just above each ear. Her face was makeup-free except for a touch of gold glitter at the corner of her pale brown eyes. I took a breath. "Have you filled out the forms, Missy?"

"Yes! That was such fun." Her eyes lit up to a yellow-ish color.

I turned to Blaine, still holding the dopey card, and exchanged my smile for a frown. "Do you have the forms?"

Blaine ignored any implied threat in my frown. "I put the forms in the interview room for you. Now I'll just go put this card in your office so you can keep it forever."

He was so dead. And Lionel Davis was so dead, too. Hell, the only man I think I liked today was Dom. And he might be gay. Forcing a smile, I said, "Missy, would you like some coffee before we get started?"

"Oh, gosh, I don't drink caffeine. Besides, I am too excited."

I thought about slipping her a couple of the Midol to bring her down. "Well, then, let's get started." I led the way into the interview room.

Thankfully, there was only a single red rose in the middle of the oak table. Ignoring it, I gestured to a chair for Missy, then sat down where Blaine had left the clipboard with the interview sheet. I skimmed the info about Missy. "It says here that you like dancing. What kind of dancing?"

She fidgeted all over her chair. "Ballroom dancing. My dream is to open a ballroom dancing studio."

I looked up. "Here? In Lake Elsinore?" Was she serious?

She nodded.

"Okay." To each his own. But I started to get an idea. Of course, first I had to make sure that I wasn't pairing Missy here up with a card-carrying stalker or lunatic.

I was exhausted. Blaine and I had discovered that every time I stumbled over a murder, Heart Mates became a popular place. We'd fielded phone calls and clients all day. I dragged myself home, determined to pull it together for Angel's party in half an hour. I didn't

want to think about what the boys' bathroom looked
like.

Frowning, I passed a paneled van leaving our prop-
erty when I pulled onto the dirt in front of the house.
Who was that? Grandpa had picked up the boys, and his
Jeep was here. So was Angel's car. The phone message
from yesterday threatening me sprang into my mind.
All kinds of thoughts tumbled around, like my sons and
Grandpa being kidnapped, bound with duct tape, and
tossed in the back of that van with no windows.

Real fear brewed in my belly. I slammed on the brakes,
put the car in park, and jumped out. Oh God, what if
they had been kidnapped? Or, been hurt and left as
some kind of warning to me?

10

I hit the front door, clutching my key ring with the little canister of pepper spray, and rushed inside to see if my family and best friend had been kidnapped.

I hurried through the empty living room with my heart hammering viciously. Ohmigod, where were Grandpa, TJ, Joel, and Angel? I made it to the small dining room when things started registering. The smell of Pledge dusting spray, the furniture moved around in the living room, the rack of covered clothes I'd raced past in the living room. Empty serving bowls set out on the dining room table that looked ready for chips and dip. I turned right into the kitchen and stopped. Grandpa was setting up the coffeemaker. Angel was arranging blenders and margarita mixes, and the boys were bickering about making onion dip.

They were fine.

I was the one having a meltdown. I needed to get a grip. Forcing my mouth in a smile, I said, "Hi. Who was in that van that just left?"

"The house cleaners." Angel walked over to the pantry in her black silk pants paired with a halter top, and bent over. She came out with a stack of plastic margarita glasses. "Everything's done, Sam. Go take a shower."

Cleaners? I couldn't afford cleaners. Finally it dawned on me. "Angel, I love you!" She'd hired a cleaning company to come in and clean the house.

She flashed her billion-watt grin. "Barney's going to take the boys over to your mom's soon. They are going to eat over there. Dom will be here to tend bar and model the men's lingerie. Roxy and I will do the rest."

"Roxy? You talked to her?" I hadn't had time to worry about her once I had gotten to work today.

Stopping to stare at me, Angel said, "Yes, I talked to her. About an hour ago, but I hired her to model for me two weeks ago. You look tired."

TJ looked over. "That's because one of Mom's loser clients was sleeping on the porch last night. He said he was protecting her and asked her if she needed Midol. Then she tried to take Gabe's gun to shoot him, but Gabe wouldn't let her."

Angel looked back at me. "Gabe was here?"

"Here and gone without quite answering my questions," I clarified. "Lionel spread loose flowers all over the office and left a large poster board card—with a bottle of Midol taped to it."

Grandpa set out a stack of Styrofoam cups by the coffeemaker, then turned to look at me. "How did he get in?"

My head throbbed at the memory, since I'd asked the exact same question. "He was waiting outside the office when Blaine arrived to work. Blaine let him in. I think I might fire him." Walking into the kitchen, I put my arm around Joel. "How was your day?"

"Boring. Angel brought us a whole bag of candy to take over to Grandma's house. Grandma will probably want to stay there with us instead of coming to your underwear party." Joel made a screwed-up, disgusted preteen face.

"Lingerie, Joel," Angel walked by and play-smacked him on the shoulder.

"Whatever," Joel rolled his eyes.

Going into my bedroom, I stripped down and got into the shower while planning what to wear. Many of the guests tonight would be the moms from my PTA and soccer days. The fact that I stepped out of that world and hardly looked back made us uneasy with one another, at best.

Ever since I could remember, I've been fascinated by relationships. That's what attracted me to romance novels and dissecting them for reviews.

And then to Heart Mates. I loved trying to successfully match people up. It endlessly fascinated me to try to assess what clients really wanted and find matches for them.

The other side of relationships—why they unravel—fascinated me just as much. Which is what drew me into the part-time PI work with Gabe. I hadn't really known the man I was married to. Okay, the truth is more like I refused to see the man I was married to.

What makes a woman refuse to see the truth? Look at the misery that denial brought.

Like Janie. She had known Chad wasn't quite the shining town hero soccer coach, but she wouldn't admit it. She let the town force her out of soccer after he dumped her for Dara. Why? Love? Even love that has died? Or something else? And now that she was trying to face the truth—including who murdered Chad and why—I wanted to help Janie do that.

But the women I'd spent years doing PTA and soccer with didn't understand what drove me. I'd done a hundred-and-eighty-degree turn in my midthirties, turning my life around. They had only known me as a committed soccer mom. I changed the rules on them and they didn't know how to respond.

I shut off the shower, got out, and dried off. I used the blow-dryer to smooth the frizzies and did my own brand of magic with mascara, blush, and lipstick. Then I slipped into my electric-blue thong panties and matching camisole. I walked out of the bathroom.

Angel sat on my bed reading my romance novel. "Don't you dare tell me the end!" I warned as I went to my closet. Of course, all real romance novels had a happy ending, but how they got there was the key. I tugged on a pair of low-cut jeans and topped that with a sheer electric-blue top that allowed my camisole to peek through. Sexy but not slutty. Hopefully. I stepped into a pair of slip-on heels and turned around. "Well?"

Angel looked up from the book. "Depends. The women will hate you, but if Gabe stops by, he'll kidnap you for hot monkey sex."

I wrinkled my face. "I could never figure out what the hell hot monkey sex is. Why would anyone want to swing from trees naked?"

Angel laughed, leaned over, and put the book on my bedside table. "So Barney mentioned a plan to get a few people drunk and pump them for info. Oh, he's got some stuff on Dara that he'll tell you tonight. He and the boys have left. Dom's in the kitchen re-doing the coffee. He brought his own coffeemakers, liqueurs, and stuff to make coffee desserts."

I went to my desk and got my yellow pad. "I made some notes. First on my list is Sophie Muffley. We want to get her drunk and find out more about Chad, the missing soccer money, and what Sophie was looking for in Chad's office." Quickly I got Angel up to date on my rendezvous with Vance in Chad's office last night.

When she stopped laughing over Gabe's changing

the tracking device to Vance's car, she said, "So you are spying for Vance now?"

I glanced over at the romance novel. How many books had heroines forced to go against their morals, but that always found a way around, a way to do the right thing? I just had to figure out what the right thing was. I'd give Vance what I thought wouldn't hurt any of the players. Chad had been murdered, and we had to find the killer.

Turning my gaze back to Angel, I answered her question about spying for Vance. "I gave him the disk for the SCOLE books. I should have done that right away. But I'm not going to give Vance information on people that could hurt them." Like if Dara had a brutal husband searching for her.

The doorbell rang. Angel leaped up from the bed. "It's show time!"

I smiled. "And you look gorgeous. Let's go launch Tempt-an-Angel lingerie. When we are finished, your lingerie will put Viagra out of business."

We hurried down the hall to answer the door and get the party started.

Twenty minutes later, I went into the kitchen. Dom had two fresh batches of margaritas ready. He glanced over at me. "How's it going in there?"

Over a loud roar of bawdy female laughter, I grinned. "Good. Really good. Angel's lingerie is a hit. Roxy just came out to show some of her full-sized line. You're next, and then Angel's going to coax some of the guests to try on the lingerie." I took a blender full of margaritas from him. "You'd better get ready."

"Sweetie, what's to get ready? I strip off my clothes and the ladies adore me."

Uh oh. I clutched the sweating pitcher and eyed Dom's clothes. He had slip-on shoes, butt-hugging jeans, and a blue and green Hawaiian print button-down shirt. "You aren't going to actually strip, are you? My mother's out there!" A twitch started in my left eye.

"Darlin', those women all came here expecting to see Dominic Danger, and I will not disappoint them." He touched my face. "Lighten up, Sam. It's all for fun. Your mom will have the time of her life." He took the second blender of margaritas and went into the living room to refill drinks.

And strip.

I looked down into the full pitcher of margaritas in my hand and seriously considered drinking it straight down. But if I was going to get Sophie drunk enough to talk to me, I had to stay sober enough to remember what she said. I forced my feet to move into the living room.

About twenty-five women were crammed into the living room, spilling over the couch, love seat, and folding chairs. They watched Roxy as she came out in her last outfit. Roxy had her blond hair cascading around her face in loose waves. She wore a black-and-white silk lounging pants set that looked only slightly suggestive, but beneath that, Angel informed us, was a very sexy bra and panty set, and she held up a matching set for the women to see.

The older women, in particular, liked the nice look of the lounging set, yet appreciated the charge from the secret knowledge of naughty clothes beneath.

I flashed a smile at Angel and went over to where Sophie sat on the love seat with—

Oh, boy. It was Iris, Gabe's mom.

What was she doing here? Panicked, I looked around the room. My mom was chatting with Linda Simpkins, the PTA president, and Molly, who owned Frank's Flowers with her husband. Dominic finished filling my mom's glass, said something that made her laugh, and headed toward me on his way back to the kitchen. He winked at me as he passed by.

He was going to strip. In front of my mom and my boyfriend's mom.

"All right, ladies!" Angel shouted out. "Does everyone have their drinks? It's time for the main event!"

Catcalls and whistles broke out.

My eyes widened. I felt like I was standing on the tracks with a fast-moving train barreling down on me. I didn't know how to stop it. I waved my free hand toward Angel, frantically shaking my head, trying to signal her to stop Dom.

A warm hand touched my arm. "Sam! Hello there. Sophie invited me and she introduced me to your mother. Is that more margaritas?"

I looked at Iris's smooth face and twinkling eyes. Then at the glass she held out. Not knowing what else to do, I filled her glass, and then topped off Sophie's glass.

While I poured the frozen drink, I wondered if Iris had finagled the invitation from Sophie to get her drunk and pump her for information to help Gabe and Dara. I hoped not, since Iris would probably have more luck than I would. Sophie had been pretty annoyed at me when I saw her in the beauty shop yesterday. It was going to take a lot of alcohol to soften her up toward me.

On the other hand, Iris could be here to check up on her son's girlfriend. I was sure a man stripping in my living room at any second would make quite an impression. Cripes, how do I get myself into these situations?

The music started. The fast, pulsing beat of "I'm Too Sexy" blared out of the stereo.

Dom burst out of the kitchen and into the middle of the living room. By the time the song hit the part about being too sexy for his shirt, Dom reached for his top button.

I stood there, seeing my life pass before my eyes.

What would my mother say? What would Gabe's mom say to him? *Your girlfriend has sex parties?*

"Sam," Iris said from her seat behind me. "You're in the way, dear."

I stepped to the side and sat down on the arm of the couch, holding the pitcher.

Dom was down to the bottom button of his shirt, swaying and teasing the women. His natural boyish charm was combined with just enough sexuality to keep the tension on the fun side. He edged the shirt off his shoulders.

Sophie shouted, "Pants."

Shocked, I turned to look at her. Her thin face was flushed to a pretty glow, and she was clapping in time to the music. The tension lines around her eyes and mouth eased. She'd had enough to drink to slide into happy giddiness. Was it enough to answer my questions?

My thoughts were interrupted when I saw Dom toss the shirt.

It landed on my mom.

My mom! The woman who had built herself into the Queen of real estate and had successfully convinced herself she did not grow up in a trailer right here where this house was. Mom worked hard to be a lady of class.

A man had just thrown his freshly stripped-off shirt at her.

Mom picked up the shirt and put it around her neck like a fine silk scarf, the bright Hawaiian print standing out starkly against her beige blouse.

Dom ripped open the buttons on his jeans and began to ease them down his hips.

Beneath was a pair of pure white satin boxers. Kind of disappointed, I watched him kick off the jeans directly into Missy's, my new client's, lap.

Missy looked down at the jeans in her lap. Then she smiled and drained her margarita glass.

The music was winding down when Dom turned around and shook his behind.

There, in a blaze of red embroidered on the white satin, read "Tempt An Angel."

Laughter and clapping broke out. Dom basked in the attention, going around and planting kisses on various women's cheeks.

Dom did a few more changes, modeling some items Angel had for the men, before Angel coaxed some of guests into trying things on for themselves and coming out to show us.

I relaxed. So far my mom and Gabe's mom appeared to be having a good time. They weren't going to make an issue of Dom's little strip show.

Dom had managed to get his jeans back to make another batch of margaritas, and then he switched to coffee with or without Kahlua.

Gabe's mom chatted with Sophie. I narrowed my focus on them. I had to separate them before Iris got the information I needed. But how? Dom? He was busy with coffee.

Angel strode up and dangled a dangerous-looking piece of lingerie from her fingers. "Sam—"

I cut her off. "No way." I glared at the thing.

Angel flashed her smile. "Come on, Sam. It's a bustier. You have the perfect figure to model it."

Iris and Sophie stopped talking to watch me. If Angel hadn't been my best friend . . . crap. "Fine. Give it to me." I grabbed the item from her hand. Turning it over, I frowned. "How the hell do I get this on?"

Sophie spoke up. "It's got eye hooks like a regular bra." She stood, took a second to check her balance, and said, "I'll help you."

She would? Was she going to yell at me again? But yesterday, when she'd demanded I stay out of the investigation into Chad's death, she'd made her case in front of the entire beauty shop. So what did Sophie want?

Lord, I didn't really want to put my enhanced breasts on display to Sophie for gossip at the next SCOLE meeting.

But this was my chance to get Sophie alone. I fixed a fake smile on my face. "Let's go in my room." She followed me down the hallway.

Once we got in my bedroom, I shut the door and started with casual conversation. "Did you see anything you liked, Sophie?" Sophie looked around my room, her gaze going to my bookcase stuffed with romances. Her brown eyes had the glazed, slightly unfocused look of snockered going toward tired. Finally she sat on my bed and answered, "Besides Dom?"

I smiled at that. "Besides Dom."

"I already ordered a few pieces from Angel. Give me that," she gestured to the bustier in my hand. "I'll unhook it for you while you take off your top."

She wasn't slurring drunk. Her speech was slightly thick, but that was it. Pulling my top over my head, I tried to think how to change the focus of the conversation to Chad. "Sophie, I know you are under a lot of pressure with Chad's death, but—"

"He was a prick."

I threw my shirt on the chair at my desk and turned around to stare at her. I hadn't expected that. I thought she was trying to protect SCOLE's reputation. Now she was telling me Chad was a prick? "Chad? I thought you liked him. I mean . . . you and Jay always supported him." Sophie's husband, Jay, was the SCOLE president. "And you worked part-time for him."

"I worked for him, but I hated him. Jay hated him. The worst part is I wished him dead, but not without knowing . . ." She trailed off, looking down at the bustier in her hand.

My thoughts spun around. *Without knowing what?* Where he put the soccer money? "What, Sophie? What don't you know?" I tried to keep my voice steady and soothing. Not desperate. "Maybe I can help you."

She looked up at me, her gaze shimmering with frustration. "I almost did that, hired you to find the pictures, but I just kept going along, thinking that eventually I'd find them." She shook her head. "I don't know where he put them."

Huh? I didn't quite follow what she was talking about. Something about finding pictures. "What is it you are looking for? Something Chad has of yours?"

Sophie turned the bustier over in her hand, concentrating on working the little hooks. "I was drunk. One night, I was drunk and that prick was there with his digital camera. If those pictures surface, if that detective finds them, it'll destroy my marriage."

Ohmigod! It slammed home fast and hard. Sophie wasn't talking about the missing soccer money. She was talking about—"Chad had pictures he was using against you, Sophie? For what?"

A tear slid down her cheek. "For whatever he wanted. Money, a secretary, sex."

Blackmail. Chad Tuggle blackmailed Sophie. Stunned, I tried to sort it out. "That's why you didn't want me digging around about Chad—you thought I'd find the pictures?" Did she think I'd let Vance have pictures like that?

Sophie wiped away the single tear. "I searched the office. His computer was wiped clean, but I'm afraid he had copies somewhere. I couldn't find them, and that detective barged in, telling me I was breaking into a crime scene."

So that's why Vance staked out the office. He knew people were looking for something, but not what. He'd caught Sophie looking. No wonder he was so frustrated.

Sophie took a breath. "Your mom . . ."

I snapped out of my thoughts about Vance. My mom! She and Sophie were good friends. My mom showed up in Chad's house. The pieces slid together. "You asked her to look in Chad's house."

She sniffed once, then leaned forward and stood holding out the bustier. "Go put it on in the bathroom. Then I'll hook you up."

Lord, she was tough. Even semidrunk she pulled herself together. I had to admire that. I could also see that she had told me as much as she was willing to right now. Taking the bustier, I went into the bathroom. I slipped off my camisole and struggled into the bustier. Holding it together as best I could, I went back out. Sophie and I spent a good five minutes fastening and arranging. Finally we decided I was as good as I was going to get. Now I was dressed in my low-cut jeans and an ice blue satin bustier with lace overlay.

Was I really going to walk out in the living room and model this?

Sophie giggled. "If anything pops open on that, the wires are going to kill someone. Even your cleavage looks dangerous."

I turned to the mirror on my closet door.

Jeez—I looked like a cartoon. The bustier had cinched in my waist and pushed up my boobs so that I looked sort of like Jessica Rabbit. "Oh, boy, I can't go out there like this!"

Sophie walked up behind me. "Why did you have implants, Sam?"

Meeting her gaze in the mirror, I only saw curiosity. I had the urge to shrug my shoulders, but that seemed dangerous. "To look better and feel better. It was part of forcing myself out of the comfortable role I was in. The role where I let my husband walk all over me. I didn't want to be that woman any more."

Sophie nodded. "Then don't be afraid to model your decisions." She turned and left the room.

I stared after her. Who would have guessed the slim, uptight Sophie Muffley would understand? But then, wasn't the same true of me? Had I really understood Sophie? She was afraid of her marriage being destroyed for one mistake that somehow got caught by Chad's camera.

Sucking up a deep breath, I was more determined than ever to find out the truth behind Chad's death and see if I could find the pictures for Sophie. It didn't take a genius to figure out she'd probably had a fling with some guy. I'd seen true remorse in Sophie's eyes.

I turned away, pulled open the bedroom door, and walked down the hallway with my head held high. It was no different than wearing a bathing suit top or a tank top.

Angel spotted me first. "Okay, ladies, now here's the key to a more curvaceous figure." Everyone turned and looked at me.

Getting courageous, I did a little turn and spotted Roxy heading for the front door with a makeup case slung over her shoulder. Stopping dead, I said a quick, "Excuse me," and raced to catch Roxy as she stepped outside.

The shock of the night air hit me. Damp and cold, I wrapped my arms around myself and remembered I was in the bustier. Damn, I should have grabbed something to throw over it. Too late now. I spotted Roxy and called her name.

Her back stiffened beneath her sweater. Slowly she turned around and fixed her green eyes, rimmed in smoky liner, on me.

I blinked. Anger shot out of her gaze. "Roxy, are you all right? You didn't show up at Smash Coffee. What happened?"

Her face iced over. "I thought you were my friend, Sam. I thought you . . . Friends are loyal. Uncle Duncan is right. I can't trust you." She turned to walk away.

"Roxy!" I raced up to her and grabbed her arm. I could feel her trembling. "What are you talking about? I was there at Smash Coffee waiting for you. Is Duncan all right? Is he sick?"

Her green eyes narrowed. "He's not sick. He just loves me. And I did show up at Smash Coffee." Tears filled her eyes and spilled over. "Then I left. I know better than to trust you now. I'll fix this myself." She pulled her arm from my hold and got into a black Jaguar.

"Fix what? Roxy, wait!"

She slammed the door, started the engine, and slid away into the dark night.

I stared after her into the blackness. What was she talking about? Why would she show up at Smash Coffee and then leave before talking to me? What the heck happened on her last date? Why did she keep saying Duncan loves her? Everyone knows that. She's his only family.

A noise jarred me out of my thoughts. Turning my head, I looked to see a large truck turning onto the dirt of our property.

Suddenly, the blinding white headlights were speeding right for me. Dust filled my nostrils. Fear kicked in, and I turned to run up to the porch. All the while, my mind stumbled over the possibilities. Gabe had a truck— maybe—but no, my impression was that it was a light-colored truck, not black like Gabe's.

The truck slid alongside of me and screeched to a halt, and I heard the door pop open. Oh, God. My heart hammered, and blood pounded in my ears. I was steps from the front porch when something was flung over my head. Panic exploded, and I tried to fight the material covering my head. I tripped, falling to the dirt, but got the covering off my head.

Fighting to breathe and control my hysteria, I looked up. A large shape loomed over me in the darkness. My control shattered, and I screamed bloody murder.

11

"**S**amantha, stop that caterwauling!"

I abruptly closed my mouth on my next scream and squinted to make out the shape standing over me. There was just enough light coming from the house to see who it was.

Lionel Davis.

I struggled to free my arms from whatever he had thrown over me. "Lionel! What the hell are you doing here? What is this?" I fought the material, worrying that my boobs were going to explode out of the bustier.

"Stop it. You're drunk." Lionel bent down on one knee and pulled the material out from under me.

I looked at what he had in his hand. A coat. A black coat, long and with a split in the back like the cowboys wore in movies.

Lionel moved to put the coat around my shoulders. "I was just trying to cover you up. You are obviously drunk and out here in your underwear."

"Drunk?" I looked at him. His soft brown eyes darted everywhere but my chest. "You think I'm drunk?" My voice rose. "What are you, some kind of asylum escapee? And what are you doing here, anyway?" I looked past

Lionel to see several people were drawn out to the front porch by my screaming.

Perfect. Just perfect. This will probably be in the newspaper tomorrow. Or at least on the PTA and soccer mom gossip vine. "Lionel—" my words stopped when he suddenly scooped me up in his arms like a rag doll. "What are you doing?"

"You're too drunk to walk. I'm going to put you to bed."

Frustration made me furious. "You are certifiable! A lunatic! Do you hear me?" He walked up the porch steps into the middle of the gathering crowd of gaping women.

"Of course I hear you. I'm not the one that's drunk and shouting."

I did not believe this guy. Once he made it to the living room, I shouted, "I need a gun!"

Iris stepped around the love seat to block Lionel. She had her gun. It was pointed at Lionel's head.

"Put Sam down. Now."

I stared at her. The first thought that slammed into my reeling brain was that her eyes looked almost like Gabe's—cold, deadly, and determined.

Lionel grunted once, then slid me to my feet. "Look, ma'am, this has nothing to do with you. Samantha will be my girlfriend so I'm—"

Iris cut him off. "Sam, get behind me."

I walked around Iris before I realized I was obeying her. But hell, she had a gun!

"Now, listen up, Lionel. Sam is my son's girlfriend. She is not your girlfriend." Iris waved the gun in front of his face. "And I don't want to see you bothering her any more. Do we have an understanding?"

Lionel's soft brown eyes filled with wet hurt. "But she's drunk and running around in her underwear. She needs me to take care of her."

Iris sighed. "Lionel, Sam is not drunk. She hasn't had

a drink all night. She is perfectly capable of taking care of herself."

I looked around. Every woman in the room, and Dom, were all staring at the unfolding drama—Iris Pulizzi holding a gun on Lionel. The only good news was that, for once, I wasn't the center of attention.

Then I saw Missy. She stood just on the other side of the love seat, and she was swaying. Her normally high color drained out of her face, leaving her skin bleached and pasty. Her eyes sort of rolled around.

Uh-oh.

"Lionel, Iris is right." He was closest to Missy. He might be insane, but I was pretty sure he was harmless. Or I hoped so. "Look to your right, Lionel. See Missy there? I think she's going to pass out." I don't think Missy was used to drinking.

Lionel turned his head to the right, spotted Missy swaying, then snapped his head back to Iris. "Excuse me, ma'am." Then he took a large step and caught Missy in his arm before she slipped to the ground.

We all watched him silently. Lionel stood there looking down at the woman in his arms. She had a china-doll look to her face even though she was passed out drunk. Lionel appeared captivated. My thoughts whirled. *Hmm, a match?* Provided Lionel wasn't insane, of course.

Finally, my mom stepped forward. "Lionel, is it? Why don't you put Missy in my car? Sophie and I will take her home." My mom turned to me. "You have her address, right, Sam?"

I nodded. I had it in my purse where I had her security release for Gabe to run the check on her. "It's in my purse." I escaped down the hall and got the paper from my purse, quickly jotted down Missy's address, and then ran back out to hand it to my mom.

Mom gave me a stern look. "Lionel is one of your clients?"

"Not officially. Gabe hasn't cleared his security check yet."

My mom shook her head. She still had Dom's shirt wrapped around her neck like a scarf. "Samantha, this has crossed the line. You simply cannot dabble in this dating service any longer. Now use the next two weeks wisely and wrap up things at Heart Mates. We'll go to the real estate convention in Phoenix and get your real estate license, and you can lead a respectable life." She turned as Lionel was coming back in from depositing Missy in the car. Sophie stayed out in the car with Missy.

I watched my mom leave. Now I knew what she had been doing at Chad's, as well as why she had avoided me, since she didn't want to tell me Sophie's secret. Mom was very good at keeping secrets—she'd kept the identity of my biological dad a secret from everyone. Lord, what a mess this whole case was. But right now I had to deal with my possible client. "Lionel?"

He looked at the old shag carpet and shuffled his feet. "I really thought you were drunk, Samantha. Why else would you be outside in that . . . getup?" A blush crawled up his neck. "I just wanted to take care of you." He sighed. "Of someone. I want someone to take care of."

God. Once I would have fallen into a man's arms who just wanted a woman to take care of. Now I wanted to take care of myself. But there were women who would adore a man like Lionel—if he learned to control himself and be reasonable. If anyone needed a dating service, it was Lionel. He was sort of a misguided knight in shining armor. He needed to learn how to be a hero without trampling on the heroine. "I got it!" Excited, I said, "Wait here," and raced back to my room. Quickly I pawed through my bookshelves stuffed with romances and selected three books that had overpowering male heroes who were tamed down by the heroines. Running back out, I stopped and panted, trying to get my breath.

It was damned hard, what with the bustier squeezing my breasts up to my nose.

Finally, I held out the books. "Lionel, read these. Then we'll talk." I held up a hand. "Not about us dating. I won't date you." I couldn't make it any more plain than that. "But those books will show you what women like in men. Then maybe we can find you some lovely women to date." Or a desperate woman.

He took the books and looked at the covers. They were clinch covers that showed a man and woman in states of semiundress draped over each other. "These look . . ." he trailed off, his face darkening even more with embarrassment.

"Read them," I insisted.

"If you say so." He turned and wandered out, looking through the books in his hands as he went.

"Romances?" Iris said, tucking her gun back into her purse. Then she smoothed her black-and-lavender print shirt down over her black slacks. "Do you think it was wise to give him that trash?"

"You don't like romance novels?"

She wrinkled her nose, making hidden age lines spring out. "A woman waiting for a man to save them? Not in my world."

I smiled. "They aren't like that anymore, Iris. A woman is just as likely to save the man in today's romances. What do you like to read?"

"Mysteries, serial killers, true crime, and celebrity autobiographies."

"Ah." I studied her. Intense and intelligent eyes. Iris had raised her brood by herself after her husband's death. And judging by Gabe's self-sufficient ways, I'd guess she didn't coddle her sons the way some Italian mothers were rumored to. Plus, to raise a brood like that, Iris would have to have been successful at a career of some sort. Gabe had mentioned that she owned a restaurant. Now she was retired . . . maybe bored. "Are you out here to get a piece of Gabe's PI business?" She seemed to be helping him. She had told Gabe about the tracking device and chatted up Sophie in the beauty shop. I'd swear she finagled the invitation from Sophie to come here tonight.

Iris laughed and shook her head. "I'm not about to start taking orders from my son. No, I came out here because of what Gabe said about you."

Uh-oh. In spite of her telling Lionel that I was Gabe's girlfriend, which she could have done only to convince Lionel to leave me alone, maybe she hated me. Or hated the idea of me for Gabe. Maybe she wanted a young woman who would give her grandchildren. "What was that, Iris?" And why was I worrying so much? I knew the score. Gabe was younger than I, and would move on to a younger woman some day.

"Ask him, Sam. I had a lovely time tonight, but I have to get going."

"Wait!" I followed her to the front door. "Iris, did you get anything out of Sophie tonight?"

She looked back at me. "Nothing helpful. Except to confirm what we knew."

I nodded. I wasn't going to get any more from Gabe's mom.

"Ask Gabe, Sam. Tonight." She left.

I went into my room to change when I heard Grandpa and the boys come into the house.

"Sam!" Grandpa called out.

I grabbed a long-sleeved denim button-down shirt and threw it over the bustier, then ran back out while buttoning the shirt. I saw Grandpa at his computer. "What? What's wrong?" Nothing would surprise me.

Angel and Dom both looked up from the table where they were drinking the Kahlua coffees. Dom said, "Wow, someone needs to chill. Why don't you—"

I glared at him. "Don't you dare say Midol!"

Dom's hazel eyes widened. "Midol? Anyone can pop a pill. I was going to suggest a day at the spa. There is nothing like a few hours at the spa to clear out the toxins that make us cranky."

I wanted a day at the spa, but the way my luck was going, the good-looking guy giving me my massage would keel over dead, murdered of course, and I'd be right in the middle of another murder investigation. Or I'd be arrested on the spot as the lead suspect. A band of stress tightened around my forehead.

Mixing around in there was Iris's cryptic comment. What brought her to Lake Elsinore was what Gabe said about me. What had Gabe said that would bring his mother running?

Grandpa looked over his shoulder at me. "Sam, I got it. Been waiting for this."

I turned from Dom and Angel to Grandpa. Then I looked around. "Where are the boys?"

"TJ's in the shower, and Joel is reading a new skateboard magazine."

After taking a deep breath, I went to the empty chair closest to Grandpa and sat. Dom picked up a can of whipped cream, shook it, sprayed it onto a cup of coffee, and then slid it across to me. "Here you are, love."

"Thanks." I picked it up, then slid around in my chair to look at Grandpa. "What do you have?"

His fading blue eyes danced with excitement. "Okay, first let me tell you what I've been doing. There wasn't much info on Dara, but I nosed around a little and discovered that Dara Reed had an Arizona driver's license."

I rolled my eyes. "What set of city, county, or state records did you break into for that? Or wait, that's DMV records."

Grandpa ignored my sarcasm. "So I figured Dara lived in Arizona before coming here to Lake Elsinore.

After that, I was able to narrow down the search to a small town. What is surprising is that the town newspaper is online and has all the marriages, births, and deaths on file."

I froze with the coffee cup halfway to my mouth. "Deaths?" Grandpa and I had wondered if she had run from an abusive husband. I had thought Dara had the look of a woman who used men. But once Grandpa had mentioned that Dara didn't appear to want to be found, I'd been rethinking that. Sure, she wore tight clothes, had a belly button ring, and appeared to steal Janie's husband, the town's hero coach, but that wasn't what really struck me.

It had been her eyes. The way she had looked at Chad when she walked in right after I'd whipped creamed him. Like she could kill him.

Grandpa broke into my thoughts. "What I found was the marriage of Dara to a Mark Reed about fourteen years ago. Then there's the announcement of their son Josh's birth about thirteen years ago. By the way, Mark Reed was some kind of scientist, either a medical doctor or a Ph.D."

I took a long drink of the coffee. It was rich with Kahlua and whipped cream. "Okay, Dara was married to some kind of doctor. Is that who she's hiding from?" I couldn't get the pieces to fit. Dara Reed didn't look like a doctor's wife. She looked a little too hard edged or . . . something. But if she'd been abused by this Mark Reed, then that could account for the strain on her face and hate in her eyes.

But why would she have hooked up with another man? Chad and Dara had been an item, like, a month after Dara turned up around Chad's soccer team. It just didn't make sense.

"No. Mark Reed is dead."

I set the coffee cup down. The rich, warm liquid congealed in my stomach. "Dead? From what? Did she kill him?" Ohmigod! Had he been abusing her and she'd finally snapped and killed him? What about their son Josh?

"That's what I've been trying to find out. I couldn't access his death certificate, so I found a contact in the Office of Vital Records for Arizona. He was able to get a copy of the death certificate, scan it, and send it to me."

The Triple M network of magicians stretched far and wide. I tried not to think of the trouble Grandpa and his friend could get into. "How did Mark Reed die? Was it murder?"

"That's not exactly clear. What is clear is that he did die of an overdose of pain medications. He had cancer. Advanced terminal cancer. He either committed suicide, or someone else helped him along."

"Dara?" I felt like I was in another world. "Would she even know how to do that? Did he die at home? How could Dara get that much medication and get it into him?" It was all so confusing.

Grandpa sighed and rubbed his eyes. "Dara was a licensed pharmacist in Arizona. She worked at a small independent pharmacy."

"Oh." My mind just sort of blanked to a wet-noodle consistency. "So she could have killed him." I tried to slog through my thoughts. If Dara was a murderer . . . But no, that couldn't be right.

Gabe would not protect a murderer.

Unless she played him. Told him a lie he believed.

But Gabe was a PI. A good PI. He would have checked it out. My thoughts bounced back and forth while I tried to work it out. What was Dara's connection with Chad, then?

Blackmail. Sophie was being blackmailed by Chad, so why not Dara?

The hate that had been in Dara's eyes when she looked

at Chad—what if that hadn't been about the whipped cream and me at all? What if that had been about blackmail?

Dom's voice broke through my thoughts. "Mercy killing."

"Huh?" I glanced over at Dom. He was staring out the sliding glass window into the dark night.

Turning his gaze back to me. "Mercy killing. Assisted suicide. It's a big controversy. Remember Oregon?"

I nodded slowly, feeling a weird sense of going from a wide angle to a tight focus. "They passed the law that doctors could prescribe medications to assist in the suicide of a terminally ill patient. Or something like that. Didn't the attorney general of the county get involved?"

Dom nodded. "I don't think assisted suicide is legal in Arizona."

The focus tightened. Things were beginning to fit. "So maybe Dara assisted her dying husband in suicide. And now she could be charged with murder." I thought of the sad cases of assisted suicide I had seen on TV programs or read about. That would explain why she kept to herself in Lake Elsinore, wasn't on the Internet much, and didn't even have a credit card.

Time for the long-overdue talk with Gabe. I stood and stepped toward the phone when Ali jumped up from where she was sleeping by the slider. A warning rumble started low in her chest and rose to a vicious growl. Turning from the phone, I saw the hair stand up in a straight line down her back. She ran to the front door, barking and snarling. Then she went to the window. Furious now, Ali shoved her nose at the window. Then she jumped down to the floor and crouched.

"Ali, no!" I screamed at her and ran to the window, grabbing her collar. She trembled.

"Mom?" Joel raced out of his bedroom.

"It's okay, Joel. Just stay back from the window." Ali kept looking between the window and me. She obeyed me, but was trying to make me understand that I needed to let her go.

Angel slipped up beside me, holding a gun. "Was Ali going to jump through the window?"

I shrugged, trying to see out in the dark. I thought I saw a shadow moving by the cars, then dart away into the darkness. But I wasn't sure.

Until I heard a car start in the distance and drive away. I relaxed slightly. "They are gone. I think."

I could feel Ali's bunched muscles, as if the act of holding herself back was the hardest thing she had ever done. She whined.

Grandpa moved up toward the door, then gazed at Ali quivering beside me. "She's really bugged, Sam. Think she knows who it was out there?" He put his hand on the door.

Hell if I knew. But I did know Grandpa. "Don't! Don't go out there, Grandpa!" I let go of Ali and rushed to push myself between him and the door. Then I saw what was in his blue-veined hands. A flashlight and I recognized . . ." I held out my hand. "Give me the switchblade!"

"Cool," Joel said from where he huddled in the hallway with TJ.

Grandpa took a single step back, his slightly milky-blue eyes fixed on mine. "What switchblade?"

I glanced down at his hand. The folded blade was gone. In spite of the circumstances, I had to fight a grin. Damn, he was good. I knew exactly what he could do, but he'd kept my eyes on his face and hid the blade with his fast hands.

But no way in hell was I letting Grandpa go outside, especially with a switchblade. Grandpa had acquired the switchblade sometime after he'd seen the one a six-pack of thugs pulled on me to try to steal my car. Gabe had tried to take it away from him once, but Grandpa had then pickpocketed the blade back without Gabe knowing.

"Grandpa, I'll take Ali and go check. I need you to stay with TJ and Joel. Please."

Angel lifted her gun. "I'll go with her, Barney."

Grandpa shifted his stare past me, to Angel, Ali, and then the boys. Then he said, "Here's what we'll do. We'll send Ali out first and see what she does."

Ali barked a short agreement and stuck her nose in the seam of the front door. Since I was pretty sure whoever had been lurking around out there was gone, I reached out and opened the door for her.

She squirmed and wiggled her way out before I got the door opened, leaped off the porch, and raced to my car. There she stopped and sniffed, then looped a full circle around all the cars. Finally she barked once and sat.

I didn't speak dog, but I took that as an all-clear signal.

Of course, she could have just been asking for a beer.

I turned to Grandpa, "Can I have the flashlight, please?"

He gave it to me. I went out with Angel and her gun at my side. Carefully, I aimed the flashlight over the dirt lot in front of the house. Then I swept the beam of light over Angel's red Trans Am, Dom's yellow Mustang, Grandpa's black Jeep, and my T-bird, finally landing on Ali sitting by my car and waiting. She barked again.

I trusted Ali. No one was hiding around the cars. I walked down into the dirt yard and straight for my car.

It seeped into my consciousness that my car looked kind of low.

When I got to Ali, I shined the beam of light on it and saw why—all four tires had been slashed. Bending down, I saw a big puncture in one of the tires. "Shit."

"Sam."

I stood up. "Grandpa! I thought you were in the house with the boys." He stood right behind me.

His steely look told me he was ignoring my comment. "Shine the flashlight on the side of the car."

I did. Spray painted in big black letters was *Talk to the police and die.*

I winced. My first thought was that Blaine was going to have a fit. Then real, butt-kicking anger slammed into me. *This was my car!* It was part of my revenge on my dead husband. He'd loved his classic cars. We'd had two, this T-bird and a Mustang. I'd sold the Mustang and used the money to pay for my breast implants and some cool stuff for the kids. Then I'd claimed the T-bird for my own.

Trent had never let me drive the classics. I'd been the type of woman who let him tell me that. I detested that woman. Fury pumped in my blood. This car represented my independence, my waking up as a new woman.

Some punk had slashed the tires and written a threat to my independence. I wasn't having any of this.

"All right, everyone back inside." I herded them in, taking a second to pet Ali. Then I locked the door, set the alarm, went to the phone, and called Vance. While the phone rang, I glanced over to see Angel, Grandpa, Dom, and the boys gathered around the kitchen table. Dom served the boys some hot chocolate. While the rest of us were debating who was going outside to face the threat, Dom had made hot chocolate. I didn't know what to think of that.

Vance's voice mail talked in my ear. I waited for the beep and said, "Vance, this is Sam. Someone slashed the tires and wrote a threat in black paint on my car that said, 'Talk to the police and die.' I'm getting damned tired of getting threatened." I hung up and stared at the phone.

It pretty much dawned on me right about then that I had just called the police. Now I was supposed to die. Jeez.

"Mom?" Joel slipped under my right arm. "Are you scared?"

I reached over with my free hand and brushed his brown hair off his forehead. "Scared? Maybe a little. Mostly I am mad."

Joel glanced at the phone then back at me. "Do you think you should call Gabe?"

I squeezed Joel gently. "That's my next call, sweetheart." It was a struggle not to let Joel know how much it cut to my heart that he didn't quite feel safe with me. I'd kill anyone that tried to hurt him, his brother, or grandfather.

Joel nodded.

"Honey, I wouldn't let anything happen to you, you know that, right?"

"Yeah, sure. But Mom, Ali's not acting right. Won't Gabe know what's wrong with her?"

My heart turned over. I looked past him to Ali. Joel was right. She had her nose pressed to the front window, but her neck sort of sank between her powerful shoulders. Ali looked—worried, depressed, confused?

I picked up the phone and dialed Gabe's cell. He answered, "Pulizzi."

"Gabe? Can you come over? We've had a little problem. And Joel's worried about Ali."

A second of silence. "I'm in my truck, so I'm on my way. ETA, five minutes. What's the situation?"

I told him about my car, struggling to control my fury and not upset Joel any more than he already was, and then I told Gabe why Joel was worried about Ali.

"Put Joel on, Sam."

I handed the phone to Joel. "Gabe wants to talk to you." He took the phone and they talked for a few minutes. Then he hung up and looked at me. "He told me that Ali is special because she was in the police dog program. She's, like, smarter than other dogs." He nodded, looking very serious.

"You were very smart to see that she was acting odd, Joel."

His seriousness slid away into bright pride. "That's what Gabe said."

I studied our dog. What was going on in her head? Ali was agitated or worried about something. Or maybe she just wanted to tell us something and we were too dumb to understand. "When Gabe gets here and makes sure it's safe, you and TJ can sit by her and see if she'll—I don't know—play with you or let you know what's bothering her."

But Ali suddenly left her post at the front window to trot over to the front door. There she barked once.

I knew that bark. I went to the door and looked through the peephole. *Gabe.* I deactivated the alarm and swung open the door. He stood there in jeans and a dark T-shirt. The porch light outlined his chiseled face and dark hair. His powerful body appeared relaxed.

But I was not relaxed. I was pissed. I didn't realize how pissed until I saw Gabe. Phoned-in threats, slashed tires, graffiti threats, and he was keeping another woman's secrets. I stepped out and pulled the door shut behind me.

Gabe didn't move, but arched a single eyebrow.

I slammed both hands down on my hips, ready for a confrontation. "Did you see my car?"

"Saw it."

Full-blown fury slammed into my chest. "That's my car! My car!" I had to get control. The car was only part of it, but where the heck was I going to get money to fix my car? I didn't just need the fee from Janie, I was desperate for it. I took my right hand off my hip and waved it between us. "I'm not doing this anymore. Vance is after me to rat out people who don't deserve it. You are after me to—hell, I don't know what you want. I never know what you want. But I know this: I have to protect TJ and Joel. So either you are going to help me or you are going to leave. Which is it?"

12

So there we were, locked in our own private battle on the front porch. Gabe reached out and caught hold of my wrist, tugging me a step closer to him. The intensity of his dark gaze slammed into me. The heat of his body spread out over me. Only an inch of night air hung between us.

"Gabe?" I was out of options here. I needed an answer.

"I have a cassette tape I want you to listen to." He used his free hand to fish the small rectangle out of his pocket.

"But . . ."

He arched his eyebrow again. "But what? Am I going to abandon you and the boys when you might be in danger? Well, shit, Sam, let me think about it. There is a goddamn game on TV tonight I don't want to miss, so I'll have to get back to you on that. Christ, what do you think?"

I shivered and felt the bite of the damned bustier shoving my boobs up practically to my chin. Trying to shift my torso, I said brightly, "Okay, then! So this tape, what—"

"What do you have on under that shirt?"

Uh-oh. His voice had dropped to a sexy throb. "It's, well, a bustier. Gabe?" I'd lost his attention to my chest. The top buttons of my shirt were open, and with his hold on my wrist there was a gap. The porch light illuminated deep cleavage thrust up with each breath I took.

"Right." He swallowed once, his Adam's apple working hard to shove down sexual hunger. Then he looked up into my face and tugged me hard into his arms.

The door opened. "There you are, Samantha!"

I jumped back from Gabe. Dom stood in the doorway holding a coffeemaker. "I have to get going. I need to load up my supplies."

Angel came up behind him. "Sam, I'm going to leave my lingerie rack here and pick it up tomorrow, okay? You will be okay, right?"

"Sure." I had no idea if I was okay. Gabe made me crazy enough to momentarily forget my vandalized car and the safety of my family. *Bad mom. Very bad mom.*

Gabe handed me the small rectangle-shaped cassette tape. "Here, Sam, go listen to this while I help Dom and keep an eye on TJ and Joel."

I nodded, feeling the weight of the little tape in my hand. The boys and Ali rushed over to talk to Gabe while I went down the hall to my bedroom to find my cassette player.

I came out of my room, holding the small tape to return to Gabe. I found him at the kitchen table, talking with TJ and Joel. Grandpa must have gone to bed. Joel's face was animated as he explained something. TJ nodded and Gabe listened.

Joel caught sight of me. "Mom, Gabe has two extra tickets to the Storm game Tuesday night. I know it's a school night, but can we go? Please?"

The Storm was Lake Elsinore's minor league base-ball team. I met Gabe's eyes over the head of Joel. He watched me but said nothing. If I said no, he'd tell the boys that he'd take them another time when it was okay. I took a breath. "Sure, you can go."

Joel jumped up. "Cool!" Then he turned to look at me. "I guess we have to go to bed?"

I walked over to them. "It's late, boys. Both of you need to go to bed."

TJ stood too. "Thanks, Gabe. Come on, Ali."

Ali got up and went with the boys, leaving me alone with Gabe.

I took a seat across from Gabe and placed the tape on the table in front of me. "Why didn't you tell me, Gabe?" I was annoyed at having been so wrong about Dara. She was not the team mom slut.

"Client confidentiality."

"Bullshit." I was done playing games.

His mouth quirked, then settled into a hard line.

I started putting things together. Gabe's mom shows up, then gives me a cryptic message. Gabe pushes me out of the loop, doesn't want me on the team. But he wants to take my kids to the game. Okay, he won't let the kids get hurt. Well, good, he's a frickin' hero. "You didn't think I'd find out as much as I have on my own, did you?"

"Not this fast. You're getting good."

I refused to acknowledge the compliment. "What did you say to your mom on the phone that had her rushing out here to save you?"

Motionless, he answered, "I told her I wanted to make you a partner."

I sat back in my chair. Partners? In business? Love? The stock market? "What kind of partner?"

"Business, babe. Finish your AA degree at community college, but shift your major to criminal justice.

Keep working for me part-time, log enough hours, pay the fees, pass the test, and you are a licensed PI."

It wasn't adding up. "Heart Mates is my business."

Gabe put his arms on the table and leaned forward. "Then exactly what are you doing for Janie, Sam?"

"Helping her. Besides, you threw me off the case." We were going in circles.

"To make a point."

"What?" I snapped forward in my seat. "You were making a point?"

He nodded. "You need me."

I blinked and narrowed my gaze. "That's what this whole thing has been all about? You were trying to prove that I need you? *You can't do it without me.*'" I mimicked him when he'd taunted me at Angel's mom's beauty parlor. "Leaving me in that pond, switching the tracking device to Vance's car."

Gabe shrugged. "What about you? You're the one who put the tracking device on my car and followed me to Chad's house. What were you trying to prove?"

I knew what I was trying to prove. I had to be independent. Men were trouble. Okay, a little truth here. My tendency to build a fantasy around certain men might add to that trouble. But damn it . . . "Clarify why your mom came running, again."

His mouth twitched again. "Let me see if I can get this exactly right. 'To smack some sense into that damned Italian head of yours.' "

"I see." No, I didn't, but what the hell could I say? "And did she?"

"Not yet. Didn't bring her wooden spoon, but she'll whap me one when she feels like it."

Right. I could get behind that right about now. "So . . . Why didn't you just talk to me about this?"

"I am," he pointed out.

I took a breath. Good thing I didn't have his mom's

gun right now. "Gabe, does this whole thing seem reasonable to you?"

He got up and came around the table. Drawing a chair out, he dropped into it. "My reaction to you is anything but reasonable. The stronger you get, the sexier you are. Trouble is, I get a little possessive and had the urge to lock you up in my house."

I studied his hard-cut face, with a nose that might have been broken, a hard mouth that could flash a heartbreaker of a smile, intense deep eyes. I could spend years locked in a room with him and still not know all of him. He was a man built on street survival, mixed with regrets, sorrow, and deep pain. Then there was his kick-ass body. Gabe was way out of my league.

And five years younger.

"Heart Mates." I took a breath, hoping to put this into the right words. "It's mine. Like my car." I pushed away the gut-cramping anger for the abuse my car suffered tonight. "I love Heart Mates, Gabe. I love working to transform my little run-down business into the dream I can see in my head."

He took my hand. "I know."

He did. And he believed I could do it.

"But I also know that you have surprised yourself with your ability to investigate. Suddenly all the mysteries in your life have shifted. The power has shifted. You are learning how to find out things." He rubbed his thumb over the back of my hand. "Like who your father is."

He knew. He's always known. Just as I knew he had to do everything in his power to save Dara for Josh's sake. Because he hadn't been able to save his own unborn son or his wife. I fought down the emotion in my throat.

"We both have a job to do here, Gabe." I glanced at the tape. "Regardless of whether or not you put me on the payroll, I have to help Janie, and it's personal now. You have to protect Dara. So let's get to work."

He folded his hand around mine. "You're on the

payroll." He let go of my hand and touched the tape. "Let's start here. You understand what Dara did?"

I looked at the little black rectangle. "Her husband was in the last stages of cancer. She helped him die when he could no longer bear it." The tape contained Mark Reed's final words of love and gratitude to his wife. He clearly stated his wish to die. Stated his desperate pain . . . I turned my thoughts away. I got it. Dara did what she did out of love. I looked up at Gabe. "She helped him commit suicide."

He nodded.

I took the leap. "Somehow, Chad found out and used this against Dara. What did he have on her?"

Gabe's jaw clenched and a vein on the side of his head throbbed before he visibly got control of himself and relaxed his tensed shoulders. "Dara was in town about a month, put her son Josh on the soccer team, and kept to herself. Chad invited her to his house, telling her that he wanted to talk about Josh. Dara and I suspect that Josh may have inadvertently said something to Chad that made him realize Dara had a secret."

I thought of TJ. He had spotted Josh's vulnerability. "That makes sense, Gabe. TJ told me that Josh is a sad kid. And he thought Chad used him to get to Dara."

"I don't think your sons are ever going to fall for that. TJ and Joel are way too sharp."

"Yeah, but they didn't move to a brand-new town. They have my mom and Grandpa. Josh . . . God, he had to be so lonely and sad. It takes time to deal with a father's death." I thought about how TJ and Joel each dealt with Trent's death differently. "Did Josh know that Dara helped his dad die?" Had Chad gotten Josh to trust him enough to tell him that? What a burden for a child.

"No. Both Dara and her husband didn't want him to know. If he ever asks specifically, she says she will tell him. We think he probably said something else that made Chad look around on the Internet. Could have been something as simple as Dara refusing to have Internet access at home because it's so easy to track people."

"Like Grandpa did." I'd known Chad for years and never suspected he was such a bastard. Probably because I had taken him at face value as the hero coach. Just like many people in town had taken me at face value as the dumb and dumpy soccer mom who didn't care her condom-selling husband was out dealing drugs and sex.

"Right. So Dara went to Chad's house, and he charmed her for a while and gave her wine. She thought she had a friend, got drunk, and told him the whole story. He used a hidden camera to videotape it, with sound, including how Dara mixed the solution of morphine and some other agents to help Mark slip away. In Arizona, there is an explicit statute against assisted suicide. Chances were good that no one would care, since Mark was obviously close to death. But a local district attorney had it in for Dara Reed because she had reported him when he tried to fill a prescription for painkillers with a forged prescription. He swore it was a mistake and nothing ever came of it, but he's wanted revenge on Dara ever since. He wants to make her an example, a test case, of the law. So she took her son and left Arizona before any charges were filed."

I finished the story. "And came here to the small suburban town of Lake Elsinore. She kept a low profile, didn't mix with the women too much where she'd be tempted to talk about her problems, her grief. She had no idea there was a monster among us who would exploit her secret." I tried to get a picture of how Chad used the information. "Chad used the video to . . . what? Get money? Force her to sleep with him?"

He glanced down at the tape, then back at me. "At first, it was just money and sex. He was still married to

Janie. Chad liked the power he had over Dara. He obviously couldn't tell everyone what his hold was, so to show off he started forcing her into a public situation."

I squirmed in my chair. I couldn't even imagine how horrible it was for her. Grieving for her husband, alone in a new town and the one person she took a chance and trusted—"He forced her to be his girlfriend?"

Gabe nodded. "Dara went along with him, sure that if she didn't, Chad would turn her into the Arizona DA and she'd be arrested. Then Josh wouldn't have any parents. Chad got a sick thrill out of forcing her to play the part of his girlfriend and casting her into the home wrecker role, as you called her."

I winced, and shifted my thoughts to Dara's hate-filled eyes when she had come into Chad's office the morning I'd whipped creamed him. It fit. Now I truly understand just how much she hated Chad Tuggle.

Vance's take on the crime scene came back to me. Self-defense. Had he and Dara gotten into an argument? "Did she kill Chad?"

Gabe fingered the tape on the table. "She didn't kill Chad. According to what I got from a source, the police determined that Chad was killed by some kind of a bookend shaped like a soccer ball. Apparently one of them is missing."

"I saw those bookends in Chad's office. They were a set of stone bookends that had been painted to resemble two halves of a soccer ball. One of those killed him?" I remembered thinking that they were probably a gift from the soccer team. The irony struck me. Hero coach killed by a gift from his team. Lord, I was getting silly. "Wait, how does that clear Dara?"

He ran his hand through his hair. "The angle of the wound indicates that it was a blow by someone at least five-foot-eight. And they had to be strong enough to kill him with one blow."

Yuck. I sat back and thought about that. "Hey! That means Vance knows I didn't kill Chad!" I was five-foot-five on my best day, with heels.

Gabe nodded. "He's manipulating you. Again."

I saw the flash of dark anger in Gabe's eyes. Vance and Gabe have a history. Vance had used me to flush out a killer, and it pissed Gabe off.

"You could have mentioned this earlier," I pointed out. I wasn't totally forgiving Gabe. "Okay, we know Dara didn't kill him. So what have you been looking for exactly, the videotape?"

"CDs. Chad had the equipment to download pictures or videos to his computer, then burn them on CDs. The CDs were his backup copies. He showed Dara that he had them, but she never knew where he hid them." Gabe used his thumb and forefinger to rub the bridge of his nose. "You saw the computer at his house. It's been wiped clean."

"So has the computer at Chad's office," I added, remembering Vance's frustration.

"I've been looking everywhere for the backup CDs. And apparently so has Rick, Sophie, and your mom."

"Yeah, the whole town's practically covering up for Chad's killer while searching for the blackmail evidence." That explained why Vance was having such a hard time getting any cooperation. No one wanted the local cops to have their secrets, I mused, when suddenly the full significance of what Gabe was looking for rammed home. I put my hand on his leg and looked into his eyes. "You have to find those CDs for Dara before Vance does!" If Vance came across Dara's confession, he would turn it over to the DA in Arizona. I didn't think Vance was cruel or mean, but he believed in the law. Now I understood Gabe's comment about how Vance blackmailing me into helping him could be a huge problem. If I had somehow stumbled over those CDs, Vance would have gotten a hold of them.

Gabe got up and went to the refrigerator, pulling out two beers. "I'm looking, Sam. Everywhere Dara and I can think of. Mom's been snooping around town, trying to come up with any leads." He came back to the table, opened a beer and handed it to me, then opened the second for himself.

I took a drink of my beer. Lord, what a mess. We were in a race against time and Vance. The pressure to crack this case built around me. Janie needed to be cleared to get the insurance money and peace of mind, and we needed to find the blackmail CD to free Dara from the possibility of prison and to free anyone else Chad was blackmailing from the cloud of doom hanging over their heads. And I was pretty sure that when we found the murderer, we'd find who was threatening me. And maybe all that would somehow lead us to the missing CDs.

I reached over to Grandpa's desk and snatched a yellow legal pad and pens. Putting everything on the table, I said, "Let's start a list and figure out who might have murdered Chad. Maybe putting down the facts we have will help us figure out where the CDs are."

He set his beer bottle down. "Very sharp, babe. Let's get to work."

"Okay, five-foot-eight or taller is first." I wrote that down, then added, "Strong enough to kill with one blow."

"Right-handed," Gabe said. "The blow was to the left temple. Since there was something of a struggle, it had to happen fast. The killer likely picked up the bookend with his dominant hand."

I added *right-handed* and *struggle*. "Do you think it was a man or woman?"

Gabe shrugged. "Not a small woman like Dara. A woman big enough and scared or mad enough could maybe do it. But the voice threatening you on your answering machine was male."

True. I wrote down *male* and put a question mark next

to it. What else did we know? "Computer skills! Both Chad's home and office computers were wiped clean."

"Right. Add blackmail victims," Gabe put in. "I'm sure there are more than just Dara. Like Rick Mesa, since he appeared to be looking for something at Chad's house. And your mother."

I had to smile. "I know why mom was there. She was looking for some pictures Chad had of Sophie Muffley. Sophie was another of Chad's victims."

He watched me with his dark eyes, then smiled. "I win ten bucks."

Lifting my pen, I said, "Huh?"

He shrugged. "I bet my mom that you would get Sophie to break first."

Cool. He bet on me. "Five of that's mine." I looked down at the list. "So how does the missing soccer money fit in?"

He looked over my shoulder. "The money was never accounted for on the books?"

I shook my head. Then it dawned on me. "Chad was going to pay it back by blackmailing someone."

Gabe nodded. "It would fit."

"Let's see what we have about our killer." I read it off:

"Five-foot-eight or taller.

"Strong enough to kill with one blow.

"Right handed.

"One rock-like bookend shaped like half a soccer ball missing. Murder weapon?

"Computer skills.

"Blackmail victim?

"Struggle between Chad and murderer. Accident? Self-defense?

"Threat on answering machine a male voice."

I was starting to get a feel for what happened. "Chad was despised. I don't know when he started stealing and blackmailing, but he got bolder with the power. It was like a drug with him. He was financing his lifestyle—big-screen TV, pool table, expensive computer equipment, and cameras. He was the hero coach. He thought he was untouchable."

Gabe touched my hand resting on the yellow pad. "That's Dara's take on Chad. She was starting to come out of her grief and guilt fog enough to fight back. Chad wanted more money from her, and she refused. She told him she was tapped out."

Dara had been married to a doctor. She had been a pharmacist. She hired Gabe. Looking up at Gabe, I said, "I take it she's okay financially?"

He nodded. "But Dara said Chad needed money. She didn't know about the missing soccer money, though."

"So he took the money from the SCOLE account, sixteen thousand dollars, maybe to buy that shiny new big-screen TV, probably with surround sound and other extras. The pool table in Chad's living room had been new, too. Then he started looking for a blackmail victim in order to put the money back."

"Not bad." He rubbed his thumb over the knuckles of my hand.

I shivered in response to Gabe's touch. His dark eyes were intent on me. I tried to stay focused. "I think we have to follow the blackmail trail to find Chad's killer." Another possibility occurred to me. "Gabe, if the killer went to all the trouble to clean off Chad's computers, including breaking into his house and cleaning off that computer, maybe he or she has the blackmail CD."

He raised a brow and looked at me while continuing to run this thumb back and forth over the back of my hand.

"You already thought of that."

"Yes. And we're out of time. If Vance finds the killer, he might stumble onto the CD if the killer has it."

The warm tingling spread from my hand. "You need me."

"Yes."

"Okay, well, Sophie is maybe tall enough to have killed Chad. She was being blackmailed. She worked part-time in his office, so it's possible that she has enough skills to wipe his computer clean."

"Okay, she's a possibility."

"Hard to imagine Sophie killing."

"Sam," he settled his hand on top of mine. "Anyone can be driven to kill. The crime scene looks more like self-defense. Things could have gotten out of hand."

I nodded. "What about Rick? He's tall enough, and he owns his own business, so maybe he knows something about computers. I thought he was Chad's best friend and the assistant coach, but he showed up at the house. I think I should try talking to him again." I had to look past my perception of Rick as a nice guy.

Gabe nodded. "Take Angel, as a precaution. Try to find out what he knows, what Chad had on him, where Chad might have hid it, and who was a new interest in Chad's life. In the meantime, I'm going to go to Chad's house later tonight and toss it."

"Be careful."

He stared at me.

"Right. You're not the one that broke into a crime scene while the homicide detective was there." I sighed. Maybe I had a few flaws in my abilities. "Okay, you search Chad's house and I'll chat with Rick Mesa. So I guess we're done here."

He smiled. Slowly. With heat. He reached his hands up, undoing a button on my shirt. Then the next. "We're just getting started. I want to see that thing you have on under this shirt."

I remembered the dangerously tight bustier. I pulled back, brushing his hands away. Then I undid the remaining buttons and let the shirt fall open.

Gabe's eyes darkened. His nostrils flared and . . .

The doorbell rang.

13

I fumbled with my buttons while Gabe got out his gun and headed for the door. Ali met him there. Still struggling to button my shirt, I heard Gabe's voice challenge, "Vance, a house call this late?"

"Pulizzi, what are you doing here? I thought Sam got rid of you."

Shit, just what I needed. Dueling cops at my front door at eleven o'clock at night. Jumping up from the chair, I fought another button through the hole. I intended to head off a confrontation between Gabe and Vance. I took a step.

A thump froze me. Forgetting about the buttons, I turned around. I had knocked the tape to the floor when I jumped up.

My stomach lurched. I had to get that out of sight before Vance—

Vance's voice came from directly behind me. "Listening to bodice rippers on tape?"

Obviously Gabe had turned at the sound and Vance took that as an invitation to come in. I stared at the little black rectangle on the yellowed linoleum floor. I couldn't let Vance get a hold of that tape. While it wasn't exactly a smoking gun, it did suggest premeditation, or whatever they would call it, of Dara planning to help her husband die.

Ali slipped her head beneath my hand. Obviously she felt my tension. Since she knew both Gabe and Vance, she didn't understand. I stroked her head and took a breath. Turning around, I looked at Detective Vance and searched for a distraction. "How can you disparage the very books you write?"

His brown eyes dropped to my chest where the bustier molded my enhanced breasts. "The term just popped into my head."

I looked down to my gaping shirt, then snapped my gaze up to Gabe. He shut the front door and moved silently behind Vance, his face a tight mask of anger. Uh-oh. Gabe and Vance had danced this dance before, and worse, I'd once seen Gabe flatten another man who insulted me right in front of Vance. To get between them, I said, "Uh, Gabe? Can you put that tape back in the boys' room? They must have left it out."

Gabe looked at me from behind Vance, then at the tape on the floor. Ali whined, feeling the tension. She didn't like it. Her fur bristled beneath my hand. Then she went to the tape on the floor and picked it up in her mouth.

Startled, I stared at my dog. I mean, sure I love her and thought she was a genius as well as an alcoholic, but did she understand every word we said?

Vance spoke first. "Whoever made the decision to dump that dog from the academy had to be a moron."

God, I loved Ali. Turning to Vance, I purposely ignored Gabe. With both hands, I carefully buttoned my shirt and said, "Did you see my car, Vance?"

Gabe slipped past Vance. "Come on, Ali. Let's put the boys' tape away and get you settled."

I saw Gabe head past the love seat and hook a right

down to the boys' bedroom, with Ali following him. Sighing with relief, I finished buttoning my shirt and focused on what Vance was saying.

". . . So come by the station tomorrow and get a copy of the report number on your car for your insurance."

Huh? "Don't you want to dust the car for fingerprints, or something?"

His brown eyes narrowed. "How much did you have to drink tonight, Shaw? Pay attention. You obviously had a party, and how many of those people do you think might have touched your car?"

"How did you—" I looked around at the empty cups, stacked folding chairs, and the rack of lingerie, and shut up. "I'm cold sober, Vance. And I'm sick of getting threatened."

He glanced toward the hallway, then back at me. "Then get smart, Shaw. Quit playing with the bad-boy PI and work with me. We had an agreement. Now was Sophie Muffley here tonight at your sex party? Did she tell you what she was looking for in Chad's office? I'm assuming Rick did not come to a woman's underwear party." He glanced over at the Angel's rack of frothy, frilly, sexy lingerie.

Crap. I was caught between really needing to find Chad's killer and protect my family; and finding the CDs to protect Dara, and finding Sophie's pictures, for that matter. All I could do was buy a little more time for Gabe to look for the CDs. I drew up my shoulders and said, "It wasn't a sex party. You are such a prig."

He dropped his gaze. I knew the bustier was safely hidden behind the fully buttoned-up shirt, but heat crawled up my neck anyway. "Answer the question, Shaw. In spite of the liberal blond streaks in your hair—"

"Chunks."

He wrinkled his forehead. "What?"

"They are called chunks, Vance, not blonde streaks."

I knew I was poking a mad bear. Vance didn't look like he'd slept more than three hours total in the days since the murder. But we needed time.

The gold in his eyes caught the lights. Vance stepped closer, reached out, and caught hold of a lock of my hair. "Are you trying to divert my attention, Shaw? Maybe you want my attention on you, not the case?" His voice had dropped to a throaty chest tone.

Swear to God, I thought I heard a crackle. Something about the general dislike Vance and I held on to for each other tended to peel back my nerves. That whole opposites-attract thing. He had this air of yachting and Martha's Vineyard, while I was at home in a trailer.

"Maybe you want to give me another little peek at your undies?"

Did he think I didn't know he was baiting me? I brought my left hand up, catching him on the inside of his right forearm and knocking it away. Fortunately he let go of my hair or I'd be missing one of those high-priced chunks. "Go home, Vance. I don't have any information for you."

He stared at me. "I wonder if you are lying to me."

"Why would I do that, Vance? I'm getting threats! Don't you think I want the murderer caught?"

He studied me. "You and your ex-cop boyfriend are up to something." His patrician nose thinned like he might actually be sniffing out the truth.

I headed for the front door and opened it. "Goodbye, Vance."

He followed, and when he was dead even with me, he looked down. "Be at the station in the morning. Don't make me come looking for you again."

I slammed the door. God, he pissed me off. He thought he could order me around. I was getting really sick of men and their games.

Men. Gabe. Sighing, I headed down the hall to fish Gabe out of the boys' bedroom.

I quietly pushed the door open. First thing I saw were Ali's eyes glowing from her spot on the floor. I looked around. Joel was asleep on the top bunk, with his magazine still in his hand, which was lying on his chest. TJ slept on the lower bunk. His magazine had a white marker and was neatly placed on the nightstand. No Gabe, though.

I left the door open an inch so Ali could get out and looked around the hallway. I took a quick peek in the kitchen. No Gabe. He wasn't in the hallway bathroom, either. Had he gone down to my room? I went to the end of the hallway and looked in.

Gabe was sprawled on my bed reading my romance novel. He had one hand tucked behind his head, pulling the shirt tight across his chest. Damn, he looked good on my bed. "Good book?" I asked. Of course, I knew it was, since I had a rockin' review planned if I could just find the time to finish the dang thing. Murder and blackmail really cut into my reading time.

His gaze rolled off the page to me. Sitting up, he put the book on the bedside table and stood. He walked toward me. "Not as interesting as you." Reaching for my arm, he tugged me into the bedroom and closed the door behind me. Pressing me up against the wall behind the door, he looked down into my face. "Vance gone?"

I leaned my head back against the cool wall. "Yep. He took off as soon as he was done threatening me and giving orders. Do you guys learn that in the academy?"

"Nah, men are born that way. We like to be in control." He slid his leg between my thighs.

"Yeah?"

Grinning, his face shifted from the hard-cop expression he'd worn when Vance showed up, to bad boy. "Oh yeah, we're real big on control." He reached up and started unbuttoning my shirt, his voice tightening. "Not that I'm against losing control in some situations."

"Gabe," I grabbed his hands, "the boys—"

"Dead asleep."

"Right." I kept hold of his hands. We could play this a couple of ways, but I knew the outcome. Hell, I wanted the outcome. But we were on a case. "Gabe, what about the blackmail CD? Don't you—"

"Later. You're driving me crazy, Sam. I want to see that thing you have on under there." His words were low, feathering over my face. He pressed his thigh deeper between my legs. But he didn't fight my hold on his hands. "How far down does it go? Do you have panties on?"

His breathing hitched on the word. Made me feel powerful, female. The urge to drive him to lose control surged up inside me. I tilted my head back. "Thong. Ice-blue thong."

He made a noise in his throat. "Want me to beg?"

Oh, God, there was a picture. Sexy, dangerous, bad-boy Gabe Pulizzi begging for a peek at my thong and bustier. I pretended to ponder the idea. "Hmm, could you beg naked?"

His eyes glittered. Freeing his hands from mine, he placed them on the wall over my head and leaned closer. "Up to a point, I'll accommodate you, sugar. But let me make the endgame perfectly clear—you'll be begging me."

God. The hot blood rushed in my ears. Intensity and need poured off him in waves of musky heat. There was a dark possessiveness in Gabe, a danger that I had only glimpsed. Tonight it was barely contained by a fraying thread. I decided to test that thread. Using both hands, I shoved him back.

He took a single step.

I reached up and undid the buttons on my shirt. I slid it off and tossed it past the bathroom door, where it landed on my desk. Then I undid my jeans and slid them down. Tight as they were, I was forced to wiggle. I kicked them off. Deliberately forcing my mind away from any body flaws, I stood in the ice-blue bustier and thong. "Want to discuss begging now?"

His gaze burned black heat in a slow path down and back up. The moment stretched out long enough for me to start thinking about cellulite and baby fat when Gabe closed the space between us. "Discussion's over." He brought his mouth down to mine, his hands sliding around my bare hips to cup my butt. He took possession with his mouth and hands, driving me to a hot need.

I pressed my hand against his jeans, getting a deep groan from him. Breaking the kiss, he reached behind his back to take his gun out and carefully put it on my nightstand. Returning to me, he ripped off his shirt and kicked off his shoes.

I freed him from his jeans, taking hold of his erection.

He circled my wrist. "Hold that thought." He took my hand away to get rid of his pants and socks. I started toward the bed, but he turned back, blocking me. His gaze drilled into mine as he pushed me back to the wall. "Hope you own these panties. Or you're going to have to buy them from Angel if they are on loan."

"Huh?"

He reached down to the silk of my thong, using his index finger to press the silk into my heat. He followed that by a hot kiss and brought me to the brink. I reached for him.

He let go long enough to catch my hands and lock them together in one of his. Then he was back, stroking me, kissing my neck. "Beg me, babe."

"Not fair," I complained.

"Tough." He moved his mouth to my breasts, which were spilling out of the bustier.

He kept stroking, the silk growing wet. The sensations welled up, making me desperate. I needed him. I needed this. When he managed to draw a nipple over the bustier and into his mouth, I cried out, "Gabe!"

He stopped. "Not good enough."

"Let go of my hands and I'll show you good enough."

His smile was small and very wicked. He held on to my hands as he slid down to his knees.

Oh, God. I wanted to . . . He touched his tongue through the silk. I slammed myself back against the wall, growing desperate. I didn't realize he'd let go of my hands until I felt him grab hold of my hips, holding me where he wanted me.

"Gabe. Please."

He looked up at me. "Please what, Sam?"

In a fog of needs, I saw the raw determination glitter in his eyes. Saw the sweat of self-control on his forehead. "I need you. God, Gabe, I want you, now. You make me need you."

His control snapped. That fast. He rose, gathering me up in his arms and putting me on the bed. Catching hold of my panties, he tugged them off.

On his knees between my legs, he bent his arms under my legs, lifted me up and entered with a hard thrust. His dark gaze snagged on mine. "Take more, Sam."

"Give me more." I dug my hands into the sheets, meeting his hard thrusts, rocking against him. Needing everything Gabe had to give.

"That's it, babe. More," he thrust deeper.

I shattered first, crying out his name, and he drove into me one last time and exploded.

Gabe stretched out, rolled me onto my side, and pulled my back into his chest.

"Probably I will have to buy this bustier now."

He laughed into the back of my neck. "Money well spent."

* * *

When my radio came on, I shot up out of bed and tried to figure out where the hell I was. It was dark. What was I doing up? Squinting at the glowing green numerals, I saw that it was six-thirty.

Right. I had to get up early on a Saturday to go talk to Rick Mesa. And my car! What was I going to do about my car? I couldn't drive it around Lake Elsinore with four flat tires and a deadly threat on it. My head was filled with cotton.

And memories of Gabe. Thinking about Gabe led me to dangerous areas. Best to focus on what I had to do.

I showered and left my hair to dry with its usual flair of frizzy waves, then tugged on my jeans and a black sweater. I figured a little mascara and lipstick would do for early Saturday morning. Then I headed out to the kitchen.

Grandpa was up, and there was coffee. I got down a mug and filled it to the top, then went to Grandpa at the computer. I kissed his cheek. "Good morning. Whatcha doing?"

"Looking in the SCOLE bank account. Chad moved chunks of money in and out of there over the last year. Those transactions don't match with the books."

I pulled up a chair and sat down. I sipped some coffee, then told Grandpa about Dara Reed and what Chad had on her. "Clearly he's been blackmailing several people. What he did to Dara was horrible. Forcing her to be his girlfriend—" I broke off.

Grandpa looked at me with his milky blue eyes. "She wasn't quite the Jezebel you thought, huh?"

I shook my head. "I was wrong."

He turned back to clicking on his computer. "So what now?"

"I'm going to talk to Rick Mesa. I know a bit about what Chad had on Sophie. She's looking for some pictures Chad somehow took of her getting friendly with a one-night stand in a bar. Mom was trying to search Chad's house for the pictures when I ran into her there. Sophie tried to search at Chad's office when Vance caught her." I tried to think it out. Where would Chad hide those things? "Gabe said that Dara's video was on a CD, so I wonder if he stored the pictures of Sophie on a CD. Is that possible?"

"Sure. He could store lots of pictures on a CD. The video is probably on a separate CD. But those would be easy to hide. Do you think Rick will tell you anything?"

"That's why I'm going early. Today is Chad's funeral, so I figure he's taking the day off work. I'm planning to get to his house early, maybe catch him off guard. And I have to do something about my car." My gut tightened just thinking about my car. How was I supposed to pay for four new tires and paint?

"Call Blaine. He'll know whom you should call to get the car towed. It'll have to be on a flatbed. Can't drive it with four flats." Grandpa clicked around on the computer then asked, "So do you think someone Chad was blackmailing killed him?"

Grandpa was right about Blaine. I'd call him as soon as I finished my coffee. Turning my attention to the case, I thought about it. "Vance described the scene as a struggle, and the murder may be even self-defense. Gabe said the weapon was a rock-like bookend that's missing. I think Chad was blackmailing Rick, too. It makes sense. Rick didn't seem to care that Chad was killed. Everyone is looking for the blackmail evidence Chad had—Gabe for Dara; Sophie; and Rick. Out of the three of them, Rick's the only male and the caller on the phone was male. . . ." I trailed off.

"But?" Grandpa stopped typing and looked at me.

I twisted my coffee cup around and around. "Rick just doesn't seem like the type to kill. He never had a temper on the soccer field. Chad would yell and throw the clipboard, but Rick would take a kid aside and work with him individually. Or talk to enraged parents and calm them down."

"Maybe he bottled his rage up for too long," he suggested. "I assume you are going to Rick's house to talk to him and see if maybe you can spot that bookend that was the murder weapon. I think I should go with you. He could be dangerous."

My automatic smile froze when I spotted Grandpa's sleight of hand. "Grandpa, no weapons!" I had to get that switchblade away from him. He had boxes of magician stuff in the garage, and he was fascinated with a switchblade. Go figure. "Anyway, I'm going to take Angel. I need you to stay here with the boys if you don't have other plans." The boys and I relied on him so much.

The switchblade disappeared back into the depths of his baggy pants. He went back to his keyboard. "Sure, Sammy, I never mind staying with TJ and Joel. Have Angel take her gun."

I shuddered at that and wondered if Gabe found anything in Chad's house. "We have to find that CD or CDs before Vance does. This whole thing is just a mess." I finished my coffee and got up to call Angel. I woke her up and told her the plan, then called Blaine about my car.

He answered a groggy, "What?"

"Blaine, sorry about the call, but I have a problem."

"Work?"

"Car."

"The T?" He was wide awake now. "What happened? Were you in an accident? Where are you?"

"Uh, no accident. More like someone slashed all four tires and spray painted the car last night. I don't know who to call . . . Should I call the garage you worked at? Can they send a tow truck? Do they still take credit cards?" Stupidly, I felt tears burning up the back of my throat. I stared hard at the yellowed linoleum and forced myself to get a grip. It's just a car. Not one of my sons. A car.

My car. Some asshole thought he could damage my car. The fury wiped out my tears.

"Boss, calm down. I'll call the garage and come out with the tow truck. Any body damage to the car?"

Deep breath. "I don't think so. Thanks, Blaine. I didn't know what to do. I have to go out, but Grandpa's here."

"Got it covered. I have your cell number if I need you. See you." He hung up.

Relief rolled over my neck and shoulders. Blaine would get my car fixed. Blaine understood what my car meant to me. I'd have to charge it and find the money later. I got a second cup of coffee and refilled Grandpa's empty cup. "Angel will be here in about a half hour."

"Gabe knows you are going to Rick's this morning?"

I set the coffeepot on the warmer and went back to the table. "Yes."

"Interesting. So the two of you are working together now?"

"We're combining our efforts." I didn't know where he was going with this.

"Good." He closed the bank files and opened something else on the computer. "I have an idea."

"What?" Relieved to be off the subject of Gabe, I leaned forward.

"Well, Chad had a lot of high tech stuff. Didn't you tell me he had a digital camera? And he obviously had some kind of video camera with which he could hide and tape Dara. And the equipment to transfer it all to the computer to burn it to a CD, right?"

My nerves tightened in my stomach. "From what Chad said to me, and what Dara told Gabe, I'd agree." I didn't know what it meant. Copying the soccer books to the disk had been the absolute pinnacle of my skills.

"Ah."

"Ah, what?" I needed to take a computer class. Or pay attention when Blaine babbled at work. Something.

"I'm thinking that Chad has an account somewhere, a place where he stores all his files on the Internet."

"Stores files on the Internet?" When I thought of files, I thought of the two old gray filing cabinets in the storage room of Heart Mates. It was hard for me to grasp files floating around out there on phone lines or whatever.

"Look here, Sam." Grandpa clicked into a site where a list showed up. "These are all Internet groups I belong to. It's an e-mail system where you send an e-mail to one address, and everyone signed up gets the e-mail."

"Okay, I follow that."

"On these sites, they also have a file area where people can put things like pictures or documents, and anyone on the list can go to that site and click on the picture or document to open it up and view it." He went into one of his magician sites and clicked on "files," and then he clicked on his name. One of Grandpa's still shots he used when he was working filled the screen.

"Wow! Anyone who belongs to this group can see your picture?" This was cool. I wondered if I should do something like that for Heart Mates. How would that work? But wait, wouldn't that make me just another Internet dating service? Part of the charm of Heart Mates was being a real live service for people who've been burned by the Internet.

"Exactly."

Grandpa's answer brought me back. "But Chad wouldn't have put his pictures on a group like that—the point was to get paid by his victims for not showing the pictures or whatever he had."

"Right, but what I'm thinking he might have done was set up one of these accounts with only one member—himself."

"But he showed Dara that he had a CD."

"Sure, which is what makes me think he had another

kind of back-up. Two reasons. One, Dara might have found that CD; then Chad would be out of his income. And two, he was a braggart. He'd be so proud of his abilities that having all those pictures buried on the Internet would secretly thrill him."

I stared at the picture of Grandpa in the traditional black cape and top hat. "But how would you find it? Can you find it?"

"Well, I have to find his e-mail name and his password. But everyone leaves a trail. I have some ideas. I'll work on it."

Angel honked her horn outside. I stood up and said, "That'd be great, Grandpa. But we'd still have to find the CD."

He looked up. "Yes, but you might also find the last person who Chad tried to blackmail. Remember—someone wiped out his computer files. It might be that his victim confronted him after he sent the files to this storage site."

The horn honked again.

"Grandpa, that's brilliant!"

He laughed. "Go on before that horn wakes up the boys. I need to work." He turned back and bent over the keyboard.

My Grandpa, the magician and Internet sleuth.

Angel and I drove through the quiet town and hatched a plan to get into Rick's house. It was important for the two of us to talk to Rick inside his house so at least one of us could nose around and see if we could find anything. Like a bloody bookend shaped and painted like half a soccer ball. Ugh.

It was too early for most people to be out. We took a left on Main Street, cut through on Franklin, and ended up on Sumner to drive up the steep climb to the Tuscany Hills community.

Tuscany Hills sprang up outside of Canyon Lake, which was a gated community with a lake and golf course. Tuscany Hills was for those folks of moderate means who didn't want to deal with guard shacks and gates but wanted an upscale environment. The people who lived up there had a fabulous panoramic view of both Lake Elsinore and Canyon Lake, as well as the ability to organize and get the city of Lake Elsinore to respond to their concerns.

We crested the long hill up to the community and found Rick Mesa's modest one-story house. I followed Angel up to the door. She had rolled out of bed, thrown on a pair of low-cut black pants and a copper sweater that flirted with her belly button, and pulled her long red-with-black-tips hair back into a ponytail. She looked fantastic. Perfect for my plan.

At the door, I rang the doorbell.

Metallic clanks and thunks came from inside. What was Rick doing in there? I hit the doorbell again and looked around. Simple landscaping. A couple of big rocks and bushes under the front window, and a flat sweep of grass. All neatly trimmed, but simple. Like a man.

The door opened.

I snapped my gaze to the door. "Hi." Rick stood there in a pair of sweatpants. Nothing else. Startled, I took in his nicely formed chest and six-pack stomach. Rick wasn't as tall or well formed as Gabe was, but he had a slim wiry build that was obviously backed up with some serious weight lifting.

"Sam, I'm kind of busy right now. What do you . . . Hi, Angel."

Rick lost all interest in me. Which was the plan.

"Morning, Rick," Angel said. "We're sorry to drop in on you like this, but . . ." she trailed off and sniffled. Like she was crying.

"Angel, what's the matter?" Rick stepped out on the porch.

"Maybe we could talk inside?" I suggested.

"Sure." Rick put his hand on Angel's back and led her in, leaving me standing there. I followed them inside and closed the door. I stopped and looked at the living/dining room on my left. It was full of exercise equipment. There was a rowing machine, weights, benches, and all kinds of other stuff. No living room furniture. Realizing I was alone, I followed the voices.

I turned right into a big kitchen that opened into a spacious family room. At least the family room had furniture. Angel was already sitting at a center island bar in the kitchen. Rick was pouring her coffee. He looked up at me. "Want some?"

"Sure. Black is fine." The bar stools had to be custom made by Rick. Beautiful to look at, but hard on the butt. Climbing up on one, I took the coffee from Rick. "I guess you are wondering why we are here."

"Yes." Rick was on the other side of the tiled island.

I glanced over at Angel. "You may have heard that Angel has started her own business. Mail-order lingerie. Well, she had talked to Chad about what kind of insurance she might need, and one thing led to another and Angel let him take some pictures of her modeling the lingerie."

Rick's face hardened. "So?"

"You don't understand." Angel jumped in. "He said he'd go to the cops and tell them that I'm a prostitute. That I propositioned him."

I almost choked on that. Angel was pretty well known by the cops because of her ex-husband. They liked Angel and detested her ex-husband. He could never pass the bar exam, and the only job he could get was helping defense lawyers discredit the cops.

Angel pulled the length of her black-tipped ponytail around and played with it. "That kind of publicity would be horrible for Tempt-an-Angel, my business. I run a legitimate business for women who want to look sexy for their husbands or whomever. But if my lingerie were connected to . . . to . . ." she broke off, unable to go on.

I kicked her under the bar. She was laying it on too thick. Rick was never going to buy it.

Rick set his coffee cup down. "Angel," he reached across the bar to cup her hand. "No one would ever believe that of you."

"But the pictures! Chad changed them on his computer, somehow. I don't know how things like that are done."

Like hell she didn't! She'd once changed Hugh's picture so that he didn't have pants on and e-mailed it around his dad's law office. I glanced over at Rick. His brown eyes were intent, his mouth tight. He was buying Angel's act.

Angel took Rick's hand in both of her own. "Please, Rick, do you know where Chad put those pictures? You were his friend." She looked down. "Did he show them to you? Maybe you saw where he put them? I have to get them back and destroy them."

"No. If Chad had ever showed me anything like that, I'd have taken them from him. I assume he was blackmailing you?"

Bingo! I thought. Now we're getting somewhere.

14

I knew Rick was being blackmailed! Why else would he suggest to Angel that Chad was blackmailing her? But did that make Rick the killer? Angel had to keep Rick talking while I made an excuse to look around.

"How did you know?" Angel's green eyes shimmered with tears.

I slipped down off the bar stool. "Rick, can I use your rest room?"

He barely glanced at me. "Down the hall."

I nodded and rushed off, hearing Angel say, "Rick? How did you know that Chad was blackmailing me? I didn't tell anyone but Sam."

I found the hallway bathroom and bypassed it. I was looking for the master bedroom or an office. I found an office first. Rick had a gorgeous desk made out of some kind of wood. There was a matching chair. His computer hummed on the desk. Going inside the room, I saw one of those Web camera things that sort of look like a creepy oversized plastic eye. He and Chad were both into some high-tech equipment. This bedroom-turned-office faced the backyard. There were heavy blackout

drapes on the window that added to the weirdness of
that Web cam. Quickly, I went to the desk and looked
through drawers.

I felt like that eye-camera thing was watching me. A
slithery feeling wrapped around my spine, but I didn't
have time for paranoia. I only had a few minutes while
Angel kept Rick busy. After seeing his workout equipment and seminaked very male body, I believed he
could have killed Chad with one blow of the bookend.
Maybe they got into a fight of some kind over Chad blackmailing Rick, and Rick lost his temper. Like Grandpa
said, maybe the rage had been building up in the calm,
quiet Rick. If Rick did kill Chad, was the bookend here?
What about the blackmail CDs? Could they be here too?

But he'd shown up at Chad's house, presumably to
look for the CDs. I found a drawer with a box of CDs. I
rifled through them quickly. Mostly they were game
and computer program CDs. I didn't see any that might
be blackmail CDs. How would I know, though? Could
he have mislabeled them? I doubt he would label them
Blackmail CDs. Panic and pressure were making me stupid.

I took a big risk and dumped them all in my purse.
I'd have Grandpa check them, then figure out a way to
return them.

The rest of the desk was neatly organized. There
were files for business stuff, neatly stored catalogs for
woodworking tools, a telephone book, and an address
book. A drawer with pens, pencils, a stapler, a Post-It
note tablet, the usual stationery-type junk. I gave up on
the desk.

Conscious of time, I rushed to the closet. Sliding it
open, I stared in, surprised.

There were four garment bags neatly lined up. Did
Rick travel a lot? I really didn't know. Maybe for business? Quickly I felt down each bag to see if I found the

half soccer ball murder weapon. Nope, just clothes. I didn't have time to look in each bag. Who knows, maybe that's where Rick stored his off-season clothes.

Nothing on the floor.

On the shelf overhead, I saw rows of stacked blue plastic boxes, each about the size of a big shoebox. He probably kept his back tax returns and cancelled checks in there. Rick was so organized he was practically anal. No wonder he had never married. Staring up at the plastic boxes, I listened hard and heard the murmurs of Angel and Rick's voices.

What better place to hide a murder weapon than in a generic plastic box, maybe beneath old tax returns? Or something else equally boring. What else could be in those neatly lined-up boxes? Maybe his baseball card collection?

I had to look in at least one to know what he stored in there. And make sure there wasn't a bloody bookend hidden away.

I reached up. The shelf had to be six feet high. Who designed this stuff—giants? Rising up on my toes, I couldn't get close to the top box. I sank down to my flat feet and counted boxes. Rick had four stacks of three. I went to the door on my right and stuck my head out into the hall.

Angel and Rick were still talking. Angel was describing her lingerie.

Taking a deep breath, I went back to the closet. I reached for the bottom of the three stacked boxes in the first row and lifted up. The stack was moderately heavy. The boxes were meant to stack. The bottom of each box fit onto the lid of the one beneath it. With both hands, I tried to lift the two top boxes and gently slide the bottom box out.

I got it halfway out when it tangled on the stack next to it. My arms started to go numb from being raised over my head. Straining to lift the top stack higher, I tugged the bottom box.

Suddenly it gave. I tumbled backward, landing on my butt. My sore hip instantly shouted pain. Before I could recover, several boxes tumbled down and crashed on top of me. I barely got my arms over my face before plastic and stuff pelted me.

"What the hell was that?" Rick's voice bellowed from down the hall.

I was afraid to open my eyes. Several points on my head, arms and chest hurt. God, I hoped Rick didn't collect knives in those boxes.

And how was I going to explain this?

Slowly, I brought my arms down. I was sitting in a big puddle of blue plastic shoe-sized boxes and—

"Ohmigod."

"Sam!" Angel said as she and Rick ran into the room. Both of them stopped and stared at me.

I gawked at the assortment of high-heeled shoes, lacy garters, silk panties, and padded bras. Looking up at Rick and Angel, I said, "My God, he's a panty thief." I lifted up a strappy black, open-toed sandal that had a row of diamonds marching across the ankle strap. "And a shoe thief. Who did you steal this shoe from, an Amazon?" This had to be, like, a size ten or twelve shoe.

"You're bleeding," Angel pointed out.

"I am? Not my head, right? Tell me I didn't cut my face again!" Really, every case I worked on, I ended up getting stitches in, or had shards of glass picked out of, my face.

I glanced at Rick. He was frozen to the spot about two feet into the room. He just stood there staring at me. All the color had leaked from his face.

Angel recaptured my attention. "No, lower."

"Lower? Oh, the cut." I looked down. My black sweater was ripped from the neck down and I had a slash over the top of my left breast, above my bra. "Damn." Now that I noticed, it burned. A lot. It was about a two-inch slash, welling and spilling blood. I grabbed up a wad of something and held it on the cut.

Then I looked at Rick. "What is all this?" I gestured with my free left hand.

His face tightened, and anger darkened his coloring. "What were you doing in here? I thought you were in the bathroom."

My shock at falling and being trampled by women's shoes and underwear cleared. Shoving all the junk off of me, I climbed to my feet. Crap, the cut over my breast really hurt. Rick Mesa was a strong man. The weight equipment in his living room meant he was serious about his workouts. I'd never been afraid of Rick. Hell, it would never have crossed my mind. But now he was cornered. I had to think fast. "I was looking for toilet paper." *Hidden in a murder weapon shaped like half a soccer ball.*

Rick took a step toward me. "Did you try under the sink?"

"Where'd you get all this stuff? What are you doing with it?" I had immediately jumped to the conclusion that Rick was stealing from women because I had found my husband's stash of panties—along with a Post-It note rating each previous owner. But I didn't think Rick was a player like that. My instincts were stirring around, trying to get a hold on some reasonable explanation.

Chad Tuggle had been a player. Probably had always been a player. But Rick? He'd been quiet, kind, and he only occasionally dated. He never bragged, and he didn't drag his current honey to the soccer field and try to suck out her tonsils the way some men did just to show the world they had sex. Rick had always treated me with respect. Both when I'd been the dumpy soccer mom, and when I redesigned the package and shortened my skirts.

Something else was going on here.

Angel kicked through the mess and reached out to move my hand holding some slinky material to my chest cut. "Let me look at that. Hmm, I wonder if it needs stitches?"

"Let me see," Rick's voice teemed with frustration.

I stepped back. "Stay away."

He stopped and glared at me. "You think I killed him, don't you?"

I looked around at the mess of silk and heels. "What did he have on you, Rick? That you stole women's clothes?"

He clenched his fists by his sweatpant-clad hips. His chest muscles bulged. "I didn't steal them. I bought them off the Internet."

"Why?" I just couldn't put it together.

Angel turned to look at Rick. "No wonder you knew so much about the lingerie business."

She didn't sound upset, but interested. Okay, was I the only one here who thought it was a little weird that a single man had a closet full of women's . . . ? "Oh."

"Yeah," Rick's shoulders relaxed and slumped. He looked down to the floor. "That's what he had on me. Chad found out I liked to . . . experiment with women's underwear and clothes. He stole pictures off my computer."

The garment bags. I bet I knew what was in them now. Rick Mesa was a cross-dresser. Fascinated, I stared at him. He was a nice-looking man. "How did he do that?" I mean if Rick did something like this in his own house, who cared? It did explain the blackout drapes, though.

Rick bent down and pulled blue plastic boxes out of the mess and lined them up. "No one will want a cross-dresser to coach their kids in soccer. They'll think I'll make their sons gay." He looked up. "I'm not gay." With the boxes lined up, he started matching up outfits. "And they'll think I'm a pervert with their daughters."

He's right. Lord, Chad could have destroyed a man who had spent years building a good reputation as a coach. The burning in my chest made me a little dizzy. I sat on the edge of Chad's desk. "Did you kill Chad? Maybe get into a fight? Self-defense?" My voice started to sound far away to my own ears.

Rick looked up. "No. I didn't kill him. I don't really care who did. Sophie and I kind of agreed to not help the police find who did. Chad had really turned to—" He suddenly stood. "Sam? You'd better let me look at that wound. I know first aid."

I shook my head and almost fell off the desk.

Rick reached out, caught my shoulders, and steadied me. "I didn't kill him. Think, Sam. The worst that could happen to me is I'd be destroyed in this town. Lake Elsinore is not the only place in the world. I could have moved and started up my business anywhere. I told Chad that. I was done paying him. But he obviously pushed someone too far."

I looked up into his eyes. "Where were you the night Chad was killed?"

He glanced over toward his computer and Web cam. "I was online with my Internet group, The Silky Men. I can show the times if I have to. I was posting and sending pictures."

I frowned, thinking. He plays dress-up on the Internet, then poses in front of his camera to send out his image? "It's like a hobby, this cross-dressing?"

"Yes, sort of. Some of us have met and are putting together little acts to take on the road to nightclubs. Dressing as women and singing. We model the outfits and show them to each other over the Internet to pick our wardrobe."

"You're an entertainer." I got it now. It really was a hobby, but one Rick didn't want to cross over into his work and soccer coaching.

"Hey!" Angel slipped up beside Rick. "Maybe I can provide the lingerie. You could mention me during your act, something like 'Lingerie provided by Tempt-An-Angel. com.' "

Rick grinned. "Why not?" Releasing my shoulders, he took hold of my hand pressing the material to my breast. "Let's take a look. By the way, this was one of my best camisoles." He pulled my hand off the wound and inspected it. "Hmm, I could butterfly it, but stitches would be better. This sweater is toast." He fingered the tear in my black sweater.

"Yeah, I usually take out half my wardrobe with each case. What the hell cut me?" I didn't want stitches.

Angel bent over and picked up a garter belt. It was a siren-red elastic belt with four long elastic pieces that had metal hooks meant to snap on the edges of stockings and hold them up. "I think one of these must have caught on something on the way down, pulled tight, then snapped and sliced you."

"Sounds right," Rick nodded.

I tried to sort out my thoughts. Time was running out. Detective Vance was good. And he had a trail of evidence that he was following. But if we didn't find those CDs Chad stored all his blackmail stuff on, a lot of lives were going to be ruined. "I'll decide later on getting this stitched. Right now I need to know what you know about Chad." I took a chance. "A woman's life, her freedom, depends on finding the CDs Chad stored all his blackmail stuff on."

He turned to look at Angel. "Chad never had any pictures of you?"

She shook her head. "We used that to get in here. Sam had a pretty good idea that you wouldn't turn away a woman in trouble."

"Actually, I said a *hot* woman in trouble." I decided to be honest here.

Rick flushed. "Okay, I don't know what I can tell you. I know Chad kept the evidence he had on CDs. He got into my house and stole stuff off my computer when I wasn't home. How he figured out my cross-dressing secret is anybody's guess."

I shifted on the desk to readjust my sore hip. I had to stop getting hurt. "How did this all start?"

Rick shifted and sat down on the desk next to me while Angel disappeared down the hall. "Before he and Janie were divorced. Somehow, Chad took some money out of his insurance company trust account. Chad had always been arrogant, but we got along. We liked kicking back with a beer, playing a game of pool, or watching a game. I didn't always like the way he treated Janie, but that wasn't my business. Anyway, with those damn championships he got more arrogant."

I nodded. I'd been team mom for the first championship. Everyone sort of tolerated Chad's arrogance because his record brought the town pride.

Rick went on, "Chad just thought he was untouchable. I guess he took some money out of his insurance trust account at work. I don't know much about how that works, but it's a huge offense. Chad could have been arrested for that. He had to get the money somehow. I think he started with Sophie. I didn't know about any of Sophie's problems until Chad was killed. Sophie and Jay were having trouble right then. They sort of separated, and Chad followed Sophie to a bar where she drank and danced with a guy and then went home with him. It was . . . just a dumb thing to do. Chad took pictures of them dirty dancing and leaving together, enough to let Jay know that Sophie slept with this guy. She was desperately trying to save her marriage, and he got money from her. But it wasn't enough."

I could picture Sophie's panic. I don't know why she went home with some stud—it was dangerous to say the least—but Chad had no business blackmailing her with it. "So Chad came to you?"

"Yes. And some others. I don't know how many for

sure. Dara Reed, I know he had to have something on her."

I ignored the part about Dara. "You said you stopped paying?"

He nodded. "Sophie did, too. She said that not only did Chad take money from her, but that he also forced her to work for him part-time for minimum wage. Chad got off on that kind of thing. The power to force Sophie Muffley to be a minimum-wage worker . . ." He trailed off, his mouth tight.

Chad and his *power trip*. I'd been out of soccer for going on a couple years, but I had wondered why Rick didn't take his own team instead of staying on as Chad's assistant coach. Now I knew, Chad forced him to stay on as his assistant coach. It fed Chad's power trip.

"Anyway," Rick went on, "Sophie stopped paying him a couple of weeks back. Told him she was quitting. She said that if he went to Jay with his pictures, she'd turn him into the police and find a way to have the watchdog agencies audit his trust account."

I smiled for the first time. "Good for her." But the smile died. "He stole money from SCOLE. That means he had to find another mark to replace that money."

Rick turned to me. "Looks like he found the wrong one this time."

"Rick, do you have any idea where he hid those CDs?"

He shook his head. "Sophie was trying to look at work, and I was trying to search his house. I ran into you, Angel, and your PI at the house."

"Gabe was going to take another look. If we find them, we will destroy them."

Angel came into the office, balancing a tray with three coffee mugs. "Here we are." She set the tray down on the desk.

Grateful, I reached out and took a mug. My hand shook. Stitches and Tylenol were in my future. I didn't want to take my hand away and look at my chest again. A long gulp of hot black coffee helped. Sort of. "Rick, any idea who Chad might have gone after?"

"The only thing I know is that he went to the Riverside Public Library to go through newspaper archives." Rick reached for a cup of coffee. "He was getting cockier, certain no one would stop him. My guess is that he went after someone who had real money, and whom it would be a real victory to control."

All kinds of little sparks went off in my head. Who would Chad know? What secrets could he find at the Riverside Public Library? And who would fit the criteria Gabe and I wrote out? Five-eight or taller, right-handed, strong, maybe male due to the voice on my answering machine, and a secret he had to hide.

Secret.

Oh, boy. I knew someone with a secret. A big secret. A secret that appeared to have made him enough money to wear pricey clothes and to smell like he belonged on a yacht.

A detective who moonlights as a romance writer.

My cell phone rang while Angel drove me to the emergency room. Figuring it was Gabe, I got the phone out of my purse and answered.

It wasn't Gabe. "Shaw, where are you?"

"Vance?" Crap, now what? "Where am I supposed to be?"

"Filing a report at the police station. Now."

"I can't. I'm on my way to the emergency room." That ought to buy me some time. I had to figure out if Vance might have been one of Chad's victims.

"Inland Valley Hospital?"

How dumb would it be to lie? Inland Valley was the closest hospital. We were heading south on the Fifteen Freeway and were about five minutes away from the hospital. There was another hospital about twenty to twenty-five minutes going north on the Fifteen to Corona. I weighed out sending Vance on a wild-goose chase, assuming he meant to chase me down, and knew that would only hurt me. "Yes."

"I'll be there ASAP." He hung up.

I leaned my head back on the headrest in Angel's car.

"What's it like?"

I moved my gaze to her. "What?"

"Being caught between two hunks like Gabe and that detective."

"It's a lot harder than it reads in romance novels." I had played that part once already, between Detective Rossi and Gabe. Rossi had turned out to be the bad guy.

The trapped-between-two-hot-guys-and-one-of-them-is-a-killer plot is overused in books, but I didn't think it was likely to happen to me twice.

So how damaging was the information that Vance wrote romances to him? Basically it was his reputation as a tough cop. Vance was a little too pretty, with his sandy blond hair he kept cut ruthlessly short, square chin, and seduce-me dimples. In the cop world, tough and loyal ruled. Vance had to prove himself, over and over, to be tough. For the cops to find out now that he was a romance writer would shred his reputation on two levels. First, romance writers are not perceived as tough. Second, some might think he was betraying cop secrets.

All right, we're talking serious problems for Vance if his romance-writing career became known.

But would that incite deadly force? Would that drive Vance to murder?

No matter which way I played it, I couldn't see it. Vance did have a ruthless streak. If Chad had tried blackmailing Vance, I had no doubt Vance would have destroyed him.

But not with the crude method of bashing his head

in. When Vance caught me in Chad's office, he'd had no problem slamming me into the counter to get what he thought was an intruder under control. He had me pinned in three seconds, with measured force. Once he'd realized it was me, he'd lightened his force.

And when he'd spotted the bruise left by Lionel's nose on my forehead, he had reacted with self-disgust that he might have hurt me unnecessarily.

No, my take on Vance was that he'd have destroyed Chad with his own game. It would be swift and brutal, probably landing Chad in prison. At that point, Vance would have dealt with the fallout if it became known he was moonlighting as a romance writer.

Then there was the fact that *I knew* Vance was a successful romance writer. I used that knowledge to gain leverage with Vance several times. Vance had never once threatened me with bodily harm.

Bodily pleasure was a different matter.

Lord, I must have lost too much blood.

Twenty minutes later, I stared at the overhead light in the curtained bay of the emergency room with a laundry-rag type of hospital gown covering my breasts while a nurse practitioner applied a few butterfly bandages. "You need to keep this dry for a few days to reduce the risk of infection. Keep neosporin on the cut." Picking up a gauze bandage, the NP glanced up at me. "Your chart indicates you are accident prone. I can see from your bruised hip that you were thrown into a stationary object. And this cut looks like a blade of some sort caused it. Take my advice and file a police report against—" she dropped her gaze to my left hand, "—your boyfriend." She finished taping the bandage and started gathering up her supplies.

I sat up, my fury blunting the pain. "Will there be a charge for your condescending leap to conclusions?"

Her starched white look-at-me-I'm-almost-a-real-doctor

coat practically crackled with her indignation. "Look, I see women like you every day in here. Get a job, and stop depending on a man to pay for your fake boobs."

Remembering the hospital gown, I reached down to where it had fallen in my lap and held it up over my breasts. Jesus. I pitied any abused woman who came across this medical professional. Hell, I pitied any man who might accidentally mistake her for a woman and date her. Talk about a ball buster. I gave her my best fake smile. "I paid for my own boobs, lady. With my dead husband's life insurance."

Her pencil-shaped mouth fell open.

The curtain jerked back. Vance stepped into the cubicle, his size dominating the tight area.

The NP snapped her head around. "You cannot come—"

Vance flashed his badge and said, "Police business. Are you finished here?"

Without another word, she stalked out.

I glared at him, transferring my anger from the NP to Vance. "Get out."

Vance stood like a cop. Legs spread, shoulders back, eyes hard. Then he flashed his smile, and a pair of dimples transformed his face to sun god. "And miss finding out how you paid for your Bimbo Barbie look?"

Did he think I cared about his opinion? "Hey, Vance, I think that woman you just chased out of here has the hots for you. Why don't you go ask her if she likes boring sex once a month?"

His dimples flattened. "Once a month? God, no wonder your husband turned into a player."

Direct hit. I looked away and searched for my sweater. Spotting it folded at the bottom of the bed, I snatched it up. Holding the gown up over my chest with one hand and the sweater in the other, I focused my gaze over his shoulder. "I need to get dressed. Get out."

He didn't move. "I have some questions. What kind of shirt were you wearing the morning you got it caught in Chad Tuggle's paper shredder?"

Pull yourself together. Forcing a deep breath, I brought my gaze to Vance's. He was all business. I thought back to the morning I'd gone to Chad's office. "White cotton men's shirt. I answered your question. Now leave."

He reached inside his coat to his shirt pocket and took out his notebook and pen, flipping through the pages. "Not silk?"

"No."

"Who do you know that wears silk? Like silk blouses or scarves?"

I watched him make a note when it dawned on me—he wrote with his left hand. Vance was left handed. He might be an anal bastard, but he was not a killer. The killer, according to Gabe, was likely right handed. And why did he want to know about my shirt anyway? "Uh, my mom . . . Lots of women wear silk. Vance, what's this about?"

He looked up from his notebook. "Silk was found in the paper shredder."

"You mean that Chad's killer got caught in the paper shredder?" Wait. I remembered Chad groping me while my blouse was caught in the shredder. Then there was what Rick said, the control that Chad got off on. He'd gotten off by my blouse being sucked in the shredder, trapping me. Had he trapped someone else by that method? I realized Vance was silent. I met his gaze to find him watching me. "What?"

"We had a deal, Shaw. You help me find out what this town is hiding. I already know you weren't home this morning, because I called there to find out when you were going to be at the police station to get a copy of the report on your car."

I narrowed my gaze. "I'm getting damned tired of all these threats. You know I didn't kill Chad since the killer was taller than I am. And I doubt you want to risk pinning tampering with a crime scene on me, since the crime scene has been trampled by most of your suspects." I was buying time to figure out where the hell Chad hid those CDs.

He stilled. Gold flecks in his brown eyes glittered with his anger. "Pulizzi. I'm going to find the Pulizzi leak and plug it permanently." He took a breath. "Working with him might get you laid, but working with me will save your ass, Shaw. Now where were you this morning?"

The fury washing off him shrank the examination cubicle. Or maybe that was my fury. "I was with Angel."

Vance shattered his stone-still exterior. He shut his notebook, slipped it into his shirt pocket inside his coat, and stepped close enough that his legs touched mine. "How did you get hurt?"

Tilting my head back, I glared at him. I knew what Vance thought of me. If he wanted to believe me a sexually dead housewife turned to oversexed bimbo, I wasn't going to disabuse him. "A garter belt. Those suckers can be dangerous."

15

I had a big silver safety pin on my sweater when Angel and I got into her Trans Am. "We need to go see Sophie."

"Does it have something to do with Vance storming out of the emergency room?" Angel turned over the car and backed out of the parking space.

I tried not to think about Vance. He was getting close. He knew something. "Whoever killed Chad may have gotten tangled up in his paper shredder like I did. They found silk in there, like a blouse or scarf."

"Sophie Muffley wears silk, but so do tons of women."

"Like my mother. And both of us. Hell, the only ones I can think of who don't wear silk are Dara Reed and Janie. It's not their style."

We got to Sophie's house at ten-thirty. Our knocks dragged Sophie out of bed. She answered the door wearing a hunter green robe that matched her complexion. "What?"

Hung over. I felt guilty about that. "Sophie, we need to talk to you."

She opened the door wide, and we followed her over

the glistening hardwood floors to the kitchen. Angel and I watched her start the coffee.

"We talked to Rick this morning, Sophie. He told us how the two of you were working together to find the pictures Chad had. How did Chad get those pictures of you?"

Sophie measured coffee into the machine. "Jay and I had a trial separation. I didn't want it, but Jay needed to find himself." She slammed the can of coffee down on the tile counter and yanked the glass carafe out of the coffeemaker. Then she just stood there, staring. "How cliché is that? A fifty-something man going off to *find himself.*

I watched Sophie. With no makeup and her weaved hair standing out around her head, she actually looked softer. Not younger. The lines in her face were vivid in the sunshine from the kitchen window, but softer. Vulnerable, maybe. I knew that Sophie had pride, the kind of pride based on other people's opinions. Jay leaving to find himself severely damaged that pride.

It also cleared up some of her animosity toward me when I went through my transformation. A man usually incorporated the help of a young, stacked bimbo to find himself. While I doubted Sophie thought I was that bimbo, I think she did see my improvements as some kind of threat. We women were complicated creatures.

"Anyway,"—she turned on the faucet to fill the coffeepot—"your mom took me out to a place in Temecula to drink and dance. I met up with a man, danced with him and . . . went home with him. Chad was there. I didn't think anything of it. With those strobe lights on the dance floor, I never saw the flash when Chad took pictures of us dancing."

"Wait." Okay, this wasn't making sense. "If you and Jay separated, how could he be angry at you for dancing with a man in a club?"

Finished making the coffee, Sophie faced me. "Jay said he couldn't do it, couldn't betray me with that other woman. Swore it on his mother's grave. Said I was too good a woman to hurt that way."

Angel groaned. "Sophie, he's a lying sack of shit."

"Angel!" I tried to hiss under my breath.

Sophie held up a hand. "She's probably right. But you see, I used Jay's guilt to get him back on track and . . ." She looked away.

"It came back to bite you in the ass." Angel filled in.

I was going to have to rethink taking Angel with me on these things. "Sophie, did you kill Chad?"

She thinned her mouth and closed her eyes for a brief second. Then she looked at me. "No. He wasn't worth that. I hated him, hated the way he was playing me, forcing me to work for him when he knew I liked not working. And the blackmail money, which meant more lying and covering up to Jay." Her mouth relaxed. "But you know, the mirror Chad held up to my face by his blackmail showed me that I didn't really like the woman I'd become. I was proud of not working, like I was better than a woman who worked? I had to guilt my man into being what I considered a good husband? I was so proud of all my charity awards, plaques, and newspaper articles, but when did I lose sight of what charity, real charity, was about? What kind of woman had I become? I told Chad to shove it, and planned to tell Jay the truth."

I believed her. But I tried a little test. "What are you going to do now that Chad's dead?"

"Want coffee?" Sophie asked, going to a cupboard to pull down white china cups.

"No." I left it at that to see what she'd say.

Sophie filled a cup and fished out a blue packet of fake sweetener. She came back to stand in front of me and tore open the packet. "I told Jay yesterday, before your party. About the man I had the one-night stand with, and about Chad's blackmail. He slept at the office."

She passed the test. She'd told Jay the truth even though Chad wasn't holding it over her any more. "I thought you'd told me that stuff too easily last night," I mused aloud. Sophie was not a dumb or sloppy woman. Sure, alcohol could loosen her tongue, and sure, she looked a little hung over this morning—or was that a night of hurt from Jay walking out to sleep at the office?

"I wanted to tell you. I'm trying to protect . . . others."

"Others?"

"Other victims that Chad was blackmailing, and the man that I . . . well, him, too. He didn't deserve to be dragged through this mess. If the police found those pictures, it would hurt a lot of people."

Amen to that, I thought. Particularly Dara and her son, but others too, like Rick Mesa. "Did you tell your . . . ah . . . friend about the pictures?"

"No." Sophie actually smiled. "He fancies himself something of a protector of women. He'd have done something rash."

"Lots of those types going around." I thought of Lionel trying to save me from Gabe, then from my own supposed drunkenness last night.

"Men always want to fix things for us little women." She paused, sipped some coffee, cleared her throat, and said, "I considered hiring you to help me find those pictures. Your mom suggested it, actually. She said you'd help me and I could pay you back by helping you get clients when you got your real estate license."

Angel laughed.

I ignored Angel. "Sophie, maybe Chad tried blackmailing your . . . ah, friend." Someone had to kill Chad. I didn't think it was Rick or Sophie. And the threat on my answering machine was male. Maybe this guy didn't take well to being blackmailed and went to Chad's office, and there the two had an altercation that left Chad dead.

Angel said, "Sam's getting threats. Serious threats. I think maybe you'd better tell us who this man is."

Sophie blinked in surprise. "He wouldn't threaten her. He's half in love with her. He's one of those types that thinks of females as *the little woman.*"

"Half in love with me? How does he know me?" Startled, I felt a slow recognition creeping up from my toes.

"He's read all about you in the newspapers. Talked about you a lot. Thought you were the type that needed a man to help you so you wouldn't keep stumbling onto dead bodies. In fact, he was even talking about signing up at your dating service."

A buzzing exploded in my ears. My mouth was so dry it was hard to pry my lips apart. "Sophie, what's his name?" But I knew.

She sighed. "Lionel Davis."

"You have a stalker!" Angel said over the hood of her car as she unlocked the door.

"Let's just hope he's not a killer, too." Getting in the car, I said, "I want to go by work and get Lionel's address. Time to have a talk with him. Are you and your gun up to it?" I wasn't taking any chances. Could Lionel have killed Chad and be threatening me to keep me from finding out? Then what? I become his girlfriend? Was he a complete lunatic?

Or just a lonely, kind of dorky, sweet man?

My cell phone rang as Angel pointed her car toward Heart Mates.

I dug the phone out of my purse. "Hello?"

"Sam, you'd better get over to the office."

"You're at work? Is this about my car?" What else could go wrong?

"Your car's at the garage. I had a buddy drop me at the office while they do the work. We have a problem here at Heart Mates."

My heart slammed down into my uneasy stomach. I'd already had enough shocks today. "Please tell me there are no dead bodies."

"No dead bodies."

"Good." I just hated finding dead bodies. "We'll be there in a few minutes."

Less than ten minutes later, we walked into Heart Mates to find Blaine sitting on the front of his desk eating a bear claw.

"So what's up, Blaine?" I looked around. Thankfully, I didn't see a dead body. Though I believed Blaine, I still was a tad worried. I glanced at the interview room. Maybe it was a client?

"You'd better see for yourself, boss." Blaine stood up and tossed the half-eaten bear claw into the trash.

Oh, shit. Maybe there was a body. When was the last time Blaine tossed away perfectly good junk food? My heart hammered, making the cut on my chest throb. "Blaine?"

He stopped at the interview room door and looked back. "Come on."

I trusted Blaine with my life, but I didn't want to see what was on the other side of that door. "What is it?" I had another bad thought. "Is my mother in there?"

"It's not your mother."

Angel stood behind me. "We'll find out faster if you stop stalling."

"Right." Angel had a good point. I followed Blaine into the interview room, with Angel right behind me. I looked around. Round oak table, four chairs, camera, camcorder, tripod, stool, posters on the wall. "What?" I asked. "Everything's normal."

"In here." Blaine reached for the door handle that led to the storage area and a tiny bathroom.

It felt like my heart was stabbing the cut on my chest. I took a deep breath. "Is there anybody in there, dead or alive?"

Blaine shook his head, then ran his blunt fingers through the feathered front of his hair and checked the ponytail in the back.

"Snakes?" I hated snakes.

He opened the door. The light was already on. He disappeared inside.

Angel got tired of waiting for me and passed me by to rush inside.

"Coward," I muttered to myself. I hated being a chicken. But I had a bad feeling. A doom feeling. The kind of feeling that was claustrophobic. "Get over it." I forced my feet to move and walked into the storage room. About the size of half a bedroom, it had several metal filing cabinets straight ahead and a sink and toilet that made up the no-frills bathroom on the right.

Nothing was out of place.

Wait, something was. I frowned and looked around. A memory teased my subconscious. The floor had the same industrial steel-gray carpet, the filing cabinets all looked—

I stopped breathing. There was one thing out of place—about three inches of a blue sheet stuck out of the bottom drawer of one of the filing cabinets.

The memory flashed vividly. Lionel Davis and I had collided head to nose, and then I had grabbed the sheet Blaine used as a drape for photos to stem Lionel's nosebleed. And finally, I'd tossed the sheet into the storage room to take home and wash.

I'd tossed it on the floor and forgotten all about it. "How did it get in there?" I looked over at Blaine. He stood by the cabinet, his jeans sagging and his blue button-down work shirt hanging out.

Blaine covered his hand with the tail of his work shirt, squatted down, and pulled open the drawer.

Gruesome curiosity pulled me over to see. I only took a few steps, then looked down.

Inside was a rock shaped and painted like half a soccer ball and splattered with—

The room spun. Sweat prickled beneath my arms and behind my neck. My thoughts scattered.

"Don't faint!" Blaine yelled.

His bellow startled me enough to take a step back and bend over at the waist with my hands braced on my knees. *Omigod* ran through my head over and over.

Angel turned and walked out of the room.

I wanted to follow, to get outside, but I was afraid I'd fall on my face and throw up. Instead, I ran a few short steps into the bathroom and turned on the cold water. I cupped my hand and I splashed the water on my face. The crisp wetness helped. A little.

Looking up into the mirror, I saw horror etched into my brown eyes and forming tight lines around my mouth.

I couldn't believe it. Who would put that in my storage room? Why?

"Breathe." I told myself.

Blaine filled up the doorway. His face had a sweaty pale look with red splotches of anger. "I came back here to use the head when I noticed the sheet." He shrugged, the rest being obvious.

"It's the bookend that killed Chad." God, it was too horrible to think of it in my filing cabinet.

Blaine touched my arm. "Did you see the scarf?"

I turned left to look at Blaine. "Scarf?"

"The bookend was sitting on a torn and blood-stained scarf."

I heard him, but my mind just couldn't grasp it. One look at the bookend had been all I could handle. "Uh, I didn't see it."

"Let's go out into the office, boss." He still had a hold of my arm. He tugged.

I followed. *Scarf?* Vance had said a blouse or scarf was found in the shredder.

Outside in the reception area, I stopped. "I'm being set up."

Blaine stopped walking and turned around. "Looks like."

Angel came in from outside carrying three sodas, indicating she'd slipped over to the liquor store that was in the same strip mall as Heart Mates. Two Diet Cokes for us, and a grape soda for Blaine. She set them on the desk. "Are you going to call the police?"

All our gazes went to the phone on Blaine's desk. Should I call the police? Would they arrest me? "Uh." I walked to the phone, telling myself I was going to do the right thing. There was probably evidence on those . . . things in the filing cabinet. If this were *CSI*, the case would break because of this discovery.

Putting my hand on the phone, I remembered that I was much more of a chicken than a good citizen.

I called Gabe.

While waiting for Gabe to show up, Angel and I pulled up chairs around Blaine's desk, and we drank our sodas.

"Got a message on the machine," Blaine pushed a button on the phone.

A recorded voice said, "This is Kevin returning Sam's call. My date with Roxy didn't happen. She never showed up. I think your service sucks." Click.

I took a sip of my Diet Coke and set it on the desk. "Roxy is self-destructing. She accused me last night of not being a loyal friend and said she can't trust me." That had hurt. I really wanted to help Roxy. I'd been trying to steer her away from hot-looking men who just wanted to date her because she was a model. I had hoped to help her find a guy who really appreciated her.

"Roxy said that?" Angel twisted the black ends of her otherwise red hair. "She was a little off when she got to your house last night. Nervous, edgy. But once she starting putting on the lingerie and modeling, she was fine."

I shrugged. Frankly, Roxy wasn't my biggest problem right now. The murder weapon in my filing cabinet had taken center stage.

"Roxy's under a lot of pressure, Sam." Blaine drained his grape soda and tossed it in the trash can. "Trusting people has to be hard for her now. How does she know if someone wants to be her friend because of her or her career? Going to a dating service can't be the best thing for her image, either."

"All right, I get the point. I'll talk to her again. And I'll call back Kevin, the jilted date. We'll get it all straightened out."

Blaine's face brightened, and he rooted around his highly organized file trays before pulling out a sheet of paper. "The new client—" Blaine looked down to read the paper, "Missy? She came up as a match for Kevin."

"Really?" Now that was interesting. Thinking about matching dates was a hell of a lot better than thinking about what was in the storage room. "Missy's a bit of a dreamer, but she's grounded enough to know how to make the dream come true." I was pretty sure of that, anyway. I pulled up Kevin's file in my mind. The financial consultant who drove limos to make ends meet. He was youngish, really cute, and a talker. "Hmm, that might work. Kevin would be attracted to Missy's optimism, while at the same time, she might sort of get him focused. He's smart enough, I think. Just impatient."

Blaine clicked open files on the computer. "Missy's dream is to open a dance studio."

I chewed on the inside of my cheeks, then finally said

what I'd been sort of thinking since yesterday. "If Lionel Davis turns out not to be a stalker and murderer, but just a sweet, dorky guy, I was thinking we could pair him and Missy up."

Blaine flashed a grin. "You'd give him up?"

"Shut up." I looked around, wondering if Lionel was going to burst in here to save me from his newest imagined threat. Could he be some kind of deranged stalker, picking his victims from the newspaper? Wouldn't that be ironic if Chad had tried to blackmail a stalker nut?

It flashed through my brain that Sophie had slept with Lionel. God, I wanted to erase that knowledge. I needed a delete key for my brain.

"The hunk is here," Angel said just as the door to Heart Mates opened.

I stood. "Gabe."

He strode to me, looking grim. By the time he reached me, he was already asking, "What happened to your sweater?"

I'd forgotten all about it. I looked down. "Uh, an accident. I . . . God, Gabe, what should I do? Should I call Vance? It's the rock that killed Chad!" Suddenly, I was terrified. I didn't know what to do.

His hands closed around my shoulders, and he bent over slightly to make eye contact. "No time for a meltdown."

It felt like a slap. He was right. I had to hold it together. I had two sons who needed a mom and I couldn't be that mom to them from jail. I forced my gaze to stay on him. "Sorry." Turning out of his hands on my shoulders, I said, "Come and see for yourself." I led the way.

It got harder to breathe when I passed through the interview room to the storage area. But I kept going. Anger fed me now. Anger at myself. One look at Gabe and I thought I could fall apart and let him take over. And anger at being set up to take the fall for Chad's murder.

Time to get a backbone and face this threat.

Stopping at the filing cabinet, I pointed at the piece of blue sheet coming out of the bottom drawer.

Gabe pulled out a set of latex gloves and snapped them on. See, I thought to myself, there's the difference between an amateur like me and a professional PI like Gabe. I'd have never thought to carry gloves.

Gabe pulled the drawer open and studied the rock. "The sheet is yours?"

I kept my eyes focused on the top drawer. I didn't want to see the rock again. "Yes, it's the drape Blaine uses over the stool to take pictures. When Lionel and I hit heads, we used it on his bloody nose."

"And where was it the last time you saw it?"

"On the floor by the door."

"Do you recognize this scarf?"

I kept staring at the top drawer. "Uh, I haven't looked at it."

"Look at it, babe."

I'd had a feeling he was going to say that. Trying to fix a professional expression on my face, I forced my gaze down to the drawer. I did my best to ignore the blood-spattered rock to see the scarf it was resting on. I'd seen scarves like that at Nordstrom's. It was made of silk and had accordion-like folds running the length of it. Shades from gray to blue blended across the width. It was designed to drape around the neck and down the front of a suit jacket or shirt to dress it up. To add a little style or panache. "I've seen ones like it in the mall."

"Have you seen anyone wear this scarf?"

I struggled to focus and shuffle through my memory. "I don't think so. Several women occasionally wear scarves. My mom likes them."

"I don't think your mom killed Chad." Gabe picked up the end of the blue sheet in his gloved hand and dropped it back in the drawer.

"What are you doing?"

"Shutting the drawer."

"But the sheet was hanging out." I'd learned the hard way how touchy the police were about crime scenes and evidence.

Gabe shut the drawer and stood up. He stripped off the gloves and stuck them deep in his jean pocket. Then he reached out and put his hand on my shoulder. "We never saw that rock, scarf, or sheet in the drawer. Got it? No one has been in the filing cabinet."

A small shiver went through me. I glanced at the filing cabinet. "Whoever put that there, they called the police, didn't they?"

Gabe nodded. "If someone went to all the trouble to plant the rock and scarf in here, they likely phoned in an anonymous tip."

"I'm going to jail." This time I said it calmly.

"No, you're not. If the police, Vance, or both arrive without a warrant, we won't let them search."

"But—"

"Pay attention, Sam. If they do have a warrant, we let them search and are surprised at what they find. Got it?"

"I guess." I looked down at the filing cabinet drawer.

His hand caught my face. "Babe, what happened to your chest?"

I looked back at Gabe. Other than the tense jaw, he appeared calm. Quickly, I summed up my morning, catching him up on Rick's hobby as a cross-dressing performer and his Internet friends, The Silky Men. I told him how I got the cut and ended by explaining Sophie's one-night stand.

"Garter belt, huh?"

"Jeez, Gabe." I snapped my fingers in front of his face. "Get your mind out of my underwear for a second, will you?"

He grinned. "You had on some hot underwear last night."

His words and touch melted some of the icy-sick terror running through me. "All right, stud. Try to focus, okay? When Vance came to the emergency room, he asked me if the shirt I wore Wednesday morning to Chad's office was silk. Do you think he'd gotten an anonymous tip about . . ." I moved my eyes to the filing cabinet.

"Hard to say. He was probably just following the evidence they had. Chances are good that since the silk scarf tore, there was a piece left in the teeth of the paper shredder, and Vance noticed it. Vance is good with facts and evidence, Sam."

I nodded. That was true.

"Did you take any Tylenol for your cut?"

"No."

He still had his hand on my face. Leaning down, Gabe kissed me, then said, "I'll kiss your chest all better later. Right now, let's go in the interview room, and I'll find you some Tylenol."

I followed him from the storage room, just glad to be out of there. He tried to get me to sit down in the interview room, but I bypassed him and headed for my office.

Where I was in control.

It was time for me to get control.

Once inside my cubicle, I went around my desk and sat in my chair. I heard Gabe talking to Blaine and Angel, but I forced out the voices to think. Folding my hands, I rested my chin on them and stared at my blank computer screen.

Who? Who killed Chad? One of his blackmail victims was the most likely culprit. Not the old victims, like Sophie, Rick, or Dara. They had all told him they were done.

No, Chad had been hunting for a new mark to replace the soccer money he took. And he was getting bolder, more brazen. How did Rick phrase it? Chad would go after *someone who had real money, and who it would be a real victory to control.*

Lionel Davis, a biochemical tech for a company in Temecula? He was a teddy-bear cowboy hooked on nose spray. Where's the thrill in that? And while Lionel was fond of cowboy string ties, I'd bet Heart Mates he never wore a silk scarf.

Gabe walked in holding a cup of coffee and two tablets. He leaned across my desk and set them down. "I didn't see any signs of forced entry."

I picked up the two tablets, popped them in my mouth, and then swallowed them down with coffee. I'd have chosen water, but why argue about trivial stuff? "How do you think they got in?"

Gabe shrugged. "It's not that hard. Could have picked the locks. You don't have an alarm system," he pointed out as he dropped into the chair across from me.

I went back to my thoughts. The silk scarf. "The killer had to be a woman."

Gabe nodded. "Unless it was your cross-dressing assistant coach."

I shook my head, then remembered, "Uh, I found some CDs at Rick's and I wasn't sure what they were, so I kind of dumped them all in my purse."

Gabe's expression didn't change. "That's one way to do it."

"Best I could think of at the time." I shrugged, dismissed the CDs, and went back to the murder. It was taking shape in my mind. "Remember I told you about getting my shirt caught in Chad's shredder?"

He nodded.

"Chad liked that. He was getting off on having me trapped. While he was supposed to be rescuing me, he was running his hand up my thigh. I think he maneuvered another woman into that situation. The shredder starts automatically when something hits its sensors. It'd be so easy to nudge the long end of a scarf in there. So let's say that happened. The woman is fighting with her scarf in the shredder, and Chad starts mauling her.

Maybe trying to force sex." I took a breath, trying to set the scene. "At Chad's office, the rock bookends were only an arm's reach away. She could have grabbed the bookend off the shelf, whirled around, and hit him." I looked at Gabe to see what he thought.

He leaned forward, reached across the desk, and snagged my coffee. A long drink later, he looked at me over the rim. "That's damn good, Sam."

"The theory or coffee?"

His face softened slightly. "Your theory. And it fits with the rip in the scarf."

I picked up the cup of coffee and started to sip when I heard the front door in the reception room open up.

My eyes locked with Gabe's. We both knew who was here.

I heard Vance's voice. Then he stepped into my office doorway. "Shaw." His gaze fell to Gabe, and his face tightened. "Pulizzi."

"What can I do for you, Vance?" I knew that sounded false. I forced my best professional smile and went on, "Are you here to sign up for a dating package? I think the Temecula Wine Tasting package would be perfect for you."

"I don't need help with my love life, Shaw. But I would like to take a look around your back room."

"What for? If you'd like testimonials of satisfied customers, my assistant will be happy to provide those." I didn't dare look at Gabe.

Vance strode into the cubicle. Ignoring Gabe, he perched his tight ass on the edge of my desk. He pursed his lips, giving the appearance of being perplexed. "Do you have something to hide, Shaw? I'm just asking to look around your storage space in the back. I was under the impression you wanted to be helpful."

Gabe stood. "Do you have a warrant to search the premises of Heart Mates, Vance?"

Vance looked straight at me. "Why don't you tell

your boyfriend to go home? Surely you don't need him to tell you how to run your business. Most small businesses like cooperating with the authorities. But rogue PIs tend to forget that."

In my peripheral vision, I saw Gabe shift. It was so subtle most people wouldn't have seen it. He came forward slightly on the balls of his feet, his shoulders went back, and his arms hung loose and dangerous at his side. But it was his eyes that gave him away.

Flat and focused. Like he could tear through a local street gang and go out to catch a ball game afterward. I stood. "I'm sorry, Vance, I must have missed your answer. Do you have a warrant?"

His eyes narrowed. "That the way you want to do this, Shaw? You sure about that? I'm trying to help you here, but if you don't work with me . . ." he shrugged an implied threat.

"Let me know anytime you are interested in signing up with us here at Heart Mates." I worked to make my mouth tilt up in a smile.

Vance stood and started to walk out. When he came even with Gabe, he glared at him. "Interesting thing about Dara Reed. She's got a real low profile, know what I'm saying, Pulizzi? No wants or warrants in California, but what about where she's from? Makes me wonder . . ." He let the sentence trail off and left.

Cripes, Vance knew about Dara Reed.

16

After we heard Vance leave Heart Mates, I said to Gabe, "How much do you think he knows about Dara?"

Gabe sat down and brought his right hand up, using his thumb and finger to rub his eyes. "Enough to be suspicious. Christ."

It struck me then how tired Gabe was. How frustrated. A sudden tenderness swept over me. Whatever he'd been doing, he'd dropped it to come running to my rescue. "Did you find anything at Chad's house last night?"

Taking his hand away from his eyes, Gabe shook his head. "Nothing to indicate where those CDs are. I searched his car . . ." he trailed off.

"The Explorer? I thought the police impounded it."

"They did."

"Oh." I could visualize it. Gabe had slipped into wherever they put impounded cars and searched it. The man had skills I couldn't begin to match. "What were you doing when I called you?"

He dropped his hands to the arms of the chair. His dark brown eyes were flat. "Arranging new identities for

Dara and Josh. Dara is all Josh has. He'll go into the system if Dara is arrested."

The weight of the boy's future rested on Gabe, a responsibility he took on without complaint. I understood that he needed to help Dara and Josh, but getting them new identities? I opened my mouth to ask Gabe if he knew what he was doing. But a look at his set shoulders, tense neck, and hard face told me that he believed he was doing the right thing. Instead, I asked, "Did you get any sleep?"

"Sure."

Sure? That sounded like the distracted answers I get from TJ and Joel when they are playing Nintendo. I got up and went around my desk to stare down at him. "Yeah? How much sleep did you get?"

Surprise shot his eyebrows up. "Hour or two."

I reacted to the need in him, reaching down and taking hold of his hand. "If Vance doesn't find that CD, he won't have any proof to give to the DA in Arizona. He'll leave Dara alone. I'll help you, Gabe. We'll find the CDs and destroy them."

His smile was slow, but sexy as hell. "Playing on my team, babe?"

"I want to help you." It was the safest answer.

"I believe you." He shifted his hand from beneath my fingers, caught my wrist, and pulled me down on his lap. "But you aren't going to be able to get between Vance and me forever."

My insides went cold. "I'm not—"

"Yes, you are. Every time the two of us are in the same room, you get tense." He slid his gaze to lock onto my face. "Vance wants you, Sam, and he is moving in on what's mine. He got the mistaken impression that you are a free woman. I am going to remedy that."

God. "I'm not a possession! You don't get to fight over me with the winner getting the prize. I'm not a prize!"

Okay, that didn't come out quite the way I meant it. "I should smack some civilization into you."

He laughed. "Don't think my mother didn't try."

I groaned. "I don't have a chance if your mom and her wooden spoon didn't work."

"It must have taken some," he said, his hand rubbing my back.

"Why?" I was curious what he was talking about. And damned glad to be off the subject of Vance.

"Because I admire your independence and determination. The way you are fighting so damn hard to help Janie, and won't let threats stop you. And trying to help Roxy find the kind of happiness she wants. You even try to understand that imbecile Lionel, who's totally in love with you. That's a lot for a man to take, by the way. But even though I want to shoot Lionel, and force you to work for me on my terms to investigate for Janie, I know that you have to do these things your own way."

I studied Gabe. "This is because I don't fall all over you and tell you my feelings every four minutes." The truth was I never told him how I felt in exact words. I tried not to even think about it. My feelings for Gabe were complicated. Big. And sometimes, they were too damned romantic.

He caught my chin, turning me back to face him. "I had that, Sam. My wife adored me. She did love me—so much that I think it crippled her."

He so rarely talked about Hazel. I put my hand around his fingers on my cheek. "You loved her, too, Gabe. You did all that you could for her."

"Except save her."

"You're only a man, Gabe, not a superhero." I wished I knew how to convince him of that, to ease the burden of guilt he carried.

His face shifted, the shadows receding. "Not a superhero? You're hell on a man's ego."

I laughed, grateful to have slipped into neutral territory. "Don't let it worry you, stud. You manage to keep up with me okay for a mortal."

He lowered his mouth to mine, making my head ring.

"Boss! Your grandpa on line one."

I jerked back. Obviously it had been the phone ringing, not my head. "Do you think they heard us?"

He did the Italian shrug.

I scrambled off his lap, reached across my desk, and picked up the phone. "Grandpa? What's up?"

"Good, you're there. You didn't answer your cell phone. Figured you might be at work."

I frowned, wondering where my purse was. Why hadn't I heard my cell phone? Wait, I left my purse in Angel's car. "Grandpa, why are you looking for me?"

"I found it, Sammy! The boys helped me."

The boys were playing with Ali in the front dirt when Gabe and I pulled up in his truck. Angel had stayed behind at Heart Mates to give Blaine a ride to check on my car. TJ and Joel ran up to the truck.

"Grandpa made us go outside," Joel complained as soon as I opened the door.

I shifted my purse, which I had remembered to get out of Angel's car, and put my arm around him. "Yeah? Grandpa told me that you and TJ were brilliant and helped him break the code."

"We got it from the soccer disk that you copied, Mom." TJ fell in on the other side of me, while Ali ran up to say hi to Gabe. TJ went on. "I saw that Coach had changed what should have been *Head Coach* to *Champ Coach*. You know where they list all the titles, like President and Secretary?"

"Sure, TJ, that was clever of you. What does Champ Coach mean?" We were at the steps to the porch.

"That was Coach's name on his Internet account. All we needed was the password." TJ's eyes got serious. "Mom, you need some new clothes."

I looked down to see he had noticed the safety pin. I ruffled his hair. "Think I should stop tearing the ones I have?"

TJ studied my face. "No car chases? No gunshots? Nothing like that?"

"Nope. Promise. It really was an accident."

"Mom, I figured out the password," Joel announced. I looked over at him. "Did you?"

He looked down. "Not totally. You know, like TJ did. I mean Grandpa found where that extra cash line . . ." he squished his eyes trying to think.

"Petty cash?"

He looked up at me. "Yeah. It had 'Chump Change' underneath it. Grandpa said that was odd and tried it for the password, but it didn't work."

"No?"

TJ said, "You know how Joel likes reading license plates? That's how he did it."

Both Joel and I stared at TJ. Had he just complimented his brother? "Uh, Joel," I turned to look at him.

His chest puffed out. "Yeah, I got a pencil and wrote down the letters like they'd shorten 'em for license plates. Chump Change spelled, c h u m p c h g e worked! That was the password!"

Gabe's voice came from right behind us. "Good job, Joel. You too, TJ."

Both my sons practically grew six inches under Gabe's praise.

I stood there with an arm around each son and wondered what I was doing chasing down blackmailers and killers when I had TJ and Joel. I should be spending my days with them.

On the other hand, Janie needed answers to move on with her life and take care of her two children. And

Dara ran the risk of being forcefully parted from her son.

"Mom," Joel got my attention. "Can we go to the skate park? Our friends are going to be there. Please, Mom?"

I stopped on the porch, turning my head to look at Gabe. I wanted to know if he thought it was safe.

He nodded.

"Sure, I guess. Uh—"

Gabe broke in, "Get your boards and I'll run you over there." The boys hurried into the house to get their skateboards.

I dug out my cell phone and managed to hand it to TJ as the boys ran by me, with their boards, to Gabe's truck.

I asked Gabe, "You think they'll be safe?"

"Yes. I'll make sure they call for a ride home. Go ahead and get started with Barney. I'll be right back." He kissed me and strode off toward his truck.

Ali sat down beside me. She hung her head and whined.

I smiled down at her. "They'll play with you when they get home, girl. But they're growing up, Ali. We're just not as important as their friends."

She licked my hand, then followed me inside. Grandpa was in the kitchen, pouring himself some coffee. I set my purse down on the kitchen table and got a cup down for myself. "Gabe's running the boys over to the skate park."

Grandpa poured some coffee into my mug. "They couldn't wait for you to get home to tell you they helped with the case."

I grinned. "They told me that you made them go outside."

"Bah! I sent them outside so they'd stop asking how long it would take for you to get home."

"Really?"

Setting the coffee pot back, Grandpa picked up his cup and said, "You always make them feel smart. Now let me show you what we found. Course, I didn't let TJ or Joel see this stuff."

I followed him back to the computer. He sat down at his rolltop desk, while I pulled up a chair from the dining room table. "TJ and Joel told you how we got into the site, right?"

"Yes, they did. Very smart. TJ even told me how Joel figured out the password like a license plate abbreviation." Fierce pride stung my eyes. TJ and Joel tormented each other, but TJ knew that Joel sometimes felt overshadowed by TJ's math brain.

"Joel's a different kind of smart. That boy could charm the rattles off a snake."

I laughed. "Yeah, well, he's just like you." I remembered Grandma saying the exact same thing about Grandpa.

"Here it is."

I looked at the screen. It was a list in blue type. Grandpa clicked on the first line on the list, and Rick Mesa in full drag popped up. I blinked. "Damn, he looks pretty good."

"Doubt he wanted the whole town to know how good he looks in one of them shiny evening gowns."

Even looking at the evidence, it was hard to believe. Rick Mesa in women's clothes? He was a soccer coach! "I wonder if he can sing?"

Grandpa closed the screen and went to the next one. They were snapshots of Lionel Davis and Sophie Muffley dirty dancing. The next screen showed Sophie and Lionel in Lionel's truck, getting hot and heavy.

What struck me about the shots was the gentleness in Lionel's gaze when he looked at her. It wasn't love—Sophie had been right.

But it was understanding.

"Chad was a monster." I thought of myself when Trent was no longer interested in me. I'd buried myself in the life of a mom. But I could have been Sophie, looking for some man to make me feel like a woman. Lionel didn't look at her like a bar conquest. He appeared kind. And Chad, the prick that he was, caught Sophie in a desperate, vulnerable moment.

"A bad seed," Grandpa agreed.

The front door opened and Gabe strode in. "What have we got?"

I looked up at him when he reached us. "So far, he's found what Chad had on Rick Mesa and Sophie Muffley."

Gabe put his hand on my shoulder. "Sam, why don't you give Barney those CDs you snagged from Rick's house? He can look at them when he has time. Then we'll return them."

I reached for my purse and dug out the CDs.

Gabe took a look at what Grandpa had on the computer. "Lionel and Sophie. Lionel doesn't look quite so clumsy there."

I thought about that as I set the CDs in a pile on Grandpa's desk. "I don't think he was. He was in his element there, Gabe. Helping someone."

"He checks out, by the way." Gabe said. "Lionel had one reported incident of possible sexual harassment, but it was dropped after he took a sensitivity class. It reads more like a misunderstanding than sexual harassment."

"Sounds like Lionel." I could imagine him coming on strong to some woman at work, trying to be a hero.

"What's the next one?" Gabe asked.

"It's the video file on Dara. I didn't watch much of it." Grandpa's voice throbbed with anger. "I'm copying it all to a CD; then I'm going to delete this entire file. Once we clear everything up, I'll wipe off the CD." He clicked on the file. An icon popped up that told us it was loading to some device or another. I didn't know how this stuff worked.

Then Dara Reed filled the screen. She was sitting on the leather couch in Chad Tuggle's house. I remembered that complicated entertainment center, and fury rushed through me like a hot flash. The video camera had been hidden in the entertainment center. Obviously the video had been edited because she was crying and explaining the drugs she gave her husband.

Gabe's hand on my shoulder tightened.

I put my hand over his. "Do we need to watch this, Gabe?"

"No. Save it." He barked it out like the ex-cop he was.

Grandpa nodded and closed down the video. I tried to erase the pain I'd seen in Dara's hard face—the wrenching loneliness, grief, and guilt. "What's next, Grandpa?"

He looked at me. "It's pretty ugly, Sam."

How much uglier could it get? Tension crawled up my back. I rotated my head around, trying to ease it. Then Gabe's hand slid behind my neck, finding a spot and kneading. I answered, "Let's see it."

Grandpa clicked, and a Las Vegas newspaper headline proclaimed:

Exotic Dancer's Daughter Kills Mom's Boyfriend

I leaned forward, straining to read the newsprint. The story was about a ten-year-old girl who witnessed her mother's boyfriend beating her mother to a bloody pulp. The mother had screamed for help. And the little girl picked up the boyfriend's gun and shot him.

The mother had been in the hospital for days with her injuries.

"Oh, lord," I said softly. That poor little girl. To have

killed a man at ten. "It doesn't look like the little girl was charged. What's the blackmail there? I see the dancer's name, Candy Temple, but not the little girl." I glanced at the date on the newspaper. "This is fifteen years old. I don't understand how Chad could have used this story."

"Wait," Grandpa said. He closed the file and opened a second one.

It was a death certificate. The mother had died of suicide. "Jesus," Gabe muttered behind. "What's the date? Two months after the murder of her boyfriend. That poor little girl."

Grandpa went through his clicks again.

The last document was a grainy newspaper photo of a young girl at her mom's funeral standing next to a tall rangy man.

I stared at the photo. And I knew. She was fifteen years older now, but I knew. "That's Duncan and Roxy." I slumped back in my chair.

Grandpa closed the file. He turned and ran his hand over the gray hairs sticking to his shiny head. "I remember when Duncan brought her home with him. Only said his sister had died. We'd heard rumors of suicide, but never a word about the shooting."

Gabe stood up. "Until Chad Tuggle somehow stumbled onto it. But would Roxy have given into blackmail over this?" He paced off a few steps to the carpeted living room, then back to the small dining room.

I knew he was thinking about the CD. "Gabe, I don't think Roxy has the CD. She hadn't appeared to be looking for the CDs in Chad's house, right? You were the one who went through those. But Roxy does have computer skills. She could have wiped Chad's computer clean both at work and at his home." I remembered that Roxy had computerized Duncan's nursery, and that meant she knew a lot about computers.

Gabe came to a stop, looking down at me. "Sam, do you think Roxy could have killed Chad?"

"I don't know. I mean she's tall enough and strong enough. She's right handed. She wears silk, but . . ." I tried to think about Roxy. Like last night. She had been paranoid, thinking I had betrayed her. Said she had shown up at the coffee shop. What could I have done at the coffee shop?

Then I remembered. Vance had showed up there, and I had handed him the computer disk. My back had been to the door since Vance insisted on sitting so that he could see it. I had given him the disk and told him it was the file off Chad's computer. What if Roxy had seen that? She wouldn't have known it was just the soccer books, and not the blackmail stuff. Had she thought I had the blackmail stuff from Chad's computer on the disk, instead of just soccer books?

And what had Angel said? She was acting odd, until she started doing her modeling thing. Because when Roxy was modeling, she was somebody the world wanted to see. Not the unwanted little girl who killed her mother's boyfriend and then suffered when her mother killed herself. How rejected and unlovable would that make a ten-year-old girl feel?

Roxy had found a way to be accepted for herself as a full-sized model. And wasn't that what Roxy was looking for at Heart Mates? A man who wanted and loved her? Not someone who would take off like her biological dad, beat her like her mother's boyfriend had beaten her mom, or worst of all, would kill himself to get away, like her mom had done? My heart ached for Roxy. But none of this meant she killed Chad.

"Babe?"

I tried talking it out to get a feel for it. "Maybe. If she's carried this horrible secret." I brought my hand up to rub my forehead. "I mean, killing a man at ten years old! And she's managed to bury it, to make a life for herself, then suddenly has it dredged back up with blackmail." I dropped my hand and looked up at Gabe. "She could be coming apart—and if she had to kill another man in self-defense . . ." I didn't know what to say. How much could one person withstand?

Gabe hunkered down, taking my hand. "We have to find out. And we have to find that CD."

I had told him I would help. And I would. "We need help, Gabe. We've been running around all over. It's time to put together an organized search. Let's pool our resources and teams and work together."

A grin rolled over his face. "Teamwork, huh?"

Gabe was on the phone, while Iris, Angel, Grandpa, and my sons, once Grandpa had picked them up from the skate park, gathered around the table. Dara and her son stayed out of sight, in case they had to make sudden use of the new identities Gabe had ready for them. I caught everyone up on the bare bones of what we knew and what we were looking for.

Gabe hung up the phone and sat down next to me. "My source is reasonably certain Detective Vance will hang around Chad's funeral for a while to see who shows up. That gives us a short time frame to search for the CDs." He looked at me. "And not get caught."

TJ and Joel laughed.

I glared at them, then shifted to Gabe. "Hey, hero, you needed your mom to tell you about that tracking device on your truck. Without her, I would have beaten you."

Joel's face sobered and he set his soda down. "That true, Gabe?"

Angel and I did a high five across the table.

Gabe looked at Joel. "It's true. I never saw Angel put

that tracking device on my truck because I was too busy fighting off your mom's lunatic client, who was trying to brain me with a tire iron. I could have just pulled my gun out and shot him, but you know—" Gabe looked down and cracked his knuckles. "—Then there would be the whole police investigation and lots of time lost. So he had a tire iron, and all I had were my skills."

Joel's mouth fell open. "Awesome."

Dang. How did Gabe do that? "I thought heroes didn't brag," I muttered.

Gabe grinned, then got serious. "Okay, I went through Chad's house last night. It's clean. So next is his office. I'll take that. Next is Janie's house. It's possible that Chad stashed the CDs there. Maybe with the kids' stuff. Mom," he turned to Iris, "think you can work your way into Janie's house and look around?"

Iris nodded. "Sophie Muffley is helping Janie by setting up all the food for after Chad's funeral. I'll go help her and look around for the CD."

I was impressed. Gabe's mom had gotten in pretty tight with Sophie.

"I can go with you," Grandpa volunteered. "I'm armed."

"No!" Gabe and I both shouted.

Grandpa frowned at me. "Now, Sammy, it's just a little knife."

TJ was standing over Grandpa's shoulder. "It's a switchblade. But Grandpa is so fast with his magic, Mom can't ever catch him with it. Makes her crazy." He grinned at me.

"Yeah," Joel added. "Gabe tried to take it from Grandpa once, but Grandpa pickpocketed it again without Gabe knowing." Pride shimmered in Joel's blue eyes.

Iris laughed. "You show him, Barney. Gabe sometimes gets a little bossy. He used to lecture me about my gun until I dragged him to the shooting range. Then he saw what an excellent shot I am."

Grandpa laughed. "Want me to go with you to Janie's house, Iris?"

Gabe jumped in. "Barney, I need you to stay here and keep everyone coordinated. You're the home base. You'll be relaying messages and directing us when we are out in the field. Plus, if any of us needs information, you are the Internet wizard."

What Gabe didn't say, but both Grandpa and I knew, was that we needed him here with the boys. They would be safe with him. "All right."

I glanced around the table. "I think I should take Ali and go to Duncan's nursery. Ali has been trying to tell me something, but I haven't understood." First she was agitated at Duncan's nursery, then last night when my car was vandalized.

Ali's ears pricked up from where she was on the other side of the table. Her toenails clicked on the linoleum as she came around the table and put her head in my lap. She was such a smart dog. "I should have realized the first time she acted weird at Duncan's nursery." I turned to Gabe. "We believe now Chad's killer was a woman, right? Maybe Roxy."

Gabe nodded, his thoughts obviously following mine. "But the threat on your answering machine was male. Slashing tires and black spray paint threats on your car lean to male as well."

"Yes, and Ali was determined to get into that trash can at the nursery. I think the murder weapon and scarf had been in the trash can." I stroked Ali's head, silently apologizing for not trusting her.

"So you think Duncan is threatening you?"

"Maybe. I think I'll take Ali back to the nursery and see what she does. If Roxy did kill Chad, it's possible that she took the CDs. I'll take a look there."

"I'll go with Sam." Angel agreed. "I can keep Duncan busy."

Gabe nodded. "Okay. Sam and Angel search the

ursery with Ali." He put his hand on my arm. "There's ne more place we need to look. Heart Mates."

I thought about that. "Why would the CDs be there? They could be incriminating to Roxy."

"I know. But what if Duncan took out anything in-riminating to Roxy and planted the rest of the CDs here?"

"Why?" I didn't get it. Framing me with the murder weapon and scarf made a sick kind of sense. Leaving he CDs didn't, especially since I wasn't on any of them, o it wasn't like they were a motive for me to kill Chad.

Grandpa spoke up then. "Sam, if it's Duncan, he's on edge. He's protecting the only family he has. He'll point everywhere away from Roxy. All the people on those CDs would be suspects."

I saw their point now. Duncan, if it was Duncan, would try anything to protect Roxy. "All right, I'll call Blaine and ask him to search there."

Gabe turned to TJ and Joel. "You two might have to be on the phone while your grandfather's on the com-outer. TJ, you are on Barney's cell, and Joel, you are on he landline, got it? You answer for your grandfather and do exactly what he says, okay?"

They both nodded, and I wanted to hug Gabe.

Gabe said, "Then we all know what we have to do. But this could get dangerous. No heroes. Everyone keeps n touch with Barney, all cell phones are on and answered. f Barney, or TJ or Joel speaking for Barney, gives the message to abort, you leave immediately, got it?"

Everyone agreed.

Angel, Ali, and I drove across town while I called Blaine. He said he'd get a ride over to Heart Mates and search for the CDs. My car would be ready in the morn-ng. I thanked him and hung up.

As Angel steered past Heart Mates on Mission Trail

Drive, I said, "I'm sorry for Roxy and Duncan. But I think Roxy knows that her uncle's going over the edge. Roxy will get off for self-defense, Duncan can get some help, and both of them can deal with all the loss they've suffered."

Angel turned toward me and opened her mouth to answer when we were hit from behind.

17

"**D**amn it!" Angel gripped the steering wheel and held the car on the road.

I swung my head around and looked behind us. A big tan truck. "I don't believe it. Lionel Davis hit us!" Okay, maybe it was more of a hard tap than a hit. But still, he hit us.

Angel pulled off on the side of Mission Trail and cut the engine. She looked at me, then in the back seat at Ali. "You two okay?"

Ali barked, then growled at Angel's car door. Before either of us could turn to look, Angel's door was wrenched open. Lionel's head popped in. "You ladies okay?" He whipped his head around to look at Ali.

I put my hand on Ali's shoulder. She was leaning through the middle of the bucket seats, aiming her teeth toward Lionel. "It's okay, Ali."

She stopped growling and licked me.

I looked past Angel to Lionel's huge teddy-bear eyes peering into the car. "Lionel, what are you doing here?" I mean, what were the odds? Of all the people in Lake Elsinore, what were the chances of getting rear-ended by Lionel, my stalking client?

"Following you. I was waiting in the Heart Mates parking lot when I saw you pass by. Sophie called me earlier to tell me all about the pictures. Samantha, this is dangerous business. A man has been murdered. You can't be running around getting involved in this."

Lionel's head looked like a caricature, filling up the doorway of Angel's car. A slow burn rode up my body. "You hit us on purpose!"

He waved his hand. "I have insurance."

I got out of the car and stomped around the back of the Trans Am and up to Lionel. He was still leaning over, but he had his head turned to watch me. I smacked his big round shoulder. "Are you crazy?"

He looked at me with watery hurt. "I'm just trying to look out for you." His gaze slipped down the bandage peeking over the top of my shirt, then back to my face. "I read those books you gave me."

I stopped one inch from Lionel. The top of my head barely hit his chin. I took a second to look at him. He was dressed in a shiny blue shirt with white piping, jeans, and boots. I could see the outline of his ever-present nose spray in his breast pocket. Finally, I tilted my head back to meet his stare. "You read all three books?"

"I speed-read. But the point is, I'll take care of this business for Sophie, not you. And I don't want you to be jealous. Sophie and I are over. You should go home. But if you want to work at your dating service, that's okay."

"What?" I just couldn't follow his thoughts. He was a bona fide nut case dressed as a harmless looking teddy-bear cowboy, addicted to nose spray. Could nose spray make a person nuts?

He shuffled his snakeskin boots in the dirt on the side of the road. "Well, in those books, the women like to be independent. Have jobs. Okay, I get that. But they don't chase down killers. So you can work at your little dating service while we're dating. Maybe when we're married. Not so sure when we have kids, though."

I heard laughter. I looked through the opened car door to see Angel with her forehead on the steering wheel. Her shoulders were shaking. Her whole body was heaving.

Hell. I wanted to laugh, too. And cry. "Lionel, I already have kids. I'm not dating you. I'm not marrying you. I don't even like you. And one of those books I gave you had a heroine who was a cop that chased killers!"

He shook his head. "I didn't like that one."

I blinked. Honest to God, if I had a wooden spoon, I'd have whapped him. "Give Angel your insurance information and go home."

"But . . ." He frowned, looking confused.

I went to my side of the car, got in, and shut the door. Once Angel had managed to breathe, she and Lionel exchanged insurance stuff and she got back into the car. I was staring straight through the front window and practicing the act of breathing. If I kept breathing, I might be able to keep from pulling my defense spray out of my purse and spraying Lionel. I was half afraid that after all the nose spray he did, the defense spray wouldn't have any effect. He'd just look hurt, with those huge brown eyes, and I'd feel worse. What the hell was wrong with me?

Lionel was a stalker, and I felt sorry for him. *A Stalker.* Crap, Lionel wasn't going to just stop. When Angel slipped back into her seat and shut her car door, I said, "Hang on." Wrenching my door open, I jumped out and stomped up to Lionel's truck. Ripping open the big cab door, I glared up at him. "Don't you dare follow us, got it?" I slammed the door and went back to the car.

Angel was on the cell phone. I groaned. "Tell me you didn't call this in to Grandpa."

"Joel," she clarified. "TJ's on the other phone to Gabe. I could hear Gabe laughing. Anyway, we are cleared to go on to the nursery."

I leaned my head back against the seat. "Why me?"

Angel started the car and headed the last mile toward the nursery. "Sam, he only dented the bumper and scratched the paint. My body shop can fix it in a day."

I couldn't help but smile. "I don't think the romance novels I gave Lionel helped." God, hitting us from behind to save us! Keeping my eyes closed, I said, "He's following us, isn't he?"

"Oh yeah. You gotta admire his determination. So, anyway, back to my question from this morning. What's it like to have three men after you?"

I looked down. I had changed into a fitted, button-down green shirt. It was low cut, revealing part of the bandage over my breast, but I didn't have to pull it over my head, which would have been too painful. "This stuff never happened to me when I wore stretch shorts and long T-shirts over my fast-food figure."

Angel turned into the nursery and glanced at me with her vivid green eyes. "Ever feel like going back to that, Sam?"

"No. At least now I feel alive. Then I felt nothing, except for TJ and Joel. I was happy only with my sons. Now I feel like a whole person as well as a mom."

"Great kids, Sam. If I could have had kids, I'd have wanted them to be like your boys." She parked the car.

I looked over at Angel. Drop-dead beautiful with her fair skin, jewel-toned eyes, long red hair—even with the black tips—and long lean figure. None of that could give her a child. I always thought the only reason Angel had stayed with her dickhead ex-husband, Hugh, was to have a baby. The day she caught him screwing her manicurist ended that.

But it didn't end her wish for a baby. I had offered to surrogate for her, but she never took me up on it. Instinctively, I put my hand on her arm. "Tuesday night Gabe's taking the boys to a baseball game. You and I are going to make a night of it for us. Deal?" I couldn't fix all her problems or hurts, but I could be her friend.

Her billion-watt smile lit up her face. "Deal." She squared her shoulders and tossed her hair back. Her black tips hit Ali in the nose and made her sneeze.

We both laughed and got out of the car. Looking back at Ali, I watched her shake her head to rid herself of the sneezes. "Come on, Ali."

She jumped out and padded over the dirt parking lot to stand with Angel and me at the back of the Trans Am. Angel said, "No one's here."

I looked past the dark trailer/office. The white truck was gone. "Maybe Duncan is making a delivery."

We both looked around. There were no customers, though we did spot Lionel's truck stopped on the street outside the nursery.

I shook my head at Lionel's tenacity. "Well, let's see what we can find. Maybe the trailer door is open. Ali," I looked down at her. She was sniffing the ground. "Show me, girl."

She took off running directly for the trash cans in front of the office. "Keep a look out for Duncan," I called to Angel and followed my dog.

Ali had her two front paws on top of the exact same trash can. Every nerve in my body sprang to life. All the hairs on my neck stood out like needles. "Down for a sec, Ali."

She jumped down and sat.

I pulled off the lid. A slight wind whipped around us, swaying the potted trees and bushes and spreading the wet earth smell of the nursery. I could hear the sound of dead leaves blowing around. Ali balanced her paws on the edges of the trash can. My heart pumped out adrenaline.

Angel came up beside us, her gaze sweeping around the parking lot. No one was here.

All three of us looked inside the trash can.

It was empty but for a few crumpled newspapers. I reached in and pulled out the newspapers. We spread them out on the ground. Ali used her powerful shoulders to push her way in and sniff the papers. Then she whined, pawing a sheet of the paper.

I turned it over.

All three of us stared at the smeared brown stain. Old blood. The bookend and scarf had been wrapped in this paper. I was sure we were on the right trail. Duncan, Roxy, or both had hidden the murder weapon and scarf here, then moved them to the storage room at Heart Mates. How did they get into Heart Mates? Was Roxy involved in that, or was Duncan acting on his own? Where was Roxy? Where was Duncan? I lifted my gaze from the newspaper. "Call Grandpa." We had to report in.

Angel was already dialing. "Joel? Hey, sport, any instructions for us? No? Okay, can I talk to Barney?"

Grandpa came on, and Angel got him up to date and then looked at me. "He's calling Gabe on the other line. He said Blaine's at Heart Mates now, searching. So far, he hasn't found the CDs. Oh, Barney checked the CDs from Rick's house, and they are all clear."

I'd have to get those CDs back to Rick. I carefully folded up the newspaper while Ali watched me. Now that I appeared to understand her, she wasn't upset. To Angel, I said, "The CDs aren't at Heart Mates. It doesn't make sense. I don't think Duncan and Roxy ever had them."

Angel's gaze focused on the trailer. "Sam, go see if the door is unlocked."

The trailer was made so that the front opened up to form an awning, leaving a big counter where the cash register was. The office was behind that. There was a regular door on the side of the trailer to get behind the counter. Today, even the front of the trailer was closed.

There were ramps all around the trailer that made moving merchandise easier. Past the side door was a little porch area with a couple of plastic chairs. Duncan could sit there and take a break while keeping an eye on the nursery. The sign on the side door said "Closed for Delivery." That meant that Duncan had to make a delivery of some plants, trees, or something himself instead of using the hired help. I glanced around, spotting Lionel's truck parked on the street, and a few cars passing by, but no Duncan. I hurried up the ramp to the side door.

Ali followed me. We got to the door. It was an aluminum framed door with white siding. I reached out and curled my hand around the cold doorknob. It was locked.

Crap. I stared at it. A cheap little lock. Gabe could open it. Looking around, I spotted the window over the two green plastic chairs. I could see that through the screen, a blue curtain fluttered from the breeze. The window was chest high. The wood ramp extended under the window. If I thought about this, I'd have a dozen reasons not to break into the office.

So I didn't think about it. I went over, used my hip to push a chair aside, and studied the screen. I put both hands on the frame of the screen and pushed up.

It slid up, the bottom of the frame popping out of the track.

Well, that had to be a good omen. I set the screen down on the porch. Ali sniffed it, then sneezed. Guess the screen was a little dusty. I looked in. There was a counter with a small sink. I reached over, pulled over the chair, and stood on it. Almost high enough.

I put my foot on the back of the plastic chair. If I timed this just right, I could get up high enough to push in through the window before the chair fell.

Or I'd fall on my ass.

I gave myself fifty-fifty odds.

I took a deep breath, supported myself on my right foot, and lunged in the window.

I heard the chair slide away and fall on the wood.

I was in, with my hands on either side of the stainless-steel sink but my legs still hanging straight out. Using my arms put pressure on my cut, making it burn.

Ali barked. I could feel her jumping around behind me. She probably thought my legs sticking out the window was hilarious.

Ignoring the pain from my cut, I pulled myself in far enough to turn around. My butt was in the sink, but I managed to drag my legs through the window. I lifted my butt out of the stainless steel sink and looked around.

The front counter was cluttered with papers, books, catalogs, the computer, and cash register—oh, boy! I hoped there wasn't some kind of silent alarm! The other end of the trailer was just a small kitchen with a table and chairs. I headed to the front of the trailer.

At the counter, I looked over everything. I rifled through the catalogs, the papers . . . nothing. I stared at the computer. Forget it—Roxy was way more advanced than I was. But the computer did make me wonder. How had Chad contacted Roxy? How had Duncan found out?

There were drawers and cupboards beneath the counter. I started looking through those. All kinds of office supplies, order forms, computer manuals . . .

Where the hell do people hide their blackmail notes? Was it a note? A phone call? What? I found nothing.

Depressed, I shut the cupboard door. The computer screen scrolled "Duncan's Nursery" as a screen saver. I hit the mouse.

The start-up screen popped up. Damn. What now?

Grandpa! Pulling out my cell phone, I called home. I listened to the phone ring and the ticking of Ali's toenails as she walked around outside the trailer. How much time before Duncan returned? "TJ, it's Mom. I need to talk to Grandpa."

"Sam?" I heard Grandpa's voice.

"Grandpa," I knew Angel had called in on her cell so Grandpa knew I was in the office. "I'm looking at the computer inside Duncan's office. If Chad e-mailed a blackmail threat, how would I find it?"

"Do you see any kind of Internet icon, Sam?"

I studied the screen. "AOL?"

"Good. Okay, now do you see something called Explorer?"

"Uh." I went down the rows. "There!"

"Click it. Then go to the C drive, then Program Files."

I went through the clicks, silently praying Duncan didn't return. "Now what?"

"See AOL?"

"Yes!" I clicked on it.

"Okay, good, now do you see download?"

"There." I clicked on it. "Grandpa, a bunch of things came up.

"Read them to me."

"Blondejokes, beautytips, scheduleforfeb, picsofsue, LasVegasdancer." My eyes shot back.

"Click it, Sam."

I clicked, and the article about Roxy's mom popped up. And the threat from Chad. *Pay twenty thousand or . . .* I closed my eyes. Chad was going to expose Roxy. "Grandpa, it's the article that was on Chad's file. And Chad wrote a threat telling her to be at his office by ten o'-clock Wednesday night." I took a second to think about it. "Grandpa, what would you do if you found something like this about me? You know, if you found out someone was blackmailing me?"

"I'd follow you. My guess was that Roxy got the note and went to Chad's like the note said. Duncan found it and went after her."

It sounded right. It made sense. How long had Duncan been protecting Roxy? For fifteen years, ever since her mother committed suicide. Grandpa's voice brought me back to the present.

"E-mail the file to me." He took me through several moves to send some more stuff to him, including the article, the picture from Roxy's mom's funeral, and the e-mail demanding Roxy meet Chad. "Sam, I think Duncan stumbled onto this because Roxy probably deleted it from her AOL account but forgot to delete it from the program files. He's driven by love for his niece. Get out of there before he returns."

I agreed and closed down the files. I didn't think I could make it back out the window. Instead I went to the side door and froze. A row of keys hung on a rack of hooks to the right of the door.

One of them was my key. I recognized it. The key to Heart Mates. It was a spare I kept in my purse because Blaine often took my car. If I gave him my key ring and then wanted to walk over to Burger King for lunch, I had to lock the office. It must have fallen out of my purse the day I struggled with Ali. It was on a key ring with my business card in a hard plastic cover. It didn't take any guesswork to figure out that was the key to Heart Mates.

Now I knew how Duncan, or Duncan and Roxy, got into Heart Mates to plant the evidence. From the minute Ali had signaled something was in that trash can, Duncan had been figuring out a way to place the blame for Chad's murder on me.

I shivered. Duncan wasn't an evil man. But he was a man who loved his niece—maybe too much for her own good. *And my good.* I left the key there and hurried out.

We had to find that CD, then turn everything else over to Detective Vance. Duncan had to be stopped before he went too far. Both Duncan and Roxy needed help. I shut the door behind me and turned to put the screen back in the window. Ali trotted up to help me.

I heard a car. Looking down, I saw Angel headed our way in her Trans Am. She stopped, leaned across to open the passenger door, and yelled, "Sam! We have to leave. Now!"

I glanced past the parking lot to the street and saw a white truck on the road. It slowed by where Lionel was parked. I left the screen on the ground and ran down the ramp. Ali raced ahead, jumping in the car before me. I slammed the door, and Angel shoved the car in reverse. When she had backed up far enough, she put the car in drive and headed for the exit onto Mission Trail.

When we got to the street, we saw Lionel out of his truck, talking to Duncan. Bless Lionel! For once, he was actually helping by stalling Duncan. We zoomed past them.

I turned my head in time to see Duncan staring at us. His weathered face was hard, his mouth grim.

Shit. A bad feeling shot up my spine and slammed into my brain. "Hurry, Angel, go to Chad's office. The CD is there. It has to be." I got Grandpa on the phone and told him about the key.

"Sam, one of Gabe's contacts just called me and said that Vance is getting restless at the funeral. He's been hanging in the back, but he's starting to move away toward his car."

"Oh, God. Call Gabe." I hung up. Of course, Gabe had a vast network, people who occasionally worked for him, that I hardly ever saw. I should have known he was having Vance watched. "Faster, Angel." Everything depended on us getting those CDs. First. Then Vance could blow the case wide open.

But I meant to protect Roxy. She was my friend. My Heart Mates client. And she was a victim.

* * *

We pulled around the back of the Stater Bros. strip mall. Gabe's truck was in the alley, but down on the other end of Stater Bros. Vance would have to actively look for his truck to spot it.

I pointed out the door for Angel to stop by, then turned to look at her. "Angel, take Ali and go back to my house, please. Duncan's going to know that it was me at his office. I'm worried about Grandpa and the boys." Angel had a gun. And she would use it to protect my sons.

She touched my hand resting on the console between the seats. "All right. But you swear to me that you and Gabe will be careful."

I hugged her. It'd be a lot easier with Angel looking out for my sons and Grandpa. Then I hurried out the door and slipped in the unlocked door to Chad's office.

Trouble had been brewing for a while between Gabe and Vance, plus Dara and Josh's future hung on those CDs. I had to help Gabe find the CDs and get out of Chad's office before Vance showed up.

Vance knew many people in town were searching for something. The odds were that Vance was putting the pieces together. How much had he researched Dara? Maybe his search warrant for Heart Mates would come through, and that would keep him busy. Blaine could handle the search. Even if Vance found the murder weapon, I had seen enough evidence at Duncan's nursery to prove the murder weapon had been planted at my office.

Gabe met me in the kitchen. "Barney called. Where's Angel and Ali?"

"I sent them home. If Grandpa called, then you know that Duncan spotted us at the nursery. I want the boys protected."

He nodded and dragged his latex-encased hand

through his hair. His dark eyes were haunted. "I've looked everywhere. Searched the desk, but there are no hidden spots. Nothing in the kitchen. Checked the bathroom, even the always-popular toilet tank."

I walked up to Gabe, putting my hand on his forearm.

"Babe, think," Gabe said. "Where would Chad hide those CDs? You knew him."

I looked around the dim kitchen. Vague strips of daylight spilled through from the closed blinds at the front of the office, and Gabe had turned on the light beneath the microwave. I took in the green cupboards, a small microwave, a coffeemaker with Chad's "Everybody Loves The Coach" coffee mug next to it, the sink, and the refrigerator. "You looked in the fridge?"

"Yes."

"Okay." Dropping my hand from his arm, I tried to think like Chad. Like a man. Like an arrogant town hero who relished his power. The kitchen? I don't think so. I went through the kitchen to the office. The strips of daylight were a bit more vivid. I ignored Sophie's desk. Trusting my instincts, I walked over to Chad's huge, U-shaped desk. The computer was gone. The printer was gone. On the credenza against the wall, part of the top had been hacked away to get the paper shredder out. A big yawning black hole gave me the creeps.

Dropping my gaze to the floor, I saw dark stains and shivered. I thought about how my shirt had been caught in the shredder that had been in the empty black hole on the credenza. How close had I been to having to fight with Chad like his killer had? I shook my feelings off and focused on Chad.

My instincts were built on my husband, the man who slept with other women and dealt drugs right under my nose. He had been arrogant and had thought he was untouchable like Chad. Then I'd discovered his stash of panties—they'd been hidden in his beloved Classic Mustang. Close at hand, tucked away in one of his prized toys.

Men and their toys.

I moved my gaze to the right end of the credenza where the soccer trophies stood on their fat plastic and fake marble bases, and the professionally framed pictures and newspaper articles hung on the walls. Both soccer ball–shaped bookends were gone. I assumed the police had the one that matched the bookend in my filing cabinet at Heart Mates.

What did Chad Tuggle prize the most? His power over people, the power that he used to blackmail his friends and get away with it. And where did Chad perceive that power came from?

Being the town's hero coach. Of soccer.

I looked back to the awards, newspaper articles, and trophies. How many books and movies had something hidden in frames? Wouldn't there be room to slip a few CDs behind the pictures or newspaper articles? Chad had had those items framed. He could even have had extra space built in. "Gabe, did you look in the frames?" I waved toward the wall.

"I took them off the wall and looked, but didn't take them apart."

I nodded, suddenly lightheaded. My vision narrowed. Stepping around the bloodstains, I went to the end of the credenza by the window and looked at the three huge trophies, with their fat bases sitting flush on the mahogany. They were symbols of Chad's hero status as the championship winning coach. Of his power. "What about the trophies? Couldn't one of those bases be hollowed out or something?"

Gabe came up beside me. "Good idea, babe. Put these on." He held out a pair of latex gloves.

I took the gloves and fought them over my clammy hands.

Gabe's natural confidence overrode his earlier frustration. "Let's take a look." He went to the trophy on the left, the closest one to Chad's desk. I started with the one on the right, the farthest from the bloodstains on the carpet. It was heavy, probably twenty-five pounds. I started by feeling all around the base. Through the gloves, the plastic felt like cold marble.

Like a cemetery headstone.

A shiver rocketed down my back. I heard a noise on the other side of the window. Was someone out there? I glanced at Gabe. "Did you hear anything?"

"Nothing." He lifted his trophy and looked underneath it.

I had probably heard someone moving around outside the window. There were several businesses in the strip mall that housed Chad's office. My paranoia ran a little high today. I tilted my trophy over. The entire base looked solid. The bottom was covered tightly in black felt to keep it from scratching the surface it sat on.

Gabe picked up the middle trophy.

"Here, let me look while you hold it up." I bent over, but the bottom was covered in the same felt as the others, securely glued all the way around. I put my hand on the back of the trophy—and felt a gap. It was a thin gap, the width of a razor's edge. "I think I found something! Turn it around."

Gabe set the trophy down and rotated it. Bending over, I carefully felt around. The top edge wasn't smooth, but had a little ridge. Through the glove, I pushed my fingernail into the ridge and pulled back.

A rectangular piece of the base pulled off.

"Oh." I held the piece, my heart beating. "I think we found it." I peered in. It was dark. I stuck my finger in and hit a sharp corner of something. With two fingers, I pressed down and pulled out.

A plastic CD case slid out. Then a second one. And a third. Three CD cases. I held them in my hand. "Gabe, we found them! Dara and Josh will be safe."

"Very impressive," Detective Logan Vance said as he strode into the office from the kitchen.

18

From my position bent over the trophy, I turned my head around to see Vance holding his gun trained on Gabe.

Damn. We were in big trouble. Still bent over, I pulled the CDs protectively toward me. Gabe and Vance had been dancing around a confrontation for months. I knew Gabe had his gun tucked in the back of his pants.

"Shaw, stand up and put the CDs on the credenza. Pulizzi, hands on your head. Interlock your fingers. You know the drill."

While Gabe raised his arms slowly, I started to stand. But two of the CDs slid from my latex-gloved grip and crashed to the ground. I jerked, trying to catch them, but instead I caught the edge of the soccer trophy.

It flew off the counter, the big cup part slammed into my chest. I screamed and fell backward. I landed hard on my back, and the trophy crashed down on top of me. My scream echoed in my ears.

"Samantha!" Another voice bellowed.

Pain shot from my back straight through to my chest, while that voice rocketed through my head. Something important about that voice . . . God, it hurt. Had to think. Then recognition slammed into me. *Lionel.*

Gabe came over, his face a mask of fury. "Sam, don't move. Christ, you cut open your chest." He picked up the trophy and tossed it aside.

Vance loomed over Gabe's shoulder. "Pulizzi, freeze! Get your hands—"

The front door crashed open.

I turned my head in time to see a huge shape spill through the door. The blue shirt registered. "Lionel!" My God, he'd crashed his body into the locked door, forcing it open.

Lionel stopped inside, swept his big teddy-bear gaze over me on the ground, moved up to Gabe standing over me, then froze on Vance with the gun. "I'll save you, Samantha!" He rushed Vance, pulling something out of his breast pocket.

Vance turned, his gun pointed at the ceiling as he assessed the threat.

Gabe had a hold on my shoulder, keeping me prone on the ground. But I was able to see Lionel rip out his nose spray, tear off the lid, and spray it in Vance's eyes.

Uh-oh.

"Fuck!" Vance screamed and went to his knees, rubbing his eyes. His gun hit the ground.

Lionel tucked his nose spray back into his shirt pocket. "I knew you needed me—" he began.

Gabe let go of me and rolled up to his feet.

"You're dead, dickhead," Vance threatened while scrubbing his eyes with his palm and wiping his runny nose.

"Samantha, oof." Lionel suddenly went quiet.

I struggled up to a sitting position to see Lionel face-down on the floor. Gabe put his knee to Lionel's back and worked a pair of cuffs around his wrists.

I climbed to my feet.

Gabe glanced up at me. "Sit down, babe."

I looked down at the blood all over my green top. My blood. Yuck. Trying not to think about it, I ripped off my stupid latex gloves and headed toward Vance. He was still scrubbing his eyes and swearing down a wrath of slow death on Lionel.

"Oh, God, what happened?" A new voice shouted.

I turned to the door. Roxy looked like she was posing for a photo shoot in a long black skirt and matching jacket. Simple hair and makeup, very subdued. "Roxy? What are you doing here?" Jeez, was there a party? I could probably really use a beer.

"My uncle called me, Sam. I'm worried about him. I have to tell you . . ." Her words died as her gaze fell to my chest. "You're bleeding. Bad." Her eyes rolled up into her head.

"Roxy!" I rushed to her, grabbing her arm. "Breathe!" She blinked several times.

I tried to get her to focus and not faint. "Roxy, why are you here?"

"Uncle Duncan. I have to talk to you. I called your house, and your Grandpa said you were here." She took a breath, her face bleaching beneath her makeup. "You should do something about that blood."

I glanced over to Gabe. He had hauled Lionel up to his feet and sat him in a chair. The CDs were no longer on the floor. Had Gabe stuck them somewhere? One crisis at a time. I felt Roxy trembling beneath my hand. "Duncan called you?" I prompted.

"At the funeral. I was at *his* funeral."

"Chad's funeral?" Was she trying to do the right thing? Or maybe she thought no one would suspect her of killing Chad if she went to the funeral?

She nodded. "Uncle Duncan called me there on my cell." Her beautiful eyes fixed on me. Huge pools of misery. Of secrets. "Sam, he's not thinking right. This is all my fault!" Tears filled her eyes and ran down her face.

"Oh, Roxy." My heart broke for her. I also wondered why her tears didn't smear her makeup.

"Roxy!" A thick, raspy voice thundered from behind me. "None of this is your fault. It's her fault."

"Duncan." I recognized the voice behind me, and my gaze flashed to Gabe. His stare fixed behind me, on Duncan. The street stamped down hard on his expression, making his eyes flat black stones of sheer danger. Gabe stepped away from the seated Lionel.

"No." Roxy slapped both her hands over her mouth.

Duncan's thick, plaid-covered arm whipped around me, pressing a cold blade to my neck. A knife.

I hate knives. I hate pain. I was really starting to hate my life.

And where the hell was Vance? Last time I saw him, he was on the floor, bellowing in pain. Had he left? Figured we could all kill each other? He didn't go out the front, but in the confusion he could have slipped out the back door through the little kitchen.

"Uncle Dun, let Sam go!" Roxy's voice strangled out through her manicured fingers, and then she broke into wrenching sobs. "It's over, Dun. I want to tell the truth."

"No." The knife pressed against my throat, the sharp cold blade a contrast to Duncan's thin, raspy voice. "We're going to get out of here. Roxy, you follow Sam and me. We'll start over again where no one knows what happened. It'll work; it worked before."

"I . . ." Roxy's voice shook with thick despair and she dropped her arms, clasping her hands in front of her black skirt. "I can't. I just can't. I killed him." She lowered her gaze to my face. "Why did he do it?"

It was a little hard to talk with a knife pressed to my throat. But when I looked into Roxy's tormented face, I couldn't help myself. "That's what you meant on the

ell phone, Roxy? *'Why did he do it?'* You meant, why did
Chad blackmail you?"

She shook her head, growing composed. Her voice
calmed. "I know why he blackmailed me—for money.
'm a target now. Public people are. I told him to go
ahead, tell everyone that I shot my mother's boyfriend
and that my mother committed suicide. I always knew it
would come out one day."

The muscles in Duncan's arm around me tightened,
digging the knife in a little deeper. I hoped that if I kept
Roxy talking, he'd begin to see the pointlessness of
what he was doing. I asked her, "What happened then?"

Roxy darted her gaze over my shoulder to Duncan,
then back to me. "He laughed at me and said, 'You'll
pay and you'll keep on paying until I decide otherwise.'
I was standing by him at his desk. He stood, so I backed
up and turned around. I was so mad that I turned and
put my hands on that credenza to take a deep breath."

Roxy's composure shattered. Her face paled and
then grew spots of deep, angry red. Her words hardened. "Somehow my scarf got caught in the shredder.
He laughed harder. Then he started tearing at my
clothes."

God, I could see it. I remembered how excited it
made Chad when he'd found me caught in the shredder. It would be easy to guide the edges of Roxy's scarf
into the automatic teeth of the shredder. He got off on
control. I asked, "So you fought back?"

She shifted her stare to the ugly black hole on the
credenza where the shredder used to be. "At first I just
struggled. He tore my blouse. I threatened to scream.
He told me to go ahead, that I probably liked it rough . . ."

Roxy turned back to me. "Just like my mother."

I winced in spite of the cold edge of the knife blade
pressed into the skin of my neck. "Oh, Roxy."

She didn't hear me. "He attacked me. He wouldn't
stop until I picked up that bookend and hit him. I—"

"Enough," Duncan shouted, practically in my ear. "Roxy, we're leaving." He pressed his arm holding the knife into my chest and forced me to walk backward. His elbow caught the cut on my chest. Pain blasted my nerve endings, paralyzing me until the instinct to protect myself slammed my brain into gear. Duncan was coming undone. He loved Roxy so much and was desperate to protect her.

Desperate enough to hurt or kill me to get Roxy away to what he thought was safety.

He dragged me back a step. "I'll cut her," he shouted.

I believed him.

"Uncle Dun! Don't!" Roxy begged.

I didn't look at Gabe. Instead, I concentrated and tried to think past the pain. I had to. I'd told Gabe he wasn't a superhero. If I wanted him to help me, I had to give him the opening. I knew what to do. Gabe had taught me how to break a hold.

It was going to hurt.

Don't think about it. Think past it. I drew air into my lungs and reacted, bringing both my hands up underneath Duncan's powerful tree-trunk arm. I wasn't strong enough to push his arm very far away, but I managed to push it back far enough to drop to the ground.

I hit the carpet and cried out at the rush of agony. Damn, that hurt. Pain exploded from the cut and fanned out like wildfire.

Gabe's bellow cut through my haze of hurt. "Stay down!"

I tucked in tighter and felt Gabe's body leap over me to tackle Duncan. They hit the wall, landed on the ground, and rolled.

Roxy screamed.

"The knife!" The realization that Duncan still had the knife shot through me. I rolled to my knees. Sweat popped out through every pore in my skin. Fear, pain, and pounding panic poured out of me. Gabe was young, strong, and street savvy. But Duncan was driven by a powerful love for his niece.

My feelings for Gabe got me to my feet. I swiped sweat out of my eyes and saw Duncan roll over on top of Gabe.

Gabe used both hands to hold the knife an inch off his throat. "Oh, God." A weapon. I needed a weapon. Searching, I saw Lionel, sitting handcuffed in a chair. His teddy-bear gaze turned grizzly as he watched me struggle. He leaned forward and said, "My nose spray!"

I ran over and grabbed his nose spray out of his pocket. The room spun. I locked my gaze on the struggling men and kept going, thinking only of saving Gabe.

Roxy screamed words, but nothing had any meaning.

Except saving Gabe.

The knife was a half-inch closer to Gabe's neck. Duncan matched him in weight. I yanked the cap off the nose spray, leaned down to aim in to Duncan's face, and squeezed the little bottle with all my might.

The spray missed Duncan, but hit Vance square in the eyes. Vance had crept in the front door and pulled Duncan off Gabe at the exact second I sprayed.

"Goddamn it!" Vance roared and sank to his knees.

"Oops." It came out a squeak. I knew this was going to be bad. For me. He was probably going to shoot me.

Gabe sprang to his feet as Vance doubled over in pain. He kicked the knife away from Duncan and pinned him to the ground on his stomach, hands behind his back. "Sam, get me Vance's cuffs."

I took a step closer to Vance. He'd already ripped his shirt off and pressed it to his eyes. His powerful swimmer's shoulders heaved in obvious pain. But I had no choice. We had to get Duncan handcuffed, and Gabe had already used his set on Lionel. I reached down to get his cuffs from his belt.

He wrapped one hand around my wrist and said

through his shirt, "I'm going to kill you, Shaw. Then I'm going to revive you just to kill you again."

I tossed Gabe the cuffs. He quickly snapped the manacles on Duncan, then sat him up. Roxy dropped to her knees, crying and hugging her uncle.

Since Vance had an iron grip on my wrist, I said, "Come on. Let's go in the kitchen and wash out your eyes."

"Then I will kill you," Vance assured me.

"Okay," I agreed.

"Pulizzi," Vance bellowed as we stumbled to the kitchen, "do not let Roxy leave. She's under arrest. You're all under arrest. The whole goddamn town is under fucking arrest!"

I heard Gabe snort.

I got Vance to the sink in Chad's kitchen. After turning on the water, I reached over and took the shirt away. Then I helped him cup cool water over his eyes to rinse them out. "You might want to see a doctor."

Vance stuck his whole head under the running water. Then he shut the tap off, grabbed his shirt, and dried his face. He lowered the shirt and tested his eyes by blinking slowly.

Satisfied, he fixed his bloodshot stare on me. "Now I know why so many men keep trying to kill you."

"I'm really sorry. I didn't realize you were there. I was trying to get Duncan off Gabe." I'd been so terrified for Gabe that I'd practically had tunnel vision. I only saw how close that knife was to Gabe's throat. My feelings for Gabe had ballooned right over the pain in my chest with the need to protect him.

"I was outside the door waiting for Duncan to drag you out. I would have been able to take him by surprise. Should have known you'd pull something. Do you ever think of crying or fainting like normal women?"

I was flirting with fainting right now. My adrenaline rush had slowed to a bare trickle. I didn't want to look at what damage the trophy did to my chest. I was afraid it had popped my implants, and that they had exploded out my chest. Ugh. Focus! "Vance, it was self-defense just like you said. Roxy had no choice."

He stared at me. "Not your problem now, is it? You'll get paid from your *client* and skip on to your next disaster." He rubbed his shirt over his short-cut hair, getting the extra water out.

I watched him for a minute, then said, "You already had it figured out, didn't you?"

He dropped his arms. "Why didn't you just let me look in your storeroom, Shaw? Yes, I knew. Roxy Gabor killed Chad in self-defense. The evidence tells the story of what happened."

"How did you figure it out?"

He slapped his hand down on the counter. "In Smash Coffee, when I came up behind you, I heard Dom say that Roxy wore silk scarves. I filed that information away. Then just minutes later, I saw Roxy Gabor open the door to the coffee shop just as you gave me the soccer disk. She froze when she saw you slide that disk across the table. Her whole face blanched. And it got me to thinking. Roxy had no connection to soccer, so what was up? It didn't take a genius to figure out that the whole town was trudging over my crime scenes looking for something. Given that Chad Tuggle had been messing with several funds, not just the soccer accounts, but also some work accounts, it didn't take long to make the leap to blackmail. He was desperate to put back the money he stole from those accounts. And we managed to reconstruct some of the activity on Chad's work computer."

A drop of water ran down from his scalp to his ear. I concentrated on that to stay conscious. "Vance, you aren't really going to arrest Roxy, are you?"

He stared down at me. "I'm going to bring her in for a formal interview."

Fair enough, I thought. "What about Duncan?"

"He assaulted you and Rambo out there," he tilted his head toward the office area. "He was behind the threats to you."

"He was protecting Roxy. The two of them need help."

"I'm not a doctor, I'm a cop."

He was a cop playing hardball. Time for me to do the same. Meeting his gaze, I said, "You can use this whole mess to your advantage, Vance. Think about it. Show the town your compassion for Roxy and file it as self-defense. Maybe Duncan has to face some charges, but they don't have to be serious. People in town will start to trust you." I was working up to the big problem.

"Like you, Shaw?"

I put my hand on his rigid arm. The room swayed a bit. Breathe, I told myself. "Look, Vance, you threatened me and tried to arrest me. But that's not the point. The town is going to feel that you are on their side if you handle this case with care." One more breath, then I said it, "And don't use any of the blackmail information to hurt people."

Fury shaded his face a dull red. "Like Dara Reed? The woman who used her pharmaceutical license and access to drugs to kill her husband? I'm sure if I search Pulizzi out there, I'll find those CDs."

Oh, Lord. What did I do? I'd promised Gabe I'd help him help Dara. "Vance, her husband was dying! The man was in agony, and he begged her to help him. Jesus, are you so heartless that you don't understand what she did? And what good would it do to send Dara back to Arizona now? You'd leave her son without any parents. Then there's the fact that the DA out there hated Dara for turning him in when he tried to get a medication with a forged prescription."

The gold points in Vance's brown eyes shimmered with hostility. Grabbing my hand on his arm, Vance pulled ne just forward enough to lean down into my face. "That's what you think, isn't it, Shaw? That I'm a heartless bastard who would destroy Dara and her son to fulfill the letter of the law. You're just like the rest of this town, thinking I'm out to get them. I watched my own mother die of cancer—" He stopped talking. His jaw throbbed. His neck muscles corded.

I had hurt his feelings. I opened my mouth with no idea what to say.

"Shut up, Shaw. Your cover-ups could have gotten someone else killed. Tuggle deserved what he got. I hate even wasting the paper to close out his murder. But you—" Once more he just cut off.

"Vance, I—" I what? I knew nothing about Vance's personal life. Hell, I'd never given a thought to his family. I knew he lived alone from town gossip. But I didn't know his mother had died of cancer or that it tore him up.

I'd never thought of Vance as compassionate. God, I screwed up. He was right. But it's not like he ever let me know he had anything but cop feelings. I softened my voice, partly to reach him, and partly because I was low on reserves. The edges of the kitchen were dissolving into gray fuzz. "How would I know that, Vance?"

"How? You're such an expert at figuring everyone else out. I thought all that romance reading was supposed to teach you about people."

I was trying to keep my thoughts in line. They were slipping around in my cottony head. Now that the adrenaline was draining, pain struggled to get my attention. "You won't notify the DA in Arizona about Dara?"

Silence. His hand around my fingers was warm and hard. "Swear to God, you drive me crazy. I can never decide if I should kill you or kiss you."

Uh-oh. I tried to pull back.

Too late, he got his arms around me. "Do you have any idea how badly you are hurt?"

He wasn't going to kiss me. That was good. "I'm jus⊣ hoping that I didn't pop anything."

He swept his gaze down to my breasts. "I think your Bimbo Barbie look is safe. But you have a hell of a cu⊣ on your chest, sort of gouged in the center from the corner of the trophy. You have an angry red line across your neck, but no actual cut."

"Oh." He always smelled like the sun and coconut. "I⊣ I'm hurt, that rules out kissing and killing, right?"

His gaze flicked up over my head to something, then back to me. He smiled, flashing killer dimples. I watched those dimples as he lowered his mouth to brush my lips.

I felt the touch of Vance's mouth at the same time a shadow fell over me. I rolled my eyes up to see Gabe. Cold, dark eyes, hair pushed back, jaw tight, and nose flared.

I tried to struggle to get out of Vance's hold. The entire room spun, hot and sick. "Let me go."

"Let her go," Gabe's voice echoed mine, only his was flat and deadly soft.

Vance unhooked his arms from around me then grasped my shoulders to steady me. "She needs to go to the hospital."

I was tired of being used. Leaning up against the counter, I brushed off Vance's hands. "Both of you, stop it. Now." Okay, that kind of came out like a plea.

"Stay out of it, Sam," Gabe snarled at me, never taking his eyes off Vance.

Vance moved like a ship over a glass lake, smooth and ready. His naked shoulders shimmered with fine drops of water from sticking his head under the faucet. "You've been a boil on my ass ever since I got here, Pulizzi."

Gabe had an inch or two on Vance, and his build was street tough. No fat. Hard. Fast. He held his ground. "You've been panting after what's mine, Vance."

Vance smiled. "Having trouble holding on to your woman?"

I barely saw him move. Gabe swung hard, clipping Vance in the jaw and knocking him back into the fridge.

Vance hit the fridge, bounced off, and headed back toward Gabe. Hands turned into fists.

"Stop it!" I shouted. Panic whipped through me, but the pain had dominance. I looked around for help and stared straight at Iris Pulizzi, Gabe's mom.

What was Gabe's mom doing here?

Iris sized up the situation, including the two men locked together in a killer bear hug, and grabbed Chad's oversized mug that read "Everybody Loves The Coach." She stuck it under the sink, filled it to the brim, and dumped the whole cup over the grunting men.

They both froze. But Iris was still moving, searching through drawers. She came out with a long-handled spoon. "What is the matter with you two!" She stalked toward the men, waving the spoon at them. "You! You're supposed to be a police officer?" She smacked Vance in the back of the head with the spoon.

Vance yelped in surprise.

Gabe smirked.

"And you," Iris turned to her son. "This is how you show your feelings for Sam? By letting her bleed to death while you prove your manhood?" Whack—she nailed Gabe just above his left ear.

Then she turned to me.

I wanted to run, but I just didn't have the energy. "Iris—"

She tossed the spoon in the sink, picked up Vance's shirt, and pressed it over my chest. "Come on, Sam. Let's get you to a hospital. Good thing your grandfather called me to come over here. He got the word Vance had left the funeral." She put her arm around my shoulder and started guiding me out the front. "Barney had the right of it. Men acting like dogs marking their territory . . ." She stopped talking.

Gabe stepped in front of us.

Iris tilted her head back. "You either move, or you act like a man. What's it going to be?"

Jeez, Gabe's mom scared me to death. I think I'd rather have Gabe yell at me all the way to the hospital. I'm pretty sure he wouldn't hit me with a spoon.

I looked up at him.

He stepped in and his mom moved.

"Gabe, I—"

He lifted me in his arms and strode through the kitchen, out the door, and into the alley. Blaring sirens meant more cops were arriving on the scene. Vance must have called for backup when he disappeared from the office. Once we got to Gabe's truck, he set me down, opened the passenger-side door, and helped me in.

I leaned my head back and closed my eyes. I felt him get in and start the truck. "I didn't kiss him. He kissed me."

Silence. He said nothing, and I kept my eyes closed.

19

Angel pulled into the narrow street that led to Janie's trailer. "Looks like a full house." She double-parked, blocking off the entire street.

I looked up at Janie's mobile home. I had to do this. Gabe had left me at the emergency room with the terse comment that he had to give a statement at the police station, and that he had a client to see.

Those were the words he'd said. What I heard was, *I can't stand being in the same room with you, and if my mom hadn't had a big spoon, you'd be bleeding to death in the gutter.*

It's all about translation.

"Sam?" Angel said softly.

Snapping out of my thoughts, I looked around. *Right. Janie's house.* I turned to Angel. "You can't double-park."

Her vivid green eyes watched me. "I'm going to the pharmacy to fill your prescriptions. I'll be back by the time you are done."

I opened the door. "Yeah, okay, thanks." Getting out of the car, I turned and looked at her through the opened door. "For everything, Angel. You know, picking me up from the emergency room, and doing this."

"Go on, Sam."

I shut the door, turned to the mobile home, and shivered. Night was falling. Angel had brought me her leather jacket to put over my bloodstained shirt, but I was still cold. There had to be at least ten cars still here. Everyone had gone to Janie's house after Chad's funeral.

Maybe I should wait until tomorrow to tell her.

No. Now. Janie deserved to hear this from me. Stuffing my hands in my pockets, I walked to the steps.

The door opened before I could get up the steps. Rick Mesa looked down at me. "Sam."

Surprised, I said, "Rick. I didn't expect you here."

His soft brown eyes rested on me. "No? I'm here for Janie and the kids."

I nodded. That made sense. I forced myself up the steps. "How is Janie? I need to talk to her."

Rick stepped back. "She's okay. Come in, Sam."

I walked in. Groups of people milled around the living room and into the small kitchen. Janie saw me immediately and walked toward me. She wore a long patterned skirt and a black sweater. Her face wore a tired strain. "Sam. Thank you for coming by."

Using my right arm, I put my hand on her shoulder. "Janie, I have some news. Can we talk in private?"

I felt Rick hovering behind me. He wanted to know about the pictures, I supposed. But this was for Janie, and Janie alone.

Her hazel gaze stared into my eyes. Then she said, "Yes. Let's go in my room."

Janie had a double bed stuffed into the small room. We sat on it and I took a breath. "It's over, Janie. We found who killed Chad. But there are some things you need to know." I told her all of it, ending with the hope that Roxy wouldn't be charged with murder.

Her gaze slid past me to the small window filled with darkness. I touched her hand. It was cold.

"Janie, I'm sorry. I know this is hard. You are worried about your kids. . . ."

Her gaze shifted to me. "I knew what Chad was, but I had been afraid of him. I guess my courage came too late."

Startled, I clutched her cold fingers. "You knew that he was blackmailing?"

"I guessed. I did his insurance books for years. I suspected he had messed with his insurance trust accounts once, but when I asked him about it—" Her eyes fell to the gold bedspread.

"He hit you." Anger burned my gut.

"I was afraid of what he'd do to me or the kids. Finally I couldn't stand myself anymore. That's when I came to you. But poor Roxy." Tears pooled in her eyes.

"Janie, it's not your fault." It hurt like a bitch, but I raised both my arms, locked my hands around her shoulders, and stared into her eyes. "Don't ever lose sight of the truth. This was Chad's fault. Not yours. Roxy is going to be okay. She's tough, and she recognized that she and her uncle were falling apart."

"Thank you, Sam," she said simply and started sobbing.

A hand came down on my shoulder before I could hug her. "I'll take care of her, Sam. Angel's waiting for you outside."

I got up. When I stopped at the door and looked back, I saw Rick holding Janie. It gave me a sense of peace to know Janie had a friend like Rick. He'd help her through it. Softly, I said, "Rick, we found and destroyed everything." Leaving him with the knowledge that his secret life was secret, I left them.

* * *

Angel and I pulled up to the house. She cut the engine, and we both looked around. "A party?" Angel asked.

I took in Grandpa's Jeep, my mom's car, Blaine's beat-up primer-paint Hyundai, and another car I didn't recognize.

No truck. No Gabe. No surprise. "If it's a party, there better be a lot of alcohol." I opened the door and got out of the car. Angel and I went inside.

Grandpa, my Mom, Blaine, TJ, and Joel were gathered around the kitchen table eating and talking. It sounded like a party. Ali was the first to spot us. She left her place between Joel and TJ and ran over to greet us.

All the chatter stopped. They turned and stared at me. I wanted to run. What was going on?

Iris Pulizzi bustled out of the kitchen carrying a plate of garlic bread. "Sam! There you are. Hungry?"

Why was Gabe's mother in my house? Why was my mother here? Why couldn't I just turn right, run down to my bedroom, and lock my door? "Uh, no. Iris, what . . ."

My mother stood up. "Samantha, what is this about Gabe hitting a police detective?"

My mother. Never mind that I had been a part of solving a crime. She was worried about image. It didn't look good to have a boyfriend who hits police detectives. No one mentioned that Iris clobbered both Gabe and Vance with a spoon.

Joel speared what looked like a piece of Parmesan chicken with his fork and said, "Gabe does that. I've seen him. A guy called Mom something bad and Gabe knocked him flat on his—"

"Joel!" I said.

He shifted his wide blue eyes to me. "*Back.* I was going to say *back*, Mom. Sheesh." He ate the chicken.

TJ nodded. "Yeah, Gabe probably had a good reason. Mom," my oldest son turned to me. "What was Gabe's reason for hitting the detective?"

Everyone looked at me. None of them had been

there. Iris had arrived seconds after Vance kissed me. Shit. "Uh, things got a little confusing." I didn't know what to say.

"I wasn't confused." Gabe's voice slid up behind me. "Vance kissed your mom, TJ."

TJ and Joel both nodded, like this made perfect sense.

This did not make sense. And what was Gabe doing here?

My mother drained her entire glass of wine. "Samantha, this isn't going to be good for your real estate career."

Gabe stood next to me. I barely heard my mom but answered automatically. "I don't have a real estate career."

"That's because you don't have your license yet. You'll get your license when we go to the convention in a couple of weeks."

Iris picked up the bottle of red wine and filled my mom's glass. "Katherine, Sophie Muffley was just telling me today how proud you are of Sam. Apparently, you were the one who suggested she go to Sam with her problem."

Proud of me? My mother? Was I in the right house? My mother hated my dating service and sideline of PI work. And what was Gabe doing here? I had to move, to start making sense of this. I walked to the kitchen and found my little white bag from the pharmacy on the counter. Ripping it open, I studied the two bottles. Antibiotics and pain pills. I could use the pain pills. Grabbing that bottle, I struggled with the childproof lid.

Gabe took the bottle from my hand and opened it with one twist. He cupped my hand in his and emptied out a pill. He grabbed the antibiotics and added that to my hand. Then he went to the sink and got a glass of water.

I decided to take charge. "What are you doing here?"

He handed me the water. "Take your pills."

I did. Probably because I was a big coward and afraid of Gabe's answer.

"Sam," Grandpa called me. "Come sit here."

Gabe took the glass from me and set it on the counter. Then he put his hand on the small of my back and pushed me to the chair Grandpa vacated. I sat. Iris came in carrying two plates, and Angel followed behind her carrying her own plate. She sat next to Blaine. We were squished around the table. Iris put the plate with some chicken, a piece of garlic bread, and a little salad in front of me. "Eat, Sam."

Blaine had finished everything on his plate and now sat back. "Boss, your car will be ready Monday afternoon. The police picked up the evidence that was, uh . . . left . . . at Heart Mates." He glanced at TJ and Joel. "I went to the station and filled out the forms and stuff."

I set my fork down. "Blaine, you are the best business decision I ever made." It was true. He believed in Heart Mates. And he was a good friend. I didn't know what I'd do without him.

He waved my words away like a bad smell. "I talked to Lionel there, too. He's fallen out of love with you."

I had to smile. "Lionel actually helped us at the nursery by distracting Duncan so we could escape. Of course, that was after he hit Angel's car." Obviously, Duncan had seen us in spite of Lionel's efforts and followed us to Chad's office. Lionel had then followed Duncan. And Duncan had called Roxy at Chad's funeral to say they were going to have to leave town and start over. What a big mess.

Gabe snorted. "See? This is what I put up with. Are there any men who don't fall in love with Sam?"

Blaine raised his hand. "She's all yours, Gabe. I just work for her." He turned to look at me. "I mentioned to Lionel that he might like Missy."

I perked up. "Really? What did he say?"

Blaine broke into a grin. "You were right. He was in-
fatuated with her from the night he caught her after
she passed out. So I called Missy, and what do you
know—all she remembers of that night is Lionel carrying her to the car. Looks like your instincts were right."

I leaned back in my chair. The pain pills were kicking
in. It felt good to be right about Lionel and Missy. I
hoped Lionel and Missy fell in love.

"Babe," Gabe said, "eat."

I turned to face him. I wanted to get everything
sorted out. "What about Roxy and Duncan?"

"Roxy will be cleared since she acted in self-defense. Duncan will face some charges, but they'll probably result in probation. He'll be required to make
restitution for your car and to get some treatment. This
is off the record, but Vance will get it through with the
DA."

"What about Dara?"

"Vance isn't interested in turning her in. She's safe
for now. And relieved."

I shook my head. "What is it with you men? You tried
to kill each other in Chad's office, and then you work
together to clear the case."

Gabe smiled. It was a killer smile. Sexy. Full of promise with an edge of danger.

Everyone got up and started clearing the table and
doing dishes. Even Joel and TJ. Without being told.

I know a setup when I see one. "What's going on
here?" I shouted over the running water, dishes clank-
ing in the dishwasher, and Grandpa issuing orders.

Gabe said with a straight face. "Everyone has plans
tonight. My mom, your mom, and Barney are going to
Perchanga."

"The casino in Temecula?" I asked, my suspicion
blooming.

He nodded. "Mom's been bugging me to go."

Angel stuck her head around the corner while she

dried a pan. "Blaine and I are going to drop off those CDs that you . . . uh . . . borrowed from Rick on our way to taking TJ and Joel to the movies."

I turned back to Gabe. "You got here after me. How do you know this?"

"The network, sugar. We've all been in contact while you were taking a break at the hospital."

Damn Italians. I ignored him and stood. A faint wash of dizziness passed through my head, but I was steady enough to walk over to TJ and Joel.

Joel eyed me. "Can we go, mom? Please?"

TJ put the last pan away and walked up behind his brother. "Mom, I'll stay home if you want. You know, to take care of you because you are hurt."

He would, too. I loved my two boys. "No, TJ, you and Joel go. Have fun. Tomorrow we'll hang out, okay?" I embarrassed them both by hugging them, grateful for the pain pill. It was an effort to let them go. Gabe followed everyone out, or maybe he herded them all out, but I knew he was coming back.

Ali padded over to me, putting her nose in my hand. I looked down at her. "Forgive me, Ali?" I asked her, petting her regal German shepherd head. "I should have known you were trying to tell me something that day at the nursery. Blood. You smelled the blood, didn't you?"

She barked and ran to the fridge.

Laughing, I figured, why not? I went to the fridge and pulled out a bottle of beer. Twisting off the cap sent a shaft of fire through my chest, but it was worth it for Ali. I poured the bottle into her empty water dish.

She slurped happily.

I heard the front door close and turned around. Gabe strode across the living room to me. God, he was something. Jeans low on his hips, cotton shirt tight across his chest. Straight black hair brushed back to reveal his hard Italian bone structure. He looked like the type of movie star that, when he walks on screen in the movies, it is impossible to tell if he is the good guy or the bad guy. He was capable of both.

He stopped a foot from me, his gaze dropping to the empty beer bottle in my hand. Then he lifted his stare to me.

I felt the impact. So did my libido. Even stitched up and wearing bloody clothes beneath Angel's jacket, Gabe had a way of making me feel sexy.

I must have hit my head. Hard. To cover, I said, "I tried to help. I mean, I wanted to convince Vance not to turn Dara in to the DA in Arizona."

"So you kissed him?"

"He kissed me!" Shut up. This was going nowhere. I was not going to defend myself. "Why don't you go home?"

He shook his head. "Sorry, sugar, but that's not how this works."

I closed both my hands around the cold, empty bottle. "Not the way what works?"

"Our partnership. The team. You and me. Us. You have a choice. Do you want to stay here, and the two of us will squeeze into your bed? Or we go to my house and sleep in my king-size bed?"

Sure, the pain pills were making me a little fuzzy, but it finally kicked in. Emotions weren't all that easy for Gabe to handle. He was a passionate, deeply physical man. I set the beer bottle down on the table and closed the space between us. Tilting my head up, I said, "This must be really hard for you. At least you got to hit Vance. You can't hit me, can you?"

His black eyes glittered. "Back off, Sam."

Revelation—pain pills make me stupid. "Back off? Ah, come on, Gabe. Admit it, you want to hit me. You probably hate me. But some weird loyalty makes you think you have to be here taking care of me while I'm hurt." Hmm, a small, detached part of my brain registered real, sweat-popping, heart-pounding fury. "But I got a news flash for you. I'm not going to die on you because you looked the other way. I'm going to recover. I'm going to be fine. I am not your wife!" I took a breath.

"Sam—"

I heard the warning. I just didn't give a shit. "You got a problem with me? Deal with it. Tell me. Scream at me. But just don't shut me out! You want to leave me, then be a man and tell me!" God dammit, I was not going to cry. I would be fine. Gabe was a free man. If he wanted to leave, I would let him go without any guilt.

Swear to God, I felt the quiver of his juiced-up muscles. "Are you done?" His jawline throbbed.

Oh, yeah. So done. But I added, "I don't like being dumped at the emergency room. Now I'm done."

He lifted his hands, latching on to the edges of Angel's leather jacket. "First off, I know Vance kissed you. I was standing there. I saw it. Vance was fucking with me. He's pissed, babe, because I have you. In Vance's orderly world, he can't figure out how I got the girl."

"Uh . . ."

He lowered his face and arched a brow.

I shut up.

"I'm not saying I wasn't pissed. I don't want another man's mouth on you. Ever." He drew in a breath and pulled me closer to him. "For the record, you are nothing like Hazel. You tried to save me with nose spray." His mouth twitched as if he still couldn't believe it. Then he sobered. "And you trusted me. You knew all I needed was that knife far enough away from your throat to take Duncan down. Teamwork, babe."

He was right. I blinked, staring up at him. At the time, I had reacted. But now . . . He was right. "Vance yelled at me for that. Said he was right outside the door—" I was trying to make light of it, to avoid what it meant. Teamwork. Trust. Us.

"Vance had signaled to me that he was going out the back and around to the front when Duncan showed up.

But Duncan was too unstable to wait for Vance to make his move, so when you gave me the opening, I took him down. I'd say you surprised the hell out of both Vance and me with the nose spray. I was intent on keeping the knife off my throat without hurting Duncan any more than necessary while waiting for Vance. I didn't expect you to charge in with nose spray. Clearly Vance didn't either, since he got an eyeful." He grinned at the memory.

"Oh." Stupid, stupid. I would have smacked myself, but Gabe had a hold of the jacket, pulling my body flush with his. "I guess I didn't take time to think. I'd noticed that Vance was gone, but when I saw that knife at your throat, all that mattered was saving you." Too much information. "Uh, blame it on blood loss."

He locked his gaze on me. "Or maybe you have deep, unmanageable feelings for me?"

"Maybe."

He rested his head on mine. "Yeah?"

"Yeah."

Gabe shifted and lifted me in his arms. We headed down the hallway. "Sam?"

"What?"

"I never wanted to hit you. I wanted to get you naked."

I could live with that.

Please turn the page for a preview of
BATTERIES REQUIRED
by Jennifer Apodaca.
A May 2005 hardcover release
from Kensington Publishing.

1

The slot machine tricked me. I dumped in my money, believing I'd win the big prize. The Daystar Indian Casino in Temecula, California, gleefully sucked up my last twenty-dollar bill and suggested, in that innocent way of machines, that I try again.

Probably I would have if I'd had any more cash on me. Since all I had remaining was my pride, I left the gambling area, swept past a long bar, and went into the Nova Room. I looked past the bathroom-size wooden dance floor in the center of the bar to see the band playing onstage, the Silky Men.

They were a group of men who cross-dressed and sang in a comic routine. One of them, Rick Mesa, was the head soccer coach for the Soccer Club of Lake Elsinore. I had found out about his secret life as a cross-dressing entertainer while working on a case earlier that year.

I'm not actually a private detective. I'm a romance expert. I own the Heart Mates Dating Service, which is what brought me to the Daystar Indian Casino that night. My best friend, Angel Crimson, had provided the lingerie for the Silky Men, and she promised to pass out flyers for the open house I was having for Heart Mates on Wednesday night.

We figured lonely people go to the casino looking for love and companionship, so maybe we could interest them in my dating service in Lake Elsinore. It was only about thirty miles or so from the casino. That's not too far to travel for love, now is it?

But Angel had forgotten to pick up the flyers I'd had made to take to the casino. That meant I had to bring them to her at the casino after work on a Friday night. I found Angel and joined her at one of the small tables ringing the dance floor. Her long red hair was shiny straight, and she wore a green satin top that matched her emerald-colored eyes. Underneath the table, her black micromini skirt showed off her long legs. Angel looked like she could model lingerie for Victoria's Secret, but she'd rather sell lingerie than model it.

She was there to get bookings for her Tempt-an-Angel Lingerie line, which she sold through home parties. Sort of like Tupperware, only a hell of a lot more fun. At some point during their set, the lead singer for the Silky Men, Rick, would mention that their lingerie was provided by Tempt-an-Angel Lingerie. I don't know how, given that the band were men dressed up as women, but several women usually booked parties off that sales pitch. Go figure.

After ordering a glass of water, I pulled the stack of brochures promoting my open house out of my purse and slid them across the table. Then I asked, "Are you coming back here tomorrow night? Don't forget, I'm coming over to your house Sunday morning to pick up the couch." Angel was giving me a brown leather couch for the waiting area in Heart Mates. That couch would be a big step up from the metal folding chairs that I currently used.

Angel glanced down at the brochures. "I decided to

get a room and stay the night, instead of driving back and forth." Then she looked up. "Why don't you stay with me? It'll be fun!"

Tempting, but . . . "I'm going to paint Heart Mates tomorrow, so I have to get up early. I want to have it all ready for the open house Wednesday night."

Angel ran her fingers down the length of her Cosmopolitan glass. "Damn, we could have heated up the place and set off the sprinklers." She grinned. "There's a rumor that a promoter might be here tonight or Saturday night, so I might be really late getting home tomorrow night. Make it ten or so on Sunday morning to pick up the couch."

Leaning forward, I said, "A promoter? To see Rick's group? That's great for them! And who knows, maybe it'll be good for your lingerie line, too." I shook my head at the way things were turning out for us. "When we made our pact to find our careers, I didn't quite imagine this for you." Angel and I had had a little party one night a couple of years ago, fueled by margaritas, where we acknowledged that we'd both married losers and had no lives. We had vowed to change that. I had found my career in Heart Mates. Angel had taken a little longer, but now she was working hard to build her lingerie line.

"Good evening, ladies."

Angel and I both looked to my right to see a doppelgänger for Richard Gere. Thin silver streaks ran through his wavy dark hair. Shaped brows over brown eyes, elegant face, and nicely draped suit—this man should have been on a private European island. He carried an expensive-looking briefcase.

Angel recovered before me. "Hello," she held out her hand, "I'm Angel."

He reached for her hand, and I swear to God, I thought he was going to kiss it. But instead, he smiled, revealing a row of white teeth. "Ah, the very woman I was searching for. I have been hearing very good things about you and your business venture. My name is Mitch St. Claire."

Angel took her hand back. "Really? And where would you have heard about me?"

"In the high-stakes gaming room. It appears you have made quite an impression on several future clients."

When had I become invisible? "Ahem."

Angel glanced at me. "This is Sam." She picked up a flyer from the stack in front of her. "Sam owns the Heart Mates Dating Service. You might be interested in attending the open house Wednesday night. She'll be serving wines from the Temecula wineries."

He turned to fix the full weight of his gaze on me. "Sam? Short for Samantha? Quite a lovely name."

I held out my hand. "I usually go by Sam." I just have a need to be contrary.

He wrapped his fingers around my palm. "I believe I may have heard of you. Perhaps you've been in the newspaper?"

Every time I stumbled onto a dead body, I ended up in the newspaper. Usually it wasn't a flattering article. I decided not to mention that. "Perhaps you've heard of my dating service, Heart Mates?" I glanced down at the flyer Angel had slid over to him.

He let go of my hand. "Perhaps. May I join you ladies?"

"Sure," Angel said.

I stifled a yawn. It had been a long week, and I wanted to get home to have ice cream with my two sons, TJ and Joel. I'd had a fast dinner with them, but there was never enough time.

Mitch pulled over a chair from another table and sat between us. He set down his briefcase and fixed his gaze on Angel. "I wanted to meet with you, Angel, to discuss a business proposition."

Angel sipped her Cosmopolitan and said, "What would that be, Mitch?"

She was mildly flirting. I wondered if she was interested in Mitch the man, his business proposition, or both? It had been a while since Angel had had a boyfriend. Stalking her ex-husband tended to cut down on her time for a social life.

"I'm in distribution and thought you might be interested in offering some of my merchandise through your home parties."

Trent Shaw popped into my head. "My dead husband was in distribution. He sold condoms." He had also sold coke sealed up in those condoms.

Mitch cut his brown eyes toward me. "Condoms have their place, certainly. But these products are of a more . . . ah . . . personal nature."

"More personal than condoms?" He had my interest now. Highly curious, I leaned forward.

"Actually, a little more embarrassing for some people to buy." Mitch turned to look at Angel. "That's why you sell your lingerie through home parties, right? To make it a fun, nonjudgmental atmosphere. A woman might not be comfortable buying overtly sexy lingerie at the mall, but at a home party where she can make her selections privately, she's more comfortable."

Angel flashed her brilliant smile. "I see you've done your homework, Mitch."

He nodded. "So why not take it a step further? What are the chances of these women going to the mall to buy sex toys?"

I blinked and took a drink of my water. *Sex toys?* "You mean like fur-lined handcuffs and vibrators?" That was the full extent of my knowledge of sex toys. And none of that was from personal experience. I'd read about the fur-lined handcuffs in a romance book I reviewed for *Romance Rocks Magazine.*

"Precisely. I can offer a very nice selection at wholesale prices. But today, what I'd like to do is give you a sample kit and a catalogue so that you can see for yourself what I have to offer."

I choked and had to slap my hand over my nose to keep water from spewing out. Tears filled my eyes. Mitch looked over at me. "Does this make you uncomfortable, Sam?"

His slightly condescending tone sparked my instant denial. Through my fingers, I said, "Of course not." *Liar!* If I had taken my hand off my nose, it would have grown two inches. Vibrators! Omigod! What would my boyfriend, Gabe, say about that?

Like I didn't know.

Discover the Thrill of
Romance with

Lisa Plumley

__Making Over Mike

0-8217-7110-8 $5.99US/$7.99CAN

Amanda Connor is a life coach—not a magician! Granted, as a publicity stunt for her new business, the savvy entrepreneur has promised to transform some poor slob into a perfectly balanced example of modern manhood. But Mike Cavaco gives "raw material" new meaning.

__Falling for April

0-8217-7111-6 $5.99US/$7.99CAN

Her hometown gourmet catering company may be in a slump, but April Finnegan isn't about to begin again. Determined to save her business, she sets out to win some local sponsors, unaware she's not the only one with that idea. Turns out wealthy department store mogul Ryan Forrester is one step—and thousands of dollars—ahead of her.

__Reconsidering Riley

0-8217-7340-2 $5.99US/$7.99CAN

Jayne Murphy's best-selling relationship manual *Heartbreak 101* was inspired by her all-too-personal experience with gorgeous, capable . . . *outdoorsy* . . . Riley Davis, who stole her heart—and promptly skipped town with it. Now, Jayne's organized a workshop for dumpees. But it becomes hell on her heart when the leader for her group's week-long nature jaunt turns out to be none other than a certain . . .

Available Wherever Books Are Sold!

Visit our website at **www.kensingtonbooks.com**.